TRUE LOVES

Also by Lester Wertheimer

AT SEA

Being an Eccentric Voyage of Discovery
In the Company of Misfits, Rogues, and Vagabonds

IT COULD BE WORSE

Or How I Barely Survived My Youth

TRUE LOVES

MY FELLOWSHIP YEAR ABROAD

A MEMOIR

LESTER WERTHEIMER

iUniverse, Inc.
Bloomington

True Loves
My Fellowship Year Abroad

iUniverse books may be ordered through booksellers or by contacting:

iUniverse
1663 Liberty Drive
Bloomington, IN 47403
www.iuniverse.com
1-800-Authors (1-800-288-4677)

ISBN: 978-1-4697-7740-5 (sc)
ISBN: 978-1-4697-8810-4 (hc)
ISBN: 978-1-4697-7741-2 (ebk)

Printed in the United States of America

Contents

Preface	1
Berkeley	7
New York	13
Across the Atlantic	25
Southwest England	34
London	46
Scotland	56
Norway	65
Sweden	75
Finland	87
Denmark	96
Germany	105
Austria	119
Yugoslavia	129
Greece	140
Turkey	149
Egypt	159
Upper Egypt	169
The Middle East	177
Rome	191
Italy	203
The Riviera	213
Spain	222
Paris	231
The Low Countries	241
Paris Encore	250
The Last Tour	259
Over and Out	269

This story is dedicated to my
intrepid companions in adventure.

B. D. Thorne
and
E. Jacobson

Talented artists both,
who lived, worked, and loved with passion.

Birds do it, bees do it
Even educated fleas do it
Let's do it, let's fall in love

Cole Porter

Preface

My first true love was sex, which made its debut when I reached the perplexing age of puberty. What a revelation! Suddenly there were unexpected emotions and thrilling gratifications that became an essential part of my life. With or without a companion I was often in blissful heaven. Three years later my first true love led me to an unfortunate indiscretion consisting of a partner's unwanted pregnancy. For someone who followed every rule of convention this was an emotional shock of major proportion. My life became one stressful event after another as I wondered, *What in God's name am I doing in the middle of a cliff-hanging soap opera of my own making?*

I survived the stressful events that followed but suddenly developed an intense desire to escape my current life. I needed to get away and find a new direction. So at the age of eighteen I ran off to become a merchant seaman. Imagine the delight in discovering my second true love—travel. During my year at sea I visited a number of exotic ports throughout the world and came home a more experienced and determined young man.

After abandoning the nautical life I decided to complete my education. I enrolled at Berkeley, and it was there I chanced upon my third true love—architecture. Who knew that creating buildings would bring such enormous and lasting satisfaction? I was also stunned to learn that one could sit around all day doodling daydreams and actually get paid for it.

The discovery of each true love was a life-changing experience that made me the person I became. I was now twenty-three years old; I had a master's degree in architecture and was now ready to face life's next adventure. I applied to the University for a traveling fellowship, since that would effectively combine all three true loves. The fellowship would enable me to travel for a year at the University's expense, it would allow me to explore historic architectural monuments, and perhaps, I fantasized, there would be memorable romantic adventures along the way. That was my plan, and a pretty good plan it was, if I do say so myself. It was so good, in fact, I didn't bother with an alternate plan; it was all or nothing. I could not imagine abandoning any one of my true loves.

The story that follows is an account of my fellowship year. Strictly speaking it's not a conventional travel story, but that's hardly a disadvantage. I suppose you know that travel stories are often predictable and dull. At least that's my opinion. I've read plenty of them, and I must say, travel writers often have no idea they're boring their readers. There have been cases where readers were rudely awakened by the sound of a book crashing to the floor, only to discover it was the travel book they were reading just before dozing off. Reading about other people's travels is nearly as deadly as watching someone else's home movies; and if you've ever sat through an evening of that, you know what I mean.

"Oh look, there's Laurie with a beach ball. It's bigger than she is. Wave to us, Laurie! Isn't she cute? Oh, she lost the ball; it's rolling into the water. Now she's crying. How sweet!"

Honest to God, it makes you shudder. How can anyone not related to Laurie sit through that kind of stuff? People who show family movies could save a lot of time if they just told their guests to go home, instead of boring the poor devils to the point of resentment.

Travel stories are much the same. Perfectly decent people take trips and believe the world must know every detail of their unique experiences. And then, almost inevitably, they sit down and write the equivalent of a home movie. Even the best of them fall into that trap.

Mark Twain wrote one of the most famous books on travel even before he wrote *Huckleberry Finn*. Just consider the following passage from *Innocents Abroad*:

> *At Pisa we climbed up to the top of the strangest structure the world has any knowledge of—the Leaning Tower. As every one knows, it is in the neighborhood of one hundred and eighty feet high—and I beg to observe that one hundred and eighty feet reach to about the height of four ordinary three-story buildings piled one on top of the other, and is a very considerable altitude for a tower of uniform thickness to aspire to, even when it stands upright—yet this one leans more than thirteen feet out of the perpendicular.*

Now just so you know, I like Mark Twain. He was a fine author, charming humorist, and a genuine American hero. But it was Twain who once said, *"The more you explain it, the more I don't understand it."* That passage is living tribute to those insightful words. What was he thinking? *"Four, three-story buildings piled one on top of the other? One hundred eighty feet?"* Didn't he realize that taking up a reader's time with long-winded descriptions, especially those requiring mental calculations, is just rude? If you don't mind, Mr. Twain, I'll just assume the Leaning Tower was tall; and with all due respect, that's what you *might* have said. I'm pretty sure that if he owned a movie camera, God help us, we'd be sitting through a six-hour epic about the Leaning Tower of Pisa.

Travel stories, most would agree, should be about experiences encountered by the writer, not physical facts about famous monuments. If you wanted facts you could consult an encyclopedia. What the reader wants to know is why the writer got into the French taxi with a broken meter, which everyone knew couldn't possibly end well. Or what he did when the last boat left the deserted island while he was still collecting seashells. Or how he escaped the charging rhino in the jungle clearing. That's the stuff of great travel stories—the kind of excitement stay-at-home travelers want to hear about.

Sorry to say, this book has no charging rhinos, but it does have a number of interesting adventures, exotic experiences, and some worthwhile romantic liaisons. Stick with it and you'll see.

The adventure began many years ago in Berkeley, California. It was the month of May, my favorite month, and—as far as I'm concerned—the finest month of the year. Now if you have a different favorite month, or no favorite month, at all, it really doesn't matter. A lot of people think the best month is the one in which they were born. But try telling a Scorpio that November's a lousy month. And some like December, when everyone's a bit nicer because it's the holiday season. A friend once suggested I listen to *September Song*, a romantic piece by Kurt Weill.

"September—now there's a *real* month," he said. "What a wonderful time of year! I mean, not only does *autumn weather turn leaves to flame*, as the song says, but it's also football season. What do people do in May? Dance around a maypole? Sorry, pal, you got it all wrong. It's September, not May."

Another friend pointed out that all great months have songs written about them, *September Song* being a good example. "But *April in Paris*," he said, "is not only a better song, it's a better month. Trees and flowers bloom, birds fly north, and the season brings hope and optimism.

Besides, the song has a great melody with lyrics that can bring you to tears. *Whom can I run to? What have you done to my heart?* Oh, God, I'm choking up."

"Okay, wonderful song," I said, "but let's face it, April in Paris can be wet and blustery and colder than a nun's kiss. Not only that, let's not forget that April was the month Abraham Lincoln was shot. It was also in April that the Titanic ran into an iceberg. Fine song perhaps, but a disastrous month. Too bad, my friend, you're mistaken. April may be a good month, but May—with or without its own song—is a *great* month, hands down, no two ways about it."

As I said, the story began in Berkeley, and—love it or hate it—the month was May.

CHAPTER ONE

Berkeley

The month of May in Berkeley gave students much to be thankful for. The University catalog warned that during winter months it could rain three days out of four. During the recent winter, however, most believed it had rained four days out of three. But now the drizzly days had passed, and the fragrance of new growth filled the air. More importantly, winter coats were put away, and shapely coeds reverted to short-sleeved, low-cut blouses and skirts that ended above the knees. It was an exciting time to be a student and to be alive! I regretted this was my last May in Berkeley; I was graduating in two weeks.

Where had the time gone? It seemed like only yesterday I discovered the department of architecture. What a revelation that was! Beautiful drawings decorated the walls and exquisite scale models were on display. Right then and there I decided that is what I wanted to do—make beautiful drawings and build detailed models. I knew I'd be good at it. Sometimes you just know things like that. For years I had sought a serious career path. I yearned to find something I would love to do for the rest of my life. When I finally discovered architecture I knew I had found the answer. As a result, I breezed through my classes with top grades and top honors. Now my school days were ending. *What do I do now?* I wondered.

Echoing my thoughts, my roommate, Billy Heston, asked, "What now?" Billy was a fellow architecture student and one of the nicest people in the Ark, as we called our school. He was good-looking with short-cropped dark hair and gray eyes that were accentuated by thick, black-rimmed glasses. Billy knew, since the age of ten, he would be an architect. His father worked as a Hollywood production designer, and Billy had inherited his father's love of drawing. He was not only a talented designer but an excellent student as well. I figured that with his background, charming personality, and positive attitude, his future was brighter than a klieg light.

"What now?" I repeated. "Well, if my fellowship comes through I'll travel until the money runs out. And if that doesn't happen . . . I don't even want to think about it."

If you want to know the truth, winning the fellowship meant I would spend the next year traveling alone through foreign countries—a prospect that worried me. And if I didn't win, I'd feel like a total flop. Either way, there was enough anxiety to go around.

"Whatever happens," said Billy, "you'll be fine. You're clever, talented, and people seem to like you, although I'm not sure why. You can be an awful pain in the ass."

"I love you too, Billy," I said. Then we both laughed.

"Why don't you come with me to Germany?" suggested Billy. "I'm joining a bunch of Cal grads working on Army facilities, and from what I hear, they're getting great experience, living the good life, and the job comes with a draft deferment. Or would you prefer going to Korea to fight?"

"Germany's not a bad idea," I said, "but the fellowship comes with a deferment as well."

Lately, the fellowship was all I thought about. Since my first year of Architectural History it was my dream to take the grand tour and visit the famous structures we studied. Money, however, was the problem; I never had quite enough of it.

"Why not apply for a traveling fellowship?" suggested Henry Stanton, the professor I most admired. Great idea, I thought; and a week later that's exactly what I did.

On a mild and fragrant evening in May some two hundred students gathered in the brick-paved patio of the architecture building for the year-end awards ceremony. I loved that patio from moment I first saw its cherry trees in bloom. It was a gathering place for students, and outdoor lectures often took place there—such as the one given by Frank Lloyd Wright a year earlier. The patio was bordered on three sides by the rustic shingled walls of the architecture building. That ancient, weathered structure was admired and venerated by every student who crossed its threshold. Since we spent most days and nights there, the Ark was almost literally our home.

I had the unusual sensation of sitting in the patio but, as in a dream, I felt like a detached observer. Billy Heston was sitting on my left, and to my right was Professor Stanton.

"Nervous?" the Professor asked.

"Not really," I answered. But it was a lie; I was ready to throw up.

The head of our school, Dean Warren Wilson, was standing at the podium shuffling through his notes. He had already recognized several honorees and bestowed various awards, one of which Billy had received. The ceremony had gone on for nearly an hour, and anticipation was building for the final award of the evening. The Le Conte Memorial Traveling Fellowship was the most highly regarded prize offered by the University. It carried the richest stipend, fewest restrictions, and at least a dozen others, besides me, were hoping to receive it.

I sat quietly, but the calm exterior was no indication of what was going on inside. I was ready to pop my cork. I suddenly felt my heart beating, as though it were trying to escape my chest. It was making an awful racket, and I thought people around me would surely hear it. Ba-bump, ba-bump, it went, but no one else seemed to notice. *Calm down!* I thought. *If you don't win, so what. Life goes on. Who am I kidding? It'll be a horrible disappointment, and I'll feel like a loser. Why does the Dean keep fussing with his papers? There he goes again. He's doing this on purpose; he must be trying to build up the suspense. He already knows who won. Why doesn't he just blurt it out? What a jerk!*

"And now," began the Dean, "for the final award of the 1952 year, the one you've all been waiting for, the Le Conte Memorial Traveling Fellowship. By the way, did I ever tell you about *my* student year at the American Academy in Rome? It was 1933, and . . ."

There was a sudden chorus of hoots and hollers.

"Stick to the script, Dean!"

"We don't care about your year in Rome!"

"Come on, Dean, who won the Le Conte?"

"All right, all right," he said laughing, "here it is. I won't keep you waiting any longer. The winner of this year's Le Conte Memorial Traveling Fellowship," there was a very long pause, "is Peter Newman!"

I suddenly felt a chill go through my body. Did I hear right? Was that my name? Maybe it's a mistake. I wasn't what you'd call lucky; whether it was a lottery or game of Bingo, I never came close to winning. I sat there in shock.

Professor Stanton grabbed my hand. "Congratulations, Peter! You certainly deserved this."

"Nice going, Newman." It was Billy slapping me on the back and grinning as though *he* had just won the prize. "I told you there was nothing to worry about, you old pain in the ass!"

"Peter," I heard the Dean call, "would you mind saying a few words to the audience?"

I rose unsteadily. My heart rate had slowed, but my legs were a bit wobbly. As I walked slowly towards the podium I heard the applause.

It was beginning to sink in. *Son-of-a-bitch! I won—I really won! Wahoo! If this is a dream, I hope I never wake up!*

I looked out over a sea of familiar faces and then began. "Dean, faculty members, and fellow students: I'm thrilled beyond belief and grateful to the fellowship committee for making this dream come true." I realized my words were trite and predictable, but what else could I say?

"Actually, my friends, it was no contest at all. I can't believe anyone is surprised by the outcome. It was certainly no surprise to me; I was obviously the best choice. I'm sorry my competitors lost, but what the hell, that's the way the cookie crumbles. Better luck next time, boys!"

Well of course you can't say things like that. The losers already hate you. Why rub it in?

I continued to speak, and as words of gratitude flowed from my mouth, my mind wandered to my home and family in Southern California. What would they think when they heard the news? They had no idea I even applied for a fellowship. I never spoke of it because the embarrassment of losing would be more than I could face. But now I was a winner, and I couldn't wait to tell the world.

"And finally, let me thank those who played such an important part over the past few years, helping me achieve this wonderful honor. To my professors and fellow students, you have my eternal gratitude. No matter how far I wander or how long before we meet again, I will keep the memory of you forever."

There was more applause, and the Dean shook my hand. "Congratulations, Newman", he said. "There's no question you've earned this wonderful honor." Then he looked up into the starry sky, and with a distant gaze—as if in a trance—he said, "As you embark on the next chapter of your life, I hope you will be up to the challenges that lie ahead. Now go forth into the world. Make our School and this University proud."

There was a moment of silence as the hackneyed message sank in, and in that moment I had the odd feeling Dean Wilson meant every word he said.

CHAPTER TWO

New York

"Fasten your seat belts, ladies and gentlemen; there's some nasty weather ahead." The calm drawl of our Captain's voice came over the intercom like some small town weatherman reporting the next day's forecast. There was little hint of the trouble to come. Ten minutes later a violent storm assaulted our plane like an irrepressible bully. The powerful engines of the DC-3 steadily droned on, seemingly unaware that we were pitching and rolling like a ship at sea. Through the small cabin windows we saw occasional flashes of lightning illuminate the ominous sky. Far more threatening were the intermittent air pockets that appeared like spatial potholes through which we plunged twenty or thirty feet at a time. Anyone without an attached seat belt would likely be plastered against the cabin ceiling. The erratic movements of our plane confirmed that the forces of nature were in control, not our pilot. The clatter of the aircraft and its wrenching movements made it difficult to carry on a conversation. The young woman next to me, however, was undeterred.

"Holy moly!" she said. "That's quite a storm out there." She was attractive but appeared, at that moment, pale and frightened. When I boarded the plane in Chicago, forty-five minutes earlier, she was already settled into the window seat, and I remember being grateful that she was my seatmate rather than some three-hundred-pound lineman from the Chicago Bears. She wore a pale blue dress, which complemented her dark, shoulder-length hair and deep blue eyes. A single strand of pearls rested lightly on her throat, and I noticed she wore no other jewelry. From what I could tell, she had a slight but pleasant figure.

"Holy moly?" I repeated. "You probably mean that's one hell of a storm out there, and you're right. It looks like the war of the worlds."

"I did mean that, but I don't have much tolerance for profanity."

"Profanity? You mean like the word 'hell'?" She nodded. *What an odd bird*, I thought. *She's probably a Sunday school teacher. I should just ignore her. On the other hand . . .*

Some time later I asked, "Is this your first flight?"

"How could you tell?"

"Well, to be honest, and don't be offended, it looks like you're ready to throw up. Are you going to be all right?"

"I'm not sure. My stomach is gurgling, but so far I've managed to keep down my lunch. It depends on how long this roller coaster ride lasts."

I wanted to help my suffering seatmate, but having seen this kind of thing before I knew there was no quick relief. Someone once said the best cure for motion sickness was to sit beneath a large tree for a while, but when traveling four miles above the earth no passenger wanted to hear that. On an impulse I said, "I'll hold your hand if you'd like." I regretted my offer the moment I spoke—afraid my remark would be misunderstood as a devious come-on. It sounded suggestive to me, and God only knows how it sounded to a Sunday school teacher. To my utter amazement, she put her hand in mine and said, "Thanks." Her hand was warm and soft, and I sensed something sensual in her touch.

After what seemed an eternity the storm passed. We suddenly saw a bright cerulean sky and the fading sun setting below us. My seatmate took her hand out of mine and said, "I think the crisis is over. Thanks for the helping hand—no pun intended. By the way, since we've been holding hands for the last twenty minutes, you might want to know who I am. My name is Deborah Wolfe; friends call me Debbie. What do friends call you?"

"Peter, Peter Newman. Pleased to meet you, Debbie, but I prefer Deborah, if you don't mind; you just don't look like a Debbie.

"Oh—and what does a Debbie look like?"

"More like a cheerleader, perhaps a tap dancer, maybe a cartoon character. You don't look like any of those. Anyway, you seem more relaxed now; is the stomach better?"

"Much improved, but now I'm getting hungry. Do you think they'll serve any food?"

"I doubt it. We'll be landing in Pittsburgh in another hour. But you're in luck. I just spent time with relatives in Chicago, and they loaded me down with a shopping bag full of food. You know how relatives are; they figured I'd starve before reaching New York. I'll be happy to share what I have."

"And what might that be?"

"Well, let's see. I have some smoked salmon, cream cheese, some noodle kugel, and a piece of apple strudel."

"You sound like a walking delicatessen."

"Make that a *flying* delicatessen. My relatives are convinced that—good times or bad—eating solves all problems."

"I think I'd like your relatives," she said.

I parceled out the food and warned, "Be careful of the kugel; if it drops on your foot, it could cause serious harm. That happened to a cousin of mine last week, and she's still in a wheelchair."

Deborah laughed. "You're making that up."

"Well, yes. Actually, she's on crutches now. By the way, it's not commonly known, but when David killed Goliath he didn't have a stone in his slingshot; he had a chunk of noodle kugel." She laughed again. It was a delightful laugh.

"Where are you from, Peter?"

"California," I answered. "How about you?"

"Waukegan, it's a small town outside of Chicago. I'm on my way to New York to study acting. I plan to take the city by storm, and within a week or two, become a Broadway star." Then she laughed at her own unlikely prediction.

"An actress? What do you know? I thought you taught Sunday school."

"Where on earth did you get *that* idea?"

"Well I suppose it was that profanity business." She ignored the comment and then asked, "Why are *you* going to New York?"

"I'm catching a ship to Europe in a couple of days. I just graduated and got a traveling fellowship. I plan to spend the next year looking around and learning a few things about the world."

"How I envy you! I've always wanted to see Europe, but first, I have to get this acting thing out of my system. I know the odds are all against me, but it's something I just have to try."

We landed in Pittsburgh and were forced to disembark while our plane was being refueled.

"Come on," I said, "we've got some time to kill. Let's have some coffee." I soon learned that my new acquaintance was twenty years old and had wanted to be an actress since the age of ten. Also, this was her first trip away from home. Her parents did not favor her career choice, nor did they approve of this audacious visit to a city they believed was fundamentally immoral. But they eventually agreed to her plan, provided she stay with a distant cousin who lived in Brooklyn. The cousin was supposed to meet Deborah when we landed at La Guardia

Airport, but, as it turned out, the cousin wasn't there; and when Deborah telephoned there was no answer.

"Oh rats," she said as she hung up. "Now what am I supposed to do?"

"I'll stay with you, if you like," I said, but after a half hour I suggested we leave.

"Look, you can't spend the night at the airport. Why don't you come into town with me? I'm at a hotel near Times Square, and I'm sure we can get you a room there as well." We caught a cab and thirty minutes later arrived at my hotel.

"Sorry," said the desk clerk, "there's nothing available. There's a convention in town, and I doubt if you'll find an empty room in the entire city." I heard a groan from just behind me. I persisted with the clerk, but he convinced me that not even a broom closet was available.

"Now what am I going to do?" asked my forlorn friend.

"Okay, this doesn't look good," I said. "Why don't you come upstairs, drop your bag, and try your cousin again." The result was the same as before; no one was home.

"It's getting late," I said, "and I'm afraid you're running out of options. As I see it, you have two choices: you can spend the night here—you can have the bed, I'll take the chair—and tomorrow we can solve your problem. Or, you can spend the night on a bench in Central Park, which I think is dangerous and a really bad idea. So what'll it be?"

"When you put it that way, I have to assume you're a better risk than somebody I might meet in the park."

"I'm almost flattered," I said, "I think I just won out over some homeless pervert."

She laughed. "I didn't mean it that way. You've really been decent about all this."

We took turns changing in the small bathroom and then crawled into our respective beds. The two chairs I put together made a narrow, uncomfortable perch, but I was exhausted and fell asleep almost immediately. A short time later I felt a hand on my shoulder.

"I can't do this," she said. "I feel so guilty I can't sleep. Let's switch."

"I've a better idea," I said, "and don't take this the wrong way. It's a large bed—plenty big enough for two—why don't we share it." I knew my suggestion was presumptuous, but in reality I was dead-tired, badly in need of sleep, and becoming annoyed with my unanticipated roommate.

"Well," she said, "I'm not sure. I really don't do that sort of thing."

"I don't either, Deborah, but let's face it, this is an unusual situation." *Why was I explaining? Let her sleep in the damn chair and forget it!*

She thought about my proposal a while longer, apparently unable to make up her mind. I finally lost patience. "Do what makes you comfortable," I said. "I'm going to sleep."

I crawled into bed, and moments later, so did she. Each of us positioned our bodies as close as possible to our respective edges. I was acutely aware of the warm body resting no more than eighteen inches away, and I found it difficult to think of anything else. But exhaustion took over, and in a few moments I was asleep. Somewhat later—I couldn't be certain how long—I felt a foot touching mine. I figured she was a bit off course, so I moved my foot away. But in a little while, I felt the foot again. *What's going on? Will this evening ever end?*

"Sorry to bother you," she said. "But I'm really feeling anxious." She *was feeling anxious? What about me? I'm sharing my bed with a total stranger, becoming increasingly sleep-deprived, and wondering why I'm lying next to some nut who wouldn't say "poop" if she had a mouthful of it.*

What do I really know about her? Could she possibly be unhinged or even crazy enough to set fire to the drapes in the middle of the night? What could I possibly know about someone I met only hours ago?

"Okay, Deborah, what's bothering you?" I asked.

"I'm frightened," she said. "Nothing seems to be working out. It's not just everything that went wrong today, it's my whole life. I don't know what I'm doing here. What makes me think I can become a successful actress? There must be thousands of girls in New York trying to do the same thing. Maybe my parents were right to discourage me. Maybe I should just give up now, go home, and avoid the grief and disappointment." *Why is she telling me this? Do I look like Miss Lonelyhearts?*

She was quiet for a while and then the woeful narrative continued. "My father warned me about strangers in the big city. He said, 'I don't want you jumping into bed with the first man you meet.' That's exactly what he said. And look at me—here I am, in bed with the first man I met. What's wrong with me?" Then she began to cry. *Now, what was I supposed to do?* A few moments later I put an arm around her. *What would her father think about that? More importantly, does he own a shotgun? Okay, try to be sympathetic, but for God's sake, don't do anything stupid.*

"Calm down, Deborah," I said. "Things are probably not as bad as you think. It's true, technically we're sharing a bed, and if your father walked in right now he probably wouldn't understand. But let's face it; this is a matter of survival. There's nothing wrong with you, and you're certainly not doing anything improper. Do you think your father would prefer you spending the night alone in Central Park? Is that what you think?

"I don't know what to think anymore," she replied. As I held her, I felt her rapid heartbeat. It reminded me of a small bird that had fallen out of its nest.

"Now about the acting," I continued. "Sure it's hard work, and there'll be some rejection and a few setbacks. But nothing in life that's worthwhile comes easily. If you quit now you'll always wonder what might have been. Do you really want to give up without a fight and maybe live a life of regret?" She listened quietly. The crying had stopped. "You know, we're not so different," I said. "I'm a little worried myself. Here I am going off alone to Europe and I have no idea how that'll work out. I'll be dealing with people whose language I don't speak, searching each night for a new place to sleep, eating every meal alone—none of that is very appealing. But I'm convinced the discomforts are worth it. I think about the marvelous sights I'll see, the historic monuments, and the exciting adventures. So you see, I understand—I have many of the same doubts."

She looked up at me and said, "Thanks for saying that." And then she kissed me on the cheek. Without another thought, I kissed her tenderly on the lips.

"Holy moly," she said. And then she kissed me again with greater passion. I felt an intimacy that was more than physical. I had been reluctant to consider negative feelings about my trip, but expressing my misgivings brought an odd relief. Sharing our fears brought us closer, and we found comfort that night in each other's arms. Who could have guessed that an emotional evening with Deborah Wolfe, Broadway star-to-be from Waukegan, Illinois, would constitute my first noteworthy experience in New York? I had barely set out on my yearlong odyssey, and holy moly, what do you know; my first true love had suddenly materialized.

When I awoke Deborah was dressed and sitting in a chair staring at me.

"Good morning," she said. "You look cute when you're asleep."

I smiled at her, and said, "Careful, Deborah, what would your father say?"

"I've some news," she said. "I spoke to my cousin. Here's what happened: she had an asthma attack yesterday and spent half the night in an emergency room. She apologized for standing me up, but it couldn't be helped. She's picking me up after lunch, so I'll be moving to Brooklyn."

"I'll miss you," I said.

"Me too," she answered. "You know, Peter, I could really fall for you, but you're running off to Europe, and for all I know, we'll never see one other again. And since you convinced me to give this acting thing a chance, I don't see much of a future for us."

"You're probably right. Anyway, we have some time this morning; let's spend it together." As we left the hotel we found ourselves in the chaotic heart of Times Square. Deborah stared in absolute wonder at the surrounding towers. "Oh my goodness," she said, "I've never seen such tall buildings. And the traffic—is it always like this?"

"That's exactly what I felt on *my* first visit," I said. "I couldn't look anywhere else but straight up. And the cars, the honking, and sirens—those are pretty much the sounds of New York."

After breakfast we headed for Central Park. "Golly," exclaimed Deborah, "don't pedestrians pay any attention to the signals? They're all crossing against the light."

"That's another New York habit. If you can avoid getting hit by a car, anything goes."

The weather was warm and humid and the fragrance of new flowers filled the air. We wandered through the park, and through it all she never let go of my hand.

"Okay," I said, "time for some culture." We headed back toward mid-town and the Museum of Modern Art. "This place has one of the best damn collections you'll ever see."

"There you go again," said Deborah. "Must you always swear?"

"I've got to say, Deborah, your view about profanity is just a bit weird. Some colorful expressions, you know, are not all that sinful. There's a word for what we did last night, and I happen to believe it's no more profane than what we actually did. I'm sorry you're offended, but 'golly gee' and 'holy moly' are just not in my vocabulary. I hope this quirk of yours won't ruin a lovely relationship, because I like you. I like you a lot."

"And I like you, Peter. I'm sorry; I'll try to be more tolerant."

We raced through the galleries and finally stopped for lunch at the museum café. Then it was time for Deborah's cousin to pick her up. "I hate to say goodbye," she said.

"Well then, don't. Meet me at the ship the day after tomorrow. We board just after lunch but won't sail until late in the afternoon. I'll give you a tour of the ship, and we can say goodbye then."

"I'll be there," she said. I started walking from the hotel and suddenly felt sad. We had known each other less than twenty-four hours, but we had made a connection.

On a hot July afternoon, I took a bus to Hoboken, where the flagship of the Holland-American fleet, the S.S. Nieuw Amsterdam, was docked. There she was, much larger and far more beautiful than I imagined. She was my transport to Europe and prologue to the endless adventures I could—at that point—only imagine. Waiting beside the gangway, as I hoped she would be, was Deborah Wolfe. She had a visitor's pass, and we boarded the ship together.

"I'm glad you're here," I said.

"Me, too," she replied. "Very glad."

"Let's find my cabin, I want to drop my bag." The ship was nearly as long as three football fields and it had eight passenger decks. Finding my cabin was not easy. With the help of a room steward, we finally located my assigned dormitory room. It was small but contained two double-decker bunks, two closets, two chairs, a washbasin, and—most importantly—a porthole. Sitting on one of the lower bunks was a young Dutchman who introduced himself as Stefan Gil.

"Hello," I said. "My name is Peter Newman. And my friend here is Deborah Wolfe."

"Oh my goodness," he said. "Is she occupying the other bunk?"

"Afraid not; she's only here to see me off. Anyway, this is an all-male dormitory."

"Too bad," said Stefan. "She would have been an attractive addition to our group. By the way, sleeping above me is Theo Laurent, but don't bother to say hello, unless, of course, you speak Flemish. He's Belgian and doesn't speak a word of English."

I waved hello to my Belgian roommate, who smiled and waved back. Then I wondered how he got along in New York without speaking a word of English? Probably, I thought, like I'll get along in Belgium. I dropped my bag and suggested we explore the ship.

"See you later," I said, and then we left.

"They seem very nice," Deborah said. "I like your roommates."

"And it's obvious they like you, too."

We spent the next two hours crawling over every inch of the ship's first, cabin, and tourist class public spaces. Small going-away parties were in progress everywhere, with champagne flowing freely and happy guests consuming large amounts of caviar and small sandwiches. "I don't ever want to leave," said Deborah. While exploring the tourist class areas, we stopped at the dining room to make a table reservation. I requested a table for six, hoping to improve my chance of meeting interesting people. "And if you can possibly manage it," I said to the steward, "make sure they're about my age. I'd really appreciate that."

"Already looking for my replacement?" asked Deborah.

"Of course not; you know you're irreplaceable."

When the gong for going ashore sounded the second time Deborah gripped my hand. "I'll miss you," she said. "I'm sorry I won't be with you, but I'll write and you'll answer and tell me what I missed. I won't forget you." We embraced and kissed and experienced a bittersweet goodbye. When I finally let go of her hand, she moved slowly down the gangway. When she reached the pier, she looked up, waved, then turned and walked away. Moments later tugs came to guide us down the Hudson River. We passed the Statue of Liberty and were soon sailing into the Atlantic. Two hours later land was completely out of sight. I stood at the rail watching the sunset as I recalled events of the past few days. But now it was time to look ahead. I glanced towards the bow. *Europe is out there*, I thought, *and so is my future. How exciting is that? I must be one of the luckiest people alive!*

CHAPTER THREE

Across the Atlantic

The S.S. Nieuw Amsterdam was launched in 1938 as the new flagship of the Holland American Line. It was the most modern and beautiful ship afloat and—undeniably—equal to the other great flagships, such as Cunard's Queen Mary and the French Line's Normandie. Two years later, at the outset of World War II, Nazis invaded Holland and British forces took over operation of the ship. It served throughout the war as a troop transport. The Nieuw Amsterdam was completely refurbished after the war and reentered transatlantic service in 1947, five years prior to my trip.

Of the twelve hundred passengers boarding the Nieuw Amsterdam on that bright July afternoon, two hundred—including me—were housed in tourist class, the least expensive of the ship's three classes. Tourist class was hardly elegant, but it was by no means austere. And it was worlds apart from the steerage class facilities experienced by my relatives who immigrated to America at the turn of the century. In those days steerage provided the cheapest form of transportation, but little more. By contrast, tourist class on the Nieuw Amsterdam was like spending time at a cut-rate country club.

I returned to my cabin and found Stefan Gil gone and Theo Laurent asleep. Since there was no one occupying the other upper berth, I assumed only three of us would share the cabin. I washed, changed clothes, and proceeded to the dining room, where the second sitting was about to begin. The dining room steward had done a remarkable job fulfilling my request. Seated together at the round table were two young and attractive American women, both recent graduates of Grinnell College in Iowa. Anne Cleary, slender, blond, and blue-eyed was from De Moines, and her roommate, Mary Lambert, short, redheaded, and robust was from Boston. Sitting adjacent to Mary was a middle-aged, heavily accented German by the name of Walter Metzger. Walter lived in Seattle for the past six years and was returning to Germany to visit relatives. Seated next to Walter were two Dutch, scholarship students, both tall and blond, who were returning home after attending the University of Ohio the past year. The young woman was named Rika Van Zandt, and the man introduced himself as Frans Schuyler. Though similar in appearance, they were merely friends, and not related or—as Rika was quick to point out—romantically involved. The sixth seat was located between Anne and Rika, and happily, that vacant seat was mine.

If there was an imperfect fit among our cheerful group, Walter seemed to be it. It wasn't just his age, but he appeared a bit grim and humorless. *Did the dining room steward think we needed a chaperon?* Though he was polite and quiet, Walter appeared less like a passenger and more like an unnecessary piece of furniture.

Introductions were made, biographies exchanged, and within moments it was clear that our mostly student group was a delightful collection of bright and amusing people. There was much conversation and laughter, and I felt fortunate to be part of this lively group. Our table steward distributed menus, and I was amazed by the variety of choices among American and Dutch dishes. We spent two hours at our first dinner, and by the time coffee was served, we had become friends. After dinner Anne and Mary decided to see the movie *Robin Hood*. I chose to accompany Rika and Frans to the small bar. Walter retired to his cabin, and his absence was hardly noticed.

We found a small table, ordered drinks, and sat quietly enjoying the piano music.

"So," began Frans, "what do you think of the Nieuw Amsterdam?"

"I'm very impressed," I said. "The ship is beautiful and the food tonight was wonderful. Now if the seas remain calm, we'll have no reason to ever leave. What do *you* think?"

"Rika and I came to the U.S. on this ship nearly a year ago. I loved it then and I still do. It makes me proud to be Dutch. By the way, what do you think of our table companion, Walter?"

"What do you mean?"

"Well, has he impressed you in any way?"

"He seems uncomfortable. Maybe he's not used to being around boisterous students, or perhaps he has a problem with the language. I don't know why the steward put him at our table."

"He says he's been in the States for six years," interrupted Rika. "Don't you think he'd be comfortable speaking English by now?"

"One of my roommates is Belgian, and after spending a few weeks in New York he still doesn't speak a word of English. Is there something here I'm missing?"

"Rika and I don't trust Germans. We saw enough of them during the occupation. We think it's odd that Walter immigrated to the States so soon after the war. How did he get a visa? Does he hold a German passport? We have many questions."

"Maybe we should ask him," I suggested. "He might have a reasonable explanation."

My drinking companions exchanged a few words in Dutch, and then there was a long pause.

"Let's change the subject," said Rika. "Tell us about that beautiful girl you were with before we sailed. You two looked wistful and very much in love."

"I didn't know we were being watched," I said. "She's someone I met on the plane to New York; I've only known her a couple of days. I doubt that it's true love, but we enjoyed our short time together. Perhaps we looked wistful because we may never see one another again."

"Do you always work so fast?" asked Rika.

"I don't know; but why do you ask? Is something going on here that I should know about?"

"Oh, good one," said Frans. "That should slow down my curious Rika."

Rika appeared embarrassed, but she smiled at Frans' comment. "I don't know you well enough," she said. "Give me another day or two."

Just then Anne and Mary came into the bar. "They canceled the movie," said Anne. "Something about a projector problem. So, what have we missed?"

"Not much," said Frans. "We were just discussing Peter's girlfriend."

"Oh, yes," said Anne, "we noticed her. Beautiful girl. Their performance on deck reminded me of a passionate farewell scene from a war movie."

"With more than a thousand passengers to look at, why was everybody watching *me*?"

"Well," said Mary, "you obviously put on the best show."

"Let's talk about something else," I said. "How about checking out the lounge?"

The lounge was the large meeting space where various activities, such as games, concerts, and dances took place. The lights were dimmed, and couples were slowly dancing to romantic music played by a small band. It reminded me of an intimate nightclub. We found a table and Frans asked Mary if she cared to dance. As they walked to the dance floor I was left alone with Anne and Rika." I'd love to dance with you both," I said, "but one at a time."

"I'll sit this one out," said Rika.

"Okay," I said, "but if you want to know me better, the next dance is yours."

As Anne and I walked onto the dance floor she asked, "What was that about?"

"Rika asked me earlier about the girl I was with on deck. When I said I only knew her for two days, she asked if I always worked so fast. I thought it was an odd question and suggested she might be thinking about me in a romantic way. It was just silly talk."

"Maybe not so silly," said Anne. "Don't you notice how she looks at you?"

Something strange was happening, and I found it both surprising and pleasant. I had spent the previous few years living the monastic life of an architecture student. As such, I dwelled in a practically all-male department, spending long hours over a drawing board. There was little time for socializing and practically none for dating. In recent years there was barely the hint of romance in my life. But in the last several days, I discovered what I had been missing—the delight and charm of female companionship. There it was again, my first true love! *What a discovery! What a thrill! Farewell to the ascetic life,* I thought. *I'm ready to rejoin the outside world.*

I held Anne more tightly as we swayed rhythmically to the melodious sounds of the small band. She held me firmly as well and asked, "What's going on?"

"I just had a sudden insight, and I'm feeling wonderful," I answered. Then, suddenly and impetuously, I kissed her. It just seemed like the right thing to do. There was a long pause. Then she smiled and said, "I think Rika was right. You *do* work fast."

The next several days were filled with the endless activities of our transatlantic country club. Our original group of five grew by several more young people attracted by our cheerful behavior. Among them was my Dutch roommate, Stefan Gil, but my other roommate, Theo Laurent, was rarely seen outside our cabin. The day before landing in Southampton we discovered that Theo was taking a faulty dosage of anti-nausea medicine, which kept him in a perpetual stupor. Poor Theo, while conquering seasickness he remained virtually unconscious during the entire crossing.

Much of our time was spent around the dining table, and when not there, we were busy working up an appetite for the next meal. We played shuffleboard, Ping-Pong, took long walks around the deck, and had a daily swim in the heated pool located deep within the ship's bowels. When the seas were a bit rough the ship's roll created small waves, and that made for a more exciting game of water-tag. So we ate well, exercised regularly, and danced until well past midnight every evening. It was a fantasy existence, and I wished the crossing would last forever. I was having the time of my life. I must also admit that I loved being at sea. I recalled the thrill of my merchant seaman days, but this was infinitely more satisfying. Standing on deck, staring at the horizon in every direction was pure joy. It was like being on top of the world. I believe there is no better way to experience unrestrained freedom than being on a mountaintop or in the middle of an ocean.

A few days after Frans brought up his suspicions concerning our German tablemate he confronted Walter Metzger. We were discussing the wartime occupation of Holland, and he suddenly asked, "By the way, Walter, what did you do during the war?" One might have thought every German would have a ready answer, but Walter appeared startled by the question. He sat quietly for a moment and then asked, "Do you mean World War II?"

"But of course; what war do you *think* I mean?"

Walter hesitated. "I was a director at an industrial company in Monowitz."

"Monowitz, Poland?" asked Frans, his voice rising. "The town near Auschwitz?"

"I believe so," answered Walter. He suddenly appeared more dour than usual.

"By any chance, was the name of that company I. G. Farben?"

"Yes, I worked there. I was a chemical engineer."

"You must know then, that's where Zyklon B was developed. That was the cyanide-based insecticide used by Nazis on humans at their extermination camps. You heard about that, didn't you, Walter?" Our tablemate was now perspiring, and he appeared agitated. "I know nothing about that," he answered. "My job was to produce synthetic oil from coal. That is what I did; that is all I did. I don't know anything about that other business. Why are you asking me these questions? What are you implying?"

"We're suggesting this," interrupted Rika. "It seems odd that you came to the States perhaps a year after the war's end. It appears you were eager to leave Germany. Were you running away, Walter? Is that what you were doing?" Anne, Mary, and I sat silently, as though watching the exciting conclusion to a wartime spy movie. I could hardly believe what I was hearing.

"I have been asked these questions by Allied investigators," said Walter. "They were satisfied I did nothing wrong, so why must I defend myself against some self-righteous Dutch students? You know nothing about the situation."

"We know this," answered Frans. "We know that I. G. Farben employed slave laborers. Were you aware of that, Walter? The company was convicted of war crimes, and several Farben directors are now rotting in jail. You were a director; where were *you* when all that was going on? Did the investigators miss something? Could they have overlooked you? And one more thing, Walter, how is it that you worked near Auschwitz but never smelled the odor of burning flesh?"

"I don't have to listen to this," said Walter. He suddenly leaped from the table and ran out of the dining room. We don't know where he went, but that was the last we saw of Walter Metzger.

"You were a bit rough on him, don't you think?" asked Mary.

"No, I don't," said Frans. "You have no idea what the Nazis were like. And those who worked behind the scenes, like our friend Walter, were just as bad—maybe worse. Incidentally, do you know what his name means?" There was a long silence. "Metzger means butcher."

I began to wonder about Walter. Was he really a Nazi? How could one possibly know? I had no idea what a Nazi in civilian clothes looked like. Most of what I knew came from Hollywood movies. But could Walter actually have murdered Jews at Auschwitz? Could he have been that evil? Yes, I suppose it was possible, but I realized it was unlikely we would ever know.

The following morning Anne, Mary, and I sat in deck chairs soaking up the bright sun and enjoying the sudden change in weather. The previous two days were so foggy we could barely see the bow of our ship when standing at the stern. Though most passengers were traveling to Rotterdam, we planned to disembark the following morning at Southampton.

"So," began Anne, "what are you plans after we land?"

"I'll probably head towards London," I answered. "But I may make a few detours first."

"You know, Mary and I are picking up bicycles in Southampton. We'll be cycling through England this summer. Why don't you join us for a few days? It might be fun, and we'd love to have you along."

I found the idea appealing. I enjoyed the company of both girls, especially Anne, with whom I had enjoyed an exciting flirtation for the past week—one of the most pleasant weeks ever. And though I was eager to explore the wonders of Europe, I was not particularly keen on facing the depressing notion of solitary travel. The prospect of loneliness still worried me.

"Do you both agree about this?" I asked.

"If you mean do I mind?" said Mary, "no, I don't." But she looked like someone who just lost an argument.

"Then it's settled," said Anne. Mary did not look pleased.

There was a farewell celebration that evening hosted by our Dutch friends. Frans provided the champagne, and we drank and danced until the music stopped at about two in the morning. Since we were docking at five o'clock, we decided to stay up for the remainder of the night. In the first light of dawn we circled the Isle of Wight and proceeded to our dock in Southampton. We had an early breakfast, said our fond goodbyes, and with great anticipation, walked down the gangway. We were now in England, and the foreign adventures were about to begin.

CHAPTER FOUR

Southwest England

At the end of the dock was a line of tall, black taxis. We piled into one and sped off to a nearby hotel previously booked by my two companions. As we drove down the left side of the narrow street it appeared we were heading for a disastrous crash into oncoming traffic. Mary covered her eyes, unable to watch the impending disaster, and Anne clutched my arm. "Is the driver trying to kill us?" she asked in a nervous whisper. "We're on the *wrong* side of the street!" But it was only the wrong side of the street in America; in Britain, the left side was the correct side.

"Take it easy," I said, "that's the way they drive here."

"Well it's scary, and I think it's silly," she said.

Ten harrowing minutes later we arrived at the hotel. I booked a room and then we took a quick walking tour of the town.

"Well, here we are," said Anne. "Merry old England! Isn't it exciting?" Indeed it was—familiar in a way, yet clearly different. Everyone spoke English, but it didn't sound like our language or even like a typical English movie. Some accents were so bizarre, certain words and phrases were completely unintelligible. Winston Churchill once said that we were two countries separated by a common language, but I never appreciated that remark until now. The streets of Southampton were teeming with bright red double-decker buses all racing down the "wrong" side of the street. They appeared so tall and unstable, I expected them to fall over when rounding a corner. Another peculiarity we noticed were the orderly files of people lined up at every bus stop. "That is the way we *queue* up," explained our doorman. "Even if alone, as the old saying goes, a proper Englishman forms an orderly queue of one."

And then there was the bewildering money—pounds, shillings, and pence. Who devised *that* convoluted system? With twelve pence in a shilling and twenty shillings in a pound, it seemed totally arbitrary. And if something cost, let's say, two pounds, five and six, what was that in dollars? Every purchase required frustrating calculations.

That afternoon the girls picked up their bicycles at the Raleigh factory in Southampton. Having had no sleep the night before, we had an early dinner, retired to our rooms, and slept soundly for the next twelve hours. The following morning I rented a bicycle at Collings Bicycle Shop, a local institution. We left the hotel late in the morning and peddled away from the city. The girls had mapped out a careful itinerary focusing on the New Forest area; and since I knew little about the region, there was no reason to question their plan. We headed south and in less than two hours arrived at Beaulieu Abbey, originally founded by King John in the thirteenth century. It must have been impressive then, but now, it was little more than a famous ruin. It was sobering to realize that this structure—or what was left of it—existed four hundred years before the Mayflower set sail for America. Beaulieu was French for beautiful place, which it was; but, in their inimitable way, the British pronounced it B'yew-lee.

After an hour, Mary said "Let's go; we've got to get to Bucklers Hard before dark." We continued cycling along the Beaulieu River as it meandered through the New Forest. It was a warm day and the magnificent countryside was in full bloom. It was also strangely quiet; there were virtually no cars, nor did we hear much more than the bleating of sheep and whinnying of the famous wild ponies. What a contrast to the previous week when we were surrounded by hundreds of passengers and occupied with the bustle of shipboard life.

Bucklers Hard was a charming village that might well have been created by a Hollywood set designer. Situated on the banks of the Beaulieu River, it was founded as a shipbuilding center to produce warships for Lord Nelson's fleet. An eighteenth century building was converted several years before into the Master Builder's House Hotel, and we soon discovered it was the only place to stay. By a stroke of good fortune, we got the last two rooms. Mine, however, was located up two steep flights of winding stairs that ended in a small attic. The room was clean, quaint, and modest in size, with a ceiling a mere inch or two above my head. Apparently, people were considerably shorter two centuries earlier. My room had a washbasin with running water, which, in a structure this old, was as modern as an atomic bomb. The toilet room, however, was a full flight below. Beyond my dormer window was a breathtaking view of the Beaulieu River, with several small boats at rest and the tranquil countryside beyond.

I met Anne and Mary in the lounge for a drink before dinner. There was little question about where to eat; the hotel restaurant was our only choice.

"I love it here," said Anne. "It's exactly the sort of place I hoped for."

"Me too," said Mary. "I had no idea it would be so charming. How's your room, Peter?"

"About as close to heaven as possible—and I mean that literally. I'm practically on the roof."

We had a satisfying dinner and then walked down to the river to watch the sunset. At that time of year twilight lasted until ten in the evening.

"I don't think I've ever seen a more romantic place," said Anne. I will certainly come back here; I may even consider it for my honeymoon. On second thought, I will *definitely* return here for my honeymoon."

"And when will that be?" I asked.

"As soon as some nice guy like you asks me."

"Why, Anne Cleary, you shameless flirt, this is so sudden."

"Oh, stop it, you two," said Mary. "This is embarrassing." She was noticeably upset.

"We were just making a joke," said Anne. "What's bothering you?"

"Both of you. Everything's a joke with you two, and it's really annoying."

We walked back to the hotel, and without another word, Mary went directly to their room.

"It's pretty clear," I said, "this has something to do with my being here. This may not have been a good idea."

"It's not you," said Anne, "the problem is Mary's. I think she's jealous. Once before, when we were roommates, something similar happened. I had a boyfriend and she seemed resentful. But I wasn't sure if she was envious of me or my boyfriend."

"Are you saying she may have romantic feelings for me *or* for you?"

"I don't want to get into that," she replied. "Let's change the subject. How about giving me a tour of your garret?"

When we reached my attic room we were both out of breath from the steep climb.

"This is it," I said. "Small, but charming, wouldn't you say?"

"I love it," she said. "Can I stay here with you?"

"I don't know; I'm not sure that's a good idea. What would Mary think?"

"At the moment, I don't care. Anyway, she's probably asleep by now."

Anne sat on the bed and then stretched out with her head on the pillow. It was provocative and impossible to ignore.

"Listen, Anne, I find you attractive, I really do, but I think this might create a problem. Besides, I'm kind of involved with that girl you saw me with in New York." I don't know why, but the thought of Deborah Wolfe popped into my head, and I suddenly felt guilty.

"Oh come on, Peter, she's in New York, and we're in England. Anyway, I was just wondering if the two of us would actually fit in this narrow bed."

I knew what was happening, but I wasn't sure why. *Maybe she's doing this to provoke Mary; and, by the way, what exactly* was *their relationship? On the other hand, maybe she really likes me. Since that kiss in the ship's lounge, there was something between us—something unresolved. But what about Deborah? How did I really feel about her?*

I sat down on the edge of the bed, uncertain, but fascinated by my uninvited guest.

"You're over-analyzing this," she said. "Why don't you just kiss me?"

Despite the alarm bells in my head, despite my apprehension and guilt, and with no more backbone than a jellyfish, I succumbed to the siren song. We embraced and kissed and it could not have been more thrilling. As far as Anne's concern about the bed's width, had it been the size of a bookshelf, there still would have been plenty of room.

As she began unbuttoning her blouse Anne said, "I know we're being naughty, but I really don't care. I like you; I like you a lot. And stop worrying—I know what I'm doing. I really do."

I awoke at three o'clock in the morning, and discovered I was alone. The memory of our time together was still vivid, but now I regretted our recklessness. I was hoping for an adventure, but this seemed too much, too soon. What would the next few days be like? How would we deal with Mary? I only hoped we hadn't screwed this up.

Later that morning the three of us met in the hotel breakfast room. Mary appeared somewhat contrite. "Good morning," she said. "I want to apologize for yesterday. I was in an awful mood, and I'm sorry for being such a grouch."

"Forget it," I said. "It was a long day; I understand."

"Did you sleep well?" she asked.

"Better than ever," I replied.

"Must have been the bicycling," she said. "You know, intense physical exercise promotes sound sleep." Anne began to giggle.

"What's so funny?" asked Mary.

"Nothing, really. I couldn't agree with you more. Why don't we pack up, hop on our bikes, and get some more intense physical exercise? I just *love* intense physical exercise."

We cycled through the New Forest, up and down gentle hills, and marveled at the incredible natural beauty of the area. We saw herds of wild ponies several times, but as we approached, they galloped away. Before noon we reached the charming village of Lyndhurst, known as the unofficial capital of the New Forest. We visited St. Michael's Church and saw the tomb of Alice Liddell, the original inspiration for Lewis Carroll's *Alice in Wonderland*. While walking along High Street, we purchased some food for our picnic lunch. Bicycling to the edge of town, we found an enormous ancient oak tree, sat beneath it, and enjoyed our simple food. Throughout the morning I had little contact with Anne; I barely looked at her. When Mary stopped at a restroom, Anne asked, "What's going on, Peter? You seem so far away."

"I think we have to be careful. We can't exactly carry on in front of Mary. Have you forgotten yesterday?"

"Of course not; but we can try to act more normal."

"I don't think normal applies anymore. Last night pretty much changed that."

When Mary returned we climbed on our bicycles and headed for Romsey. We arrived late in the afternoon and found rooms at the old White Horse Hotel. The town was drab, compared to the beauty of the countryside, but the well-preserved ruins of the thousand-year-old Abbey was worth the visit. After dinner that night, Anne came to my room. "We've got to talk," she said.

"You want to discuss the architecture of Romsey Abbey?" I asked.

"This is not a joke," she answered. "We have to talk about us. What's going on?"

I thought about the past twenty-four hours and said, "What's going on is this: we like each other, and we're attracted to one another. But there are complications. First, you have a jealous roommate, and we're not even sure which one of us she's jealous of. Besides, you're spending the summer bicycling through England, and I can't be a part of that. I've got to get going on my own. So, as I see it, this relationship hasn't much of a future."

"I suppose you're right," she said, "but I hate to admit it. When do you plan to leave?"

"We'll be in Winchester tomorrow; I thought I'd set out on my own from there."

"Well then, I'd like to spend the night here. I didn't plan on this happening, but since it's turning out to be the highlight of my summer adventure, I'd like to be together one last time."

I suddenly visualized Deborah Wolfe again. *Why does the thought of her make me feel so guilty? We were together such a short time, and we may never see each other again. On the other hand, here is Anne, seductive and so very appealing.* Since discovering my first true love, sound, practical judgment was clearly out the window. I was simply unable to resist an attractive woman.

A heavy rainstorm awakened me the following morning. When the storm abated, we climbed on our bikes and pedaled to Winchester. A chilly, light rain accompanied us all the way. We headed directly for the famous medieval Cathedral and saw the tombs of Jane Austen and Isaak Walton. We also visited the nearby Palace of William the Conqueror. With all the emotion created by my first true love I found it difficult to concentrate on my other true loves.

By mid-afternoon it was time to go. I was heading back to Southampton to return my bicycle. That was a fifteen-mile jaunt; and, glancing at the gray skies, it would be a wet one at that.

"Goodbye, Mary," I said. "Thanks for letting me tag along."

We hugged, and she said, "No hard feelings, Peter." I had no idea what she meant.

Then I hugged Anne. "What a delight it's been to know you. I hope we meet again, because you're very special."

"And so are you, Peter. I'll miss you and I'll write to you." Then we kissed goodbye. "I wish I could go with you," she whispered.

I hopped on my bike, waved goodbye, and headed south.

I returned to Collings and, to my great surprise, that kind old chap refused payment for the use of my bicycle. "You Yanks did so much for us during the war; this is my way of saying thanks."

I caught a bus to Salisbury and arrived there around dinnertime. Since the town was crowded with tourists celebrating the Bank Holiday, there was not a room to be had. My final rejection was at the Red Lion Hotel, where I decided to stay for dinner. Before I finished eating, the sympathetic manager approached and said, "I know you're in a bit of a fix, so let me suggest you use the couch in my office this evening. I'm afraid the space won't be available until ten o'clock, and you'll have to be out by eight in the morning; but it's much better than sleeping in the barn." It was a kind offer that was impossible to refuse.

Salisbury was a delightfully quaint town. I visited the Cathedral early in the morning and realized immediately why it was considered the greatest example of English medieval architecture. Once inside I discovered its structural magnificence along with its rare artistic treasures. I spent hours there and enjoyed every moment. The manager switched me to a real room that afternoon. It could not have been more than seven-feet wide, but it had a bed!

While sitting in the lounge before dinner, an elderly gentleman said, "Be a good chap, would you, and pass that receptacle next to you." As he was smoking a large pipe I assumed he was referring to the standing ashtray. This led to a conversation in which I learned he was on holiday with his wife. "If you have no other plans," he said, "why don't you join us for dinner." Little did he know I had no other dinner plans for the entire year. We spent a pleasant evening exchanging views on travel, English architecture, and more; and when we finished dinner this kind couple insisted on paying the entire bill. I was drowning in British generosity.

I took a bus to Amesbury the following morning and walked the remaining two miles to Stonehenge—that marvelous prehistoric development that we studied during my first year at school. I was completely unprepared for the size of the megaliths and the emotional power of their simple geometry. The stones were enormous and arranged in a circle in the middle of the Salisbury Plain. How they got there, nobody knows. Nor can anyone be certain whether Stonehenge was a burial ground, a religious site, or an ancient observatory. Equally mystifying was that, more than three thousand years ago, people were able to erect and arrange individual stones that weighed thirty tons each! I could not imagine how they did that. I spent two hours at one of the oldest structures in the world, and it was almost a religious experience.

I walked back to Amesbury in the rain and, soon afterward, returned to Salisbury. After lunch I caught a bus to Bath, pronounced "Bawth" by the British, which was a popular resort town founded by ancient Romans. The curative powers of the natural hot springs were recognized years earlier, but it took Roman creativity and resources to develop the first public bath.

As the three day Bank Holiday continued, so did my challenge to find a place to spend the night. I finally settled on a sleazy rooming house whose only advantage was its modest price. I spent the afternoon walking around town and found it impersonal and depressing. Most structures were built of local stone, which had weathered over the years to a deep charcoal color; and viewing these in the rain gave new meaning to the word "gloomy". I visited the ancient Roman bath, which was remarkably well preserved. It was believed that Roman baths represented the first, as well as the last time in English history, that bathing attained any degree of popularity.

I had a tasteless dinner, which did little to cheer me up, and then returned to what Charles Dickens would have described as a "hovel". I found everything about Bath to be dismal, and I was sinking into a deep depression. Then I considered—*maybe it's not Bath; maybe it's me.* I had been alone for a couple of days; and except for dinner at Salisbury, I had not spoken to a soul. The persistent English drizzle certainly didn't help. I was not really homesick; I was simply lonely. *If I can't survive on my own for two days, how on earth will I last a year? Maybe I should give up now and avoid the grief. Avoid the grief, but face utter failure. Holy moly, now I'm beginning to sound like Deborah Wolfe.* Those thoughts depressed me even more.

It occurred to me that some people were comfortable traveling alone, but I was not one of them. When viewing an architectural monument I needed to say to someone, "How about that? Isn't that the most wonderful thing you've ever seen?" And sitting alone in a restaurant, reading a book and trying to eat, made me uneasy. I needed to discuss things; my thoughts and observations were like itches that needed scratching. Clearly, I was emotionally unprepared to be a hermit. But what was I to do?

After an unusually good night's sleep, I awoke refreshed and in a somewhat better mood. But I'd had enough of Bath. I caught the noon bus to Stratford-Upon-Avon just as the rain stopped. The countryside was suddenly bathed in brilliant sunlight. At each curve of the narrow road I marveled at the sight of wild flowers, grazing cattle, and quaint thatched roofed cottages. I arrived at Stratford late in the afternoon and found the town teeming with people celebrating the three-day Bank Holiday. After finding an inexpensive room I wandered through the crowded streets. What a contrast with Bath! Stratford was largely composed of old, shamelessly quaint, half-timbered cottages. The entire town derived its popularity from Shakespeare, and without connection to the old bard it probably would be just another charming village along the Avon River.

The following morning I walked two miles to Shattery to visit Anne Hathaway's cottage. I also visited Shakespeare's birthplace. Both structures were picturesque, but they appeared incredibly austere, totally devoid of physical comfort, and somewhat depressing. Under those challenging conditions, I understood how Shakespeare could have written enduring tragedies, but how do you account for the comedies? At a pub that evening I met an American student who attended the London School of Economics. His name was Philip Monroe, and he had come to Stratford for a day's visit. I told him about my wandering around Southwest England for the past week. "You might consider," he suggested, "going directly to London and make it your headquarters. You can take side trips from there, as I'm doing today."

Sometimes the most practical ideas are the least obvious. "Terrific idea," I said. "I don't know why that never occurred to me. Can you suggest a place to stay?" He gave me the address of the student hostel where he was staying. "It's just basic shelter," he admitted, "but really cheap." I now had a viable plan and suddenly felt motivated. *Enough of the one-night stands*, I thought. *Tomorrow it's off to London.* I celebrated my new plan that evening by attending a performance at the Shakespeare Memorial Theater. I saw *Macbeth* with Ralph Richardson and Margaret Leighton, directed by John Gielgud. I loved the performance and admired the architecture of the modern theater. Altogether, it had been a heartening day.

Early the next morning I was on a bus to London. Since leaving New York, all my activities seemed to be prologue; I was now heading for one of the world's great capital cities. I suddenly felt energized and eager to become serious about my travels.

CHAPTER FIVE

London

Within my first hour in London I bumped into Philip Monroe, my acquaintance from Stratford. He was in the reception room of the Student Hostel in Tavistock Square.

"I see you took my advice," he said. "I think you'll like it here."

"I'm sure I will. Where do I sign in?"

Philip led me to the registration desk, where the receptionist verified my student documents and directed me to one of the men's dormitory rooms. The room contained four double-deck bunks in a clean, austere space lit by two large windows. The windows overlooked a rear garden that featured seasonal flowers and fruit trees. The bathroom was located down a short hall and appeared recently modernized. It contained two showers, which, in a two-hundred-year-old building, was as rare as eggs in post-war London. I selected one of the two empty lower bunks, put my things in the adjoining locker, and sat down on my bed. It felt like a relic from a medieval dungeon. The mattress was about an inch-and-a-half thick and felt like it was filled with shredded wheat. But what did I care; the Hostel was inexpensive, well located, and finally, here I was in London!

"You'll get used to the bed," said my upper-bunk neighbor. "It's not as bad as it looks."

"No," said the student in the adjacent bunk, "it's worse."

The first young man introduced himself as Luc Dubois, an exchange student from Bordeaux. The other person was Roger Austin, a sardonic American from San Francisco.

"At six shillings a night," I said, "it's hard to complain; that's about eighty cents U.S."

"It's not the money," answered Roger. "It's not even the pathetic mattress. Nothing in post-war England works very well." He paused and then said, "Wait 'til you flush the toilet."

"Don't pay attention to Roger," said Luc. "He has no idea what went on in Europe during the war. After the endless bombings it's a miracle that London is still here."

Ignoring Luc's comment, Roger continued. "Just remember this bit of advice: when pulling the flushing chain, you must simultaneously jump off the toilet in one swift motion. If you don't, I can assure you, you'll wish you had.

Later that afternoon, Roger asked if I'd like to join him and a couple of other Hostel students for dinner. I was delighted to have company, especially since the others turned out to be attractive young women. Diane Holden from Florida and Susse Krog, a Danish beauty from Copenhagen, were both residents in the women's section of the hostel while they attended summer school at Chelsea College of Art and Design.

"Where to?" asked Diane.

"Since Peter is new in town," said Roger, "why don't we introduce him to The Delhi?"

"They have a delicatessen here?" I asked. The others burst out laughing.

"Afraid not," answered Diane. "It's an Indian restaurant. Have you ever had Indian food?"

"I don't suppose you're talking about Apache or Navajo."

"We're talking about India," said Roger, "where curry comes from. Indian food is the best and most affordable food in London. Typical English food is not only unimaginative, but it's invariably overcooked, and flavorless. You'd be better off avoiding it."

"I had a perfectly poached egg with bacon this morning," I said. "It was delicious."

"Well," said Roger, "I'll give you that; the British do a passable breakfast. But on the other hand, they also consider smoked kippers and baked beans on toast tasty breakfast treats. And don't get me started on their other culinary oddities. They've got some that shouldn't even be mentioned in mixed company. Take, for example, Toad in the Hole; that's Yorkshire pudding and sausage. Then there's Cock-a-Leekie, Bangers and Mash, and Spotted Dick? I mean, really, can you imagine naming a pudding—or anything else for that matter—Spotted Dick?"

"I think Peter gets the point," said Susse. "You don't particularly like English cooking,"

"Right you are," answered Roger. "I don't think it should even be called 'cooking'."

I thought it odd that Roger Austin settled in London. He criticized everything about it; the weather, the culture, even the people themselves. "They're not all Lord Byron and Jane Austin," he said. "Most, in fact, are just hillbillies with a different accent."

I enjoyed the delicious Indian food, as well as the company of my fellow students. We remained at the Delhi for two hours, talking and drinking warm English beer, which, surprisingly, was the one thing about which Roger didn't complain. It had been another long day, and despite my shredded wheat-filled mattress, I slept soundly that night for more than ten hours.

Early the next morning I went to the American Express office and found seven letters awaiting me. Among them was one letter each from

Deborah Wolfe and Anne Cleary, my recent romantic companions. I could not wait to read my letters, but when I turned to leave the counter I bumped, almost literally, into Jim Elwood, an acquaintance from Berkeley.

"Woody!" I shouted, "What are you doing here?"

"I might ask the same of you," he answered.

"No, I mean, I thought you left Europe."

"Not yet. I won't be leaving for a while. How about you? I didn't even know you were coming here."

"Well, it happened pretty quickly. I won a traveling fellowship and plan to be here until the money runs out."

"Lucky bastard! Say, have you eaten? Let's get some coffee and catch up."

Marion James Elwood, known to all as Woody, was a fellow architecture student who graduated from Berkeley the previous year. He was tall, slender, and had a distinctive personal style most would describe as casual. His clothes hung loosely on his flexible frame, and he generally allowed the prevailing wind to dictate the arrangement of his reddish-blond hair. Woody moved quickly and decisively, like a commander leading men into battle. His most distinctive quality, however, was an infectious exuberance for life. Woody was an intrepid optimist.

Since we were in different classes at school, Woody and I were not particularly close; but as we became reacquainted over breakfast, it felt as though we were the dearest of old friends. I think we represented to each other the familiarity of home, and we both felt comfortable being together.

"How long have you been here?" I asked.

"I got to London two weeks ago. I would have left by now, but I'm waiting for money that was supposed to arrive last week. That's what I was checking on when we met."

"Where are you staying?"

"You're going to love this," he answered. "It's a place called Clapham Deep. It was a bomb shelter during the war, but now it's a hostel. You take the Underground to the Clapham station, and then take an elevator about five stories—straight down. It's like sleeping in a submarine, but—get this—it's less than forty cents a night. Honest to God, it feels like stealing!"

"Sounds a bit claustrophobic."

"It's not so bad, and I only sleep there. Did I mention—it's less than forty cents a night?"

We continued talking the entire morning, and at noon I said, "I promised to meet some people at the National Gallery. Would you like to come along?"

"Been there and done that—a few times. But how about dinner?"

"Great," I said. "I happen to know a terrific Indian restaurant."

"Oh, I just had Indian food last night."

"Well believe it or not, people in India eat Indian food three times a day—every day."

The following weeks were filled with serious sightseeing. Before leaving home I had prepared a list of architecturally important sights, and Roger Austin suggested an even brighter strategy. "Just check out the tourist postcards," he said, "and you'll immediately know the greatest attractions any city has to offer." That was advice I would value for years to come.

Often with Woody, but sometimes alone; and occasionally in sun, but frequently in rain, I visited every popular tourist sight from St. Paul's Cathedral to the Regent Park Zoo, in addition to several developments on my list of *Not to be Missed Modern Buildings*. We discovered that among the curious eccentricities of Londoners was their enthusiasm to give directions, whether or not they knew what they were talking about. It happened on an almost daily basis. With great confidence a stranger would say, "St. Swithin's Church? Why of course; nothing to it. It's at the top of the road, first turning on you right. Then continue straight for thirty yards, take the second turning to your left, and there it is, in all its glory." After diligently following such directions, not only was there no St. Swithin, there was no church at all, or—for that matter—any other building of interest. And then I would wonder: *what on earth was he thinking?*

After ten days of continuous sightseeing I took some time off to digest the myriad visions that filled my mind. I also needed to write some letters, do laundry, and, not least of all, get a haircut. It would be my first since leaving home. On a cloudy afternoon I found myself on Jermyn Street, which catered almost exclusively to fashionable gentlemen outfitters. It was there I discovered Ronald's Hairdressing Establishment for Gentlemen. The shop appeared extravagant, but I was undeterred.

"Do you have an appointment?" the receptionist wanted to know. *Uh oh,* I thought, *this is nothing like Marty's Clip Joint in Berkeley.*

"No," I answered. "Is that a problem?" The receptionist shuffled through the pages of her appointment book and finally said, "I'll check with Mr. Ronald." Several minutes later Mr. Ronald appeared. He was tall, slender, and wore a moustache so thin it appeared to be applied with an eyebrow pencil. He also wore a white, three-quarter-length smock and a paisley ascot. A perfect, pink rose bud appeared in the smock's lapel.

"Good-day," he said. "Kindly follow me." He led me to a washbasin, sat me down, put a towel around my neck, and asked me to tilt my head back.

"I don't need a shampoo," I said. "Just a haircut."

"We do *not* cut unwashed hair," he answered. I suddenly felt radioactive.

In the next few minutes I was advised that, for most of my adult life, I had worn my hair inappropriately. However, Mr. Ronald would be happy to remedy that distressing imperfection. He proceeded to clip and trim as if he were Michelangelo and my head was a block of marble. Forty-five minutes later Mr. Ronald removed my apron with the flourish of a matador. I looked in the mirror and was shocked by the image staring back at me. Noting my look of apprehension, Mr. Ronald said, "The effect of my work is rarely evident until after the second visit." I hadn't the heart to tell him there would be no second visit.

Returning to the Tavistock Square Hostel I bumped into Susse Krog, the Danish art student. "What happened?" she asked. "Are you trying to change your image?"

"Oh, the haircut. No, just some bad luck with a creative barber. It'll grow out—I hope."

I had dinner that evening with Woody, and his first reaction was sidesplitting laughter. "What's that all about?" he asked. "Looks like your head got caught in a pencil sharpener."

"Not funny," I said. "I met up with Mr. Ronald, the wicked barber of Jermyn Street."

"What did you do to make him so angry?"

"Forget it," I said. "I just spent five shillings, and I'm not very happy about getting clipped—if you know what I mean."

The following night I had dinner with Arnold Whittick, a writer and the biographer of my architectural professor, Erich Mendelsohn. Mendelsohn was a world-renowned architect who had given me letters of introduction to several notable people. This was my first opportunity to meet one of them. Whittick, his wife, and daughter were charming hosts, and the conversation that evening was stimulating. Mrs. Whittick served a roast that was about the size of a child's fist. She explained that this was their meat ration for the week—for the three of them! I almost lost my appetite.

"Please don't be concerned," she said. "We like to say, it's fortunate you've come on the night we're serving meat."

World War II ended more than six years earlier, but severe rationing continued. Each week a person was entitled to one egg, two ounces each of butter and cheese, and about twenty cents worth of meat. Sugar and sweets were also rationed. Those who could afford to do so, ate out; others, according to Whittick, grumbled and went home to their fish and chips.

On my first day in London, Roger Austin suggested that I apply to the Ministry of Food for a month's worth of ration coupons. "You can't even buy a candy bar without coupons," he said. Happily, I had the book with me that evening. I immediately whipped it out and presented it to Mrs. Whittick. "Please take this." I said. "I'll be leaving London soon and I'd like you to have it." You would have thought, by the look on her face, I had just presented her with the Hope Diamond.

As the money owed Woody remained *en route*, we continued to see the sights and enjoy the pleasures of London. We had more or less agreed that when his money arrived we would travel together, at least as far as Scotland. The Edinburgh Music and Drama Festival would begin in another week, and we both wanted to attend some of the performances.

As we wandered the city we were surprised to see the vast piles of rubble that remained. The Nazi blitz had been so pervasive it would be years before the city was restored to pre-war condition. Considering the overwhelming destruction of their city, the incredible loss of life, and the severe rationing that existed, it was remarkable how cheerful

Londoners remained. Most of those we met had a charming sense of humor, and there was optimism about the future that seemed to defy logic.

At the beginning of August, Woody's money finally arrived. We met at our favorite cafeteria and he greeted me, "Good news, lunch is on me. My money showed up and I'm richer than Croesus!" The next evening I had dinner with Anne Cleary and Mary Lambert, my former shipmates and bicycling friends from what seemed a lifetime ago.

"How did you find me?" I asked.

"Your letter mentioned the Tavistock Hostel," answered Anne, "and the rest was like following a trail of breadcrumbs. In fact, we decided to stay there."

"Unfortunately, I'm leaving London tomorrow," I said. "A friend from Berkeley and I are heading for Scotland."

"What a pity," said Anne. Mary didn't comment. After dinner at the Delhi, which had become one of my favorite spots, Mary said, "I'm going back to the Hostel; you two may want some time alone. Goodbye again, Peter, and good luck with your travels."

"So long, Mary, and no hard feelings." That was her mysterious sendoff to me a few weeks ago, and I was still unsure of its meaning.

"So here we are again," said Anne. We were walking back to the hostel and she put her arm in mine. "Who would have guessed we'd meet so soon?" We entered the gardens of Russell Square. The evening was warm, and the aroma of fresh flowers filled the air. We selected a secluded bench and sat down in the nearly deserted park.

"How have things been going with Mary?" I asked. "Any problems?"

"No, once you left she had me all to herself, and her attitude changed for the better."

"Well, I certainly admire her taste in women."

"You make it sound tacky. You know, there's nothing sexual between us."

"Too bad; she has no idea what she's missing."

Anne frowned but said, "Come closer." As I leaned towards her she embraced me. It brought back memories of our earlier romantic encounters. She must have had the same thoughts, because she suddenly said, "Let's do it, Peter. Let's do it right here, right now."

"Are you crazy? This is London; we could be arrested."

"Only if we're caught. But we won't be caught. Please, Peter, be a good sport."

Good sport? What was she talking about? This wasn't baseball, but it seemed to be a game to her. Apparently, all she wanted was one more sizzling page in her diary. On the other hand, wasn't this every guy's fantasy—unemotional sex with no strings attached? Well, why not?

We stretched out on the bench, rushed through the preliminaries, and completed the daring act in record time. We sat there quietly, breathing hard and regaining our composure.

"Now wasn't that worth the risk?" she asked. Perhaps it was, but it was impersonal and strangely unsatisfying and there was nothing more I could say.

The following day Woody and I caught a bus for St. Albans. As we left the city of London the sun abruptly appeared. "That's got to be a happy omen," I said. But Woody didn't hear me; he was already asleep—purring softly in his comfortable seat.

CHAPTER SIX

Scotland

Before leaving London I replaced my heavy leather bag with an inexpensive suitcase. Having *schlepped* my heavy bag for over a month, I realized, despite ample warning, I had packed too many clothes. The new case was actually high-grade cardboard, but it was small, lightweight, and far more appropriate for efficient traveling. I also discovered that fashion standards in Europe differed considerably from those in the U.S. If one wore the same outfit every day, week after week—provided one bathed regularly—no one really cared. I sent the excess baggage to Paris, where American Express would store it until my arrival next spring. Now I was really traveling light, but nowhere near as light as Woody, the undisputed travel pro. Almost everything he owned, he wore; and the rest of his possessions fit into an aluminum photographer's case, which was the size of a large briefcase. "Ideally," he said, "one should carry a toothbrush and traveler's cheques." That was the goal to which I aspired.

It was almost a pleasure to lug my new bag as we searched for—and quickly found—an inexpensive room in St. Albans. That afternoon we explored the famous Cathedral and Abbey Church, which dated from Norman times. It was noted for having the longest nave in England. Its history, however, was even more compelling.

St. Alban, after whom the town was named, was Britain's first Christian martyr. He lived an uneventful life in the Roman city of

Verulamium. In those days Early Christians were persecuted for their belief; thus, the local priest feared for his life. Alban befriended the priest and sheltered him in his own home. In return the priest converted Alban to Christianity, which, as it turned out, was a dubious favor. When Roman soldiers came looking for the priest, Alban exchanged identity with the priest and was arrested. He was brought before the Roman magistrate, where he avowed his faith and was summarily condemned to death. According to legend, Alban was beheaded on the hill where the cathedral now stood, and his severed head rolled down to a spot where a well sprang up. What a way to go! He was sainted many years later.

I had plenty of questions. First of all, why would Alban, a Roman citizen, befriend a priest? That was just asking for trouble. Didn't he realize the priest was toxic? And why would he give up his life for this guy? It might be irreverent to ask, but what was going on between these two?

For the life of me, I couldn't shake the image of Alban's head bouncing down the hill. I dreamed about it for weeks. Was his mouth open in horror? Were his eyes able to see? Did his brain even comprehend what was going on? Woody's response was far more pragmatic. "If you ask me, Alban had a few screws loose."

That evening we caught a train for Cambridge, the city known for its famous university. By the time we found a place to stay, it was ten o'clock and dinner was no longer available.

"What say we slow down?" suggested Woody. "Let's sleep in tomorrow." I agreed; it was time for a day of rest. We enjoyed a late, leisurely breakfast and by noon we were punting down the River Cam. It was exactly what we needed. We took turns poling down the river in our rented flat-bottomed boat while viewing the famous Backs of the various colleges. "Now this is what I call touring," said Woody. Fifteen minutes later he was fast asleep.

Like almost everything else in England, Cambridge had a two thousand year-old history. Romans originally settled the area, and the first college dated back to the thirteenth century. The place was dripping with tradition. Former students included dozens of notables, people like Isaac Newton, John Milton, and King George VI. Historical events, whether significant or trivial, were memorialized on brass plaques that were applied like wallpaper. Some seemed utterly frivolous. I mean, who really cared in which specific building Charles Darwin first displayed his extensive beetle collection? Certainly not me.

That afternoon we began a frenetic tour of English medieval cathedrals.

"We can't see them all," I said, "but let's visit as many as possible."

"Nonsense," said Woody. "How will the Fellowship Committee ever know *what* you see or if you see anything at all? Let's say we skip the cathedrals and spend the next month on a Greek island? Who, would know?"

"It's a matter of principle," I replied. "How can I ignore my responsibility to the University? Anyway, the guilt would kill me." I also had to admit that racing around seeing new structures was hardly a burden. Architecture, after all, was one of my true loves. Nevertheless, I thought about Woody's suggestion several times afterwards, and just *contemplating* a month on a Greek island made me feel as guilty as Bonnie and Clyde combined.

Our first stop was Ely, and after a couple of hours we continued to Peterborough. Both structures were built more than seven hundred years earlier by builders who had little more than a few simple hand tools and a great deal of faith. It was utterly inspiring. Our next stop was Lincoln, and by the time our bus arrived, it was ten o'clock and there was not a room to be had.

"What now?" Woody asked. "Do you suppose there's a park with an empty bench?"

"Too cold for that. We'd be frozen by morning. But I once read that the Church of England never closes; its doors are always open to wayfarers. What the hell—we're wayfarers. Why don't we hike up to the Cathedral and curl up in a pew?" That may have been the plan, but pity the poor wayfarer. The place was locked up tighter than a vault at the Bank of England.

"Well, it's too late to go back down the hill," I said. "I think we should stay here."

Thus began one of the most miserable nights of my life. The porch was roofed, but the stone paving was so cold, it was like curling up on a block of ice. We each selected a corner of the porch, sat on our cases, and tried to sleep while leaning against the wall. I quickly fell asleep but was soon shocked into consciousness by the church bells. Each hour on the hour the relentless bells announced the time. It was like Chinese water torture—brutal, painful, and with deafening frequency.

The church doors were unlocked at seven o'clock, and I asked about the nighttime closure. "It used to be open round the clock," said the attendant, "but they gave that up just after the war ended." After touring Lincoln Cathedral, we hiked back down the hill to get some breakfast. Sitting at an adjacent table were two lorry drivers. We noticed their large truck outside.

"Good morning," said Woody. "Where you fellows headed?"

"North," said the older of the two, whom we assumed was the driver.

"Would you care for some company?" asked Woody.

"I've got company," said the driver. "This lad sitting next to me. But if you're looking for a ride, I might be able to help. Just tell me this: are you American or Canadian?"

"American," we answered in unison.

"Good answer," said the driver. "I have an ex-wife in Canada, and I want nothing to do with anything or anybody Canadian." And that's how we ended up in Doncaster, a pleasant town, but one lacking any interest whatsoever.

We remained on the shoulder of the Great North Road, stuck out our thumbs, and immediately scored a ride to York. After a delicious lunch of roast beef and Yorkshire pudding—what else would one eat there—we toured the beautiful town of York and its stunning cathedral. Two more rides and we reached Durham. We found a quaint room in a four-hundred-year-old house run by a small, gray-haired widow by the name of Molly Finch. Both the house and the widow belonged in a folk museum. Electricity was available until an hour after sunset, and candles were used after that. It mattered little; most lights appeared to be less than a full watt. At one point a moth flew in our room, circled the bare bulb, and flew back out in apparent disappointment. The house had no heat, and hot water came from a pot on an ancient coal stove. Molly Finch proclaimed several times, "I wouldn't have a new-fangled gas stove in my kitchen, even as a gift". She appeared firmly rooted in the nineteenth century.

Primitive though the place was, it was remarkably clean and comfortable. We slept wonderfully well and awakened to the aroma of frying sausage. Molly Finch had prepared a delicious breakfast with eggs—our first in over a week—various cheeses and freshly baked bread.

"I've got to say, Mrs. Finch, you sure make a fine breakfast," said Woody. "Maybe we should extend our stay. What do you think, Peter?"

"Perhaps Mrs. Finch would consider adopting us," I suggested. Molly just blushed.

Durham Cathedral was the finest example of early Norman architecture we had seen, and for the first time I recognized the power and simplicity of that style. It was a remarkable experience to wander through this eight-hundred-year-old structure and admire the bold, abstract decoration. But there was little time to linger. By mid-morning we were on our way to Edinburgh. Since it was impossible to go anywhere directly, we soon found ourselves in Newcastle; where we waited another hour for a bus to our final destination.

This is what I found so odd: Though the length of the British Isles was less than that of California, the English perception of distances differed considerably from ours. When an Englishman spoke of a town thirty miles away, he did so with a faraway look in his eye, as if the town were on another planet. It was a provincialism that developed more than a thousand years earlier when England consisted of independent kingdoms. This same provincialism affected our ability to obtain reliable information. The English were generous with their help, but unless the information we sought concerned something within a one-mile radius, it was invariably wrong.

During the next five hours we passed through some of the loveliest scenery imaginable. The skies were clear, and the wildflowers, green hills, and heather-covered fields produced one exceptional sight after another.

Upon our arrival in Edinburgh we checked into the Scottish Youth Hostel. The Festival was in full swing, and the town was as crowded as Piccadilly Circus. That evening we attended an exhibition of Scottish Highland dances accompanied by a bagpipe band. I had no idea that I'd find bagpipe music irresistible. I just couldn't get enough of it.

"I don't get it," said Woody. "That stuff sounds like geese being strangled. Hell, it's nearly as bad as accordian music."

"Hate to admit it," I said, "but I love that too."

We soon discovered that our Hostel had no hot water, and what flowed from the tap was a couple of degrees above freezing.

"That's what you get for thirty-five cents a night," said Woody. "No wonder so many British men have beards; ice water discourages shaving."

It occurred to me weeks earlier that the principal difference between our cultures was not the language or even the stiff-upper-lip tolerance for suffering; it was the plumbing! While in London, I discovered that an Englishman, Thomas Crapper—a name one could not possibly make up—invented the flush toilet. Others claimed it was Sir John Harrington. When you realize that one refers to the appliance—in the vernacular—as both a "crapper" and a "john" you might think: So what—who cares?

Personally, I give all credit to Mr. Crapper, because his is simply a better name. However, I wish he would have taken one more step in that innovative direction and made it easy for one to wash his hands or—God forbid—take a shower.

After two days we were forced to leave the Hostel, because the director claimed every bed was previous booked by other students.

"I thought you couldn't reserve accommodations," I said.

"Not normally," answered the director, "but during the Festival the rules change."

"So what are we supposed to do now?" asked Woody.

"You might try the YMCA," the director replied, but it was clearly not *his* problem.

Our nightly fee leaped to forty-five cents, but suddenly we had an endless stream of hot water! Hallelujah! Had we known that, we wouldn't have bothered with the Hostel in the first place.

We spent half of the next day arranging passage to Norway. The only way to get there was from the port at Newcastle. Since every ship that week was completely booked, we ultimately purchased third-class tickets to Bergen for the following week.

During the next few days we experienced the beauty and charm of Edinburgh. The city's main thoroughfare, Princes Street, had shops on one side, while a park on the opposite side led to a sloping hillside crowned by the elaborate Edinburgh Castle. It was a majestic sight. The Scots were friendly and helpful and often displayed a charming sense of humor. And although they claimed to be speaking English, we often had doubts. Specialties of this area included tweeds and cashmere goods. I purchased a cashmere scarf, and in coming, cooler months, I would be thankful I did.

Another student at the YMCA suggested we attend the Highland Games. He said, "You're going to love it." What we saw was essentially Highland dancing, a track meet, a bagpipe competition, bicycle races, and several marching bands. It was an odd blend of the Olympics and a three-ring circus, with athletes vying for attention with entertainment stars. What an exciting and colorful afternoon! That evening we attended a performance of the Sadler's Wells ballet company starring Margot Fonteyn. The following evening we saw another spectacular event called the Tattoo. It took place on the Castle grounds and was reminiscent of a Cecil B. DeMille production. Participating were eight pipe bands in full kilts, the RAF marching band, and the Royal French Guard riding horses and playing hunting horns—an incredible feat in itself. All this music and marching took place under floodlights, and the sounds and colors were extraordinary.

The next day we caught an early bus to Glasgow and spent the day touring the famous lakes, including Loch Ness. It was a rare, sunny day, and the surrounding hills were covered with lush foliage as well as a profusion of cows and sheep. The animals seemed to be everywhere, including, quite often, the middle of the road. That evening, our last in Edinburgh, we attended a performance of Swan Lake by the New York City Ballet. It was the finest company I had ever seen. We were fortunate to see so many wonderful Festival events, and all credit went to the people at the YMCA. Every performance was sold out weeks before the Festival began, so our tickets were cancellations acquired by the Y and resold to students.

In the cold rain of the following morning we took a train to Newcastle, where our ship to Norway was docked. We boarded the M.S. Venus, flagship of the Bergen Steamship Company, found our dormitory room, and settled in for the overnight voyage across the North Sea. It had been a month since landing in Southampton, and I was finally leaving the island.

"I love crossing borders," said Woody; "it's like a new beginning."

Indeed it was. We were off to a genuinely foreign country—a country about which we knew little and in which neither of us could speak a single word of the language. Nor could we possibly anticipate the remarkable adventure we were about to experience.

CHAPTER SEVEN

Norway

The M.S. Venus left port as the cold rain continued, and within an hour a violent storm assaulted our ship. Torrential rains, winds, and huge swells crashing over our bow made it perilous to remain on deck. The Venus rolled, pitched, and bounced about like a cork in a washing machine. Several passengers, as well as some crewmembers, began to feel queasy and took to their bunks. Oddly, I felt well enough to attempt dinner. The dining room was about one-quarter full, which was fortunate, as only a handful of waiters were able to work. I shared a large table with three Australian students, two young women and an uncomfortable-looking man. Just as the soup course was served, the young man excused himself and was not seen again.

"Rupert is the sensitive one in our group," said the young woman named Claire. She was tall, attractive, and emitted an aura of energy and confidence.

"Rough seas are indiscriminate," I replied. "Even Horatio Nelson would have trouble with today's weather."

"I think this is rather fun," said Jane, the other member of our group. "After all, we were hoping for an adventure, and what's more exciting than a storm at sea?" Jane exhibited a relentlessly cheerful disposition, but appeared a bit vacant. The next course served was steak and kidney pudding; but before taking a bite, Claire made her exit. She suddenly became pale and said, "I must leave now. Sorry." And then she was gone.

"Which of us is next?" I asked a bit nervously.

"Not me," Jane replied. "I have no intention of becoming ill."

"Let's hope for the best," I said, "but look around; we *are* in the middle of a nasty storm. I wouldn't bet against the odds of us joining Rupert and Claire."

Just then the ship rolled, and glassware flew off the next table and went crashing to the floor.

"This is becoming dangerous," I said.

"Oh, nonsense," answered Jane, ignoring the obvious. "This is thrilling."

Moments later there was an enormous clatter from the pantry as dishes and glasses flew off their shelves. Almost simultaneously our dinner plates jumped from the table and landed in a heap a few feet away. Waiters rushed about the room cleaning up debris and trying to maintain order, but it was a futile battle. The erratic lurching of the ship knocked down waiters, passengers, and furniture alike. Ultimately, we were hanging on to the table for survival.

"Had enough thrills yet?" I asked. Jane suddenly appeared a bit more frightened. Her perpetual smile vanished, as our predicament slowly penetrated the shallow recesses of her mind.

"Perhaps you're right," she said. "We might be safer in our rooms." She arose just as the ship pitched; and, losing her balance, fell in an awkward heap. "I don't feel very well," she said in a weak voice. "Would you help me to my room?" We staggered out of the dining room, but before reaching the deck below, poor Jane lost every morsel she had downed just moments before.

"Oh, God," she moaned, "how embarrassing! I'm sick, really sick. Help me, Peter."

I half-carried her to the women's dormitory, where we found Claire, who looked dreadful.

"We need some help," I said. "Jane is in terrible shape."

"*Everyone's* in terrible shape," she answered. "This place is like an infirmary."

Persistent moans of discomfort filled the room, and the aroma of nausea was enough to make one ill. I left the ladies and headed for the deck above to get some fresh air. I was beginning to feel a bit queasy myself. The ship was jumping about so vigorously it was difficult to maintain my balance. I made it to the rail where I was drenched by a surge of water blowing off the sea. I clung to the rail gasping for air; and—without warning—violently expelled my dinner into the sea. My retching continued long after there was nothing more to throw up. As a merchant seaman, some years earlier, I survived several storms at sea, including a hurricane off the Brazilian coast; and I was familiar with the discomfort of seasickness. But nothing I suffered before seemed as dreadful as this North Sea storm.

While grasping the rail I heard a voice yell in English, "For God's sake, man, get away from the rail; you could be washed overboard!" It was a Norwegian deck hand.

"You'll have to excuse me; I'm busy throwing up."

"Well, do it below deck," he ordered. "It's dangerous up here."

When I reached the men's dormitory, the stench of nausea hit me like a cloud of poison gas. I couldn't find Woody and I certainly couldn't remain in that miserable snake pit, so I went back on deck to breathe some fresh air. I suddenly saw Woody hanging on to a cable near the bow.

"What the hell are you doing here?" I asked. "This is dangerous."

"This whole damn ship is dangerous," he answered. "But an old seaman told me to stand near the bow, as close as possible to the middle of the ship. I'm soaked and freezing, but not yet sick. You, on the other hand, look terrible. How are you feeling?"

"Nothing left to throw up, so I guess I'm okay. But this storm is getting worse. I don't know how long I can stay out here."

Thirty minutes later, soaked by rain and frozen from the icy wind, I retreated to the ship's lounge. The room was littered with suffering passengers, but it was warm, dry, and considerably more bearable than the dormitory. I spent the remainder if the night there listening to the moans of fellow passengers and creaking of the ship, as the endless pitching and rolling continued.

By the gray light of dawn I found that nearly every passenger was seriously ill and miserably unhappy. The Purser announced that breakfast would not be served, and nobody seemed to care. The storm abated late in the morning, but by then the damage was done; the M.S. Venus was in shambles. Land was sighted a short time later, and the joy of that announcement must have rivaled the centuries-old reaction of every seaman aboard the Niña, Pinta, and Santa Maria.

We arrived in Bergen two hours late, a new and unenviable record for the Bergen Steamship Company. There was a cold drizzle falling, but it looked to us like a tropical paradise. Passengers rushed down the gangway, happy to escape the floating torture chamber and feel again land beneath their feet. As we were leaving I heard someone refer to our ship as the *Vomiting Venus*, and the nickname stuck. I bumped into Rupert, Claire, and Jane in the Customs Office. Looking ill and bedraggled, Claire proclaimed, "When our holiday is over, we're flying back to England. No more Vomiting Venus for us ever again!"

Woody and I headed towards town and took a funicular up a mountainside to the Bergen Youth Hostel. The Hostel was situated a thousand feet above the city in a beautiful, heavily wooded area. The small, pine-covered structure appeared like a remote mountain camp, complete with outdoor plumbing. We had a cup of hot tea and sat in the lounge before a roaring fire. Staring at the light rain outside we sat quietly, and, for the first time in over twenty-four hours, began to relax.

"I never want to do that again," Woody said. "That was brutal!"

"The absolute worst," I answered. "What a treat to sit here quietly without the floor moving. But my stomach is still not right."

"Let's skip dinner and get some sleep," suggested Woody. "I didn't sleep at all last night."

We awoke ten hours later in a room that was a few degrees above freezing. As the endless rain continued, we explored the charming town of Bergen. We visited the old city, the famous fish market, and, near the outskirts of the city, a nine-hundred-year-old stave church. The church was constructed entirely of wood and was in a remarkable state of preservation.

Our plan was to go directly to Oslo, but a British professor we met at the hostel that evening persuaded us that a visit to the fjords was an absolute must. He even outlined our itinerary. The next morning we headed for the quaint village of Gudvangen. Moments after leaving Bergen the sun appeared, and the trip through forests and lakes was stunning. Among the dozen or so buildings in Gudvangen was a Youth Hostel, where we had dinner and shared a room that night with two British students, the only other people there. The dinner was buffet style and included all varieties of fish, sausages, cheeses, pâtés, and several kinds of bread—all this for about forty cents. We ate steadily for over an hour. Told that breakfast was the same price as dinner, we could not imagine how the two meals could cost the same. The answer was revealed the next morning, when we discovered it was precisely the same buffet.

Our Hostel had no hot water or electricity, but the spectacular scenery made up for much of the discomfort. We were situated on the Naerøyfjord with sheer mountains rising on both sides and small waterfalls everywhere. It was incredibly dramatic. We boarded a boat the next morning and spent two hours sailing down the narrow channel of water, hemmed in on both sides by sheer cliffs topped with snow. We arrived at Aurland late in the day, just as the rain reappeared. It continued to rain the entire afternoon, so we sat in the cozy lounge of our Hostel listening to American programs on the Armed Forces Radio Network. An amiable Norwegian couple ran the Hostel, and we were the only two guests that night. Nevertheless, they prepared a wonderful dinner of fresh fish, homegrown vegetables, and a lingonberry torte. I slept more soundly that night than I had since leaving home.

We spent the following day traveling to Oslo. We caught the Bergen-Oslo Express at Myrdal and began one of the most beautiful train rides in the world. The nine-hour trip comprised forests, lakes, waterfalls, glaciers, and rivers. We also saw small farms with herds of cows, sheep, and goats, as well as occasional patches of snow. It was a spectacular visual treat. The long journey provided an opportunity for conversation with Woody.

"Let's talk about our plans," I began. "When we left London we figured we'd travel together as far as Scotland. Now here we are in Norway, heading for Sweden. I'm happy to be traveling with you, but I'm curious about your plans after Scandinavia."

"You probably know by now I don't plan too far ahead," Woody began, "but here's what I think. It's September, and I figure my money will hold out until early next year. By then, I'll have to go home." He paused, as if recalling the past few weeks. "I have to say it's been great traveling with you, and I'd like it to continue. Why don't we stick together for the next few months and hope for more of the same?"

I could not have agreed more! So Marion James Elwood and Peter Newman, two young architecture students, agreed to remain partners in adventure while riding the Bergen-Oslo Express on an autumn afternoon in 1952. It turned out to be one of the wisest decisions either of us ever made.

At about the halfway point of our journey, Woody brought up the subject of lunch.

"I doubt if we stop before Oslo," I said. "This is an express. But maybe there's a dining car on the train. I'll check it out." I left our third-class compartment and headed towards the first-class cars. Before reaching the end of our car I heard someone call my name. Just three compartments away from us were Claire and Jane, the two Aussie girls from the Vomiting Venus.

"What a pleasant surprise!" I said. "It's great to see you. But where's Rupert?"

"Rupert returned to England," said Claire. "He was so distressed by our North Sea crossing he decided to stay with relatives in Newcastle until we return. Like I said, he's the sensitive one."

"Too bad," I said. "Listen, I was just going to find some lunch; can I get you anything?"

"Oh," said Claire, "don't go to the dining car. Their prices are outrageous, and the food looks awful. Stay here; we have plenty to eat."

"Even enough for my traveling companion?"

When Woody and I returned to their compartment, the girls were pulling out of their immense backpacks enough food to feed a regiment. It was apparently typical for traveling Australians to carry on their backs every convenience of home. I almost expected they would next pull out a waffle iron or upright vacuum cleaner. Woody contributed a large chocolate bar, and the spontaneous picnic lasted for the remainder of the trip.

As in Bergen, the Oslo Hostel was situated high above the city in a former ski-hut. It was large, reasonably comfortable, and featured heat and running water. It was also filled with students from around the world. We began our tour of Oslo with a visit to the Bygdøy peninsula, site of three, fascinating nautical museums. The first of these housed ancient Viking ships that dated from the ninth century. The second museum contained The Kon-Tiki, Thor Heyerdahl's rafts and other items from his famous expeditions. Finally, the Fram Museum featured the ship Amundsen sailed during his exploration of the South Pole. We also visited an outdoor folk museum that contained two-hundred-year-old wooden houses. That fascinating excursion took the entire day.

"What's up for today?" Woody asked the next morning.

"We're going to see one of Erich Mendelsohn's friends," I answered. "I have a letter of introduction to Olaf Platou."

"Is he a Norwegian architect?" asked Woody. "I've never heard of him."

"I think he's pretty well known around here, and I'm sure he's never heard of us either."

Platou greeted us warmly. "Tell me," he said in perfect, unaccented English, "how is my old friend Mendelsohn? When I last saw him he appeared quite heavy."

"That hasn't changed," I answered. "He still loves food nearly as much as architecture."

"It's not healthy to weigh so much," said Platou, who stood over six feet tall and was fashionably slender. It occurred to me that thin people were often contemptuous of overweight people, as if the world would be a far better place if only they ate less.

Platou had planned our day, which began with a city tour conducted by a young staff member named Edvard Bang. Like most Norwegians, male and female, Edvard was tall and slender, blond and blue-eyed, and very good-looking. We were driven around town in a chauffeured limousine and shown every significant piece of architecture, including sites from the Winter Olympics held earlier that year. We stopped for a late lunch at an elegant fish restaurant where Platou awaited us.

"Has everything been satisfactory?" he asked.

"Everything has been more than we hoped for," I answered.

After we were seated, Platou said, "Don't bother with the menu; you must absolutely have the boiled trout. This place is famous for trout."

"How do you feel about boiled trout?" I whispered to Woody.

"It's suddenly my favorite fish."

Our trout was plucked out of a fresh water tank, cooked to perfection, and incredibly delicious. It was one of the best meals I ever had. We finished lunch, thanked Platou and Edvard for their generous hospitality, and returned to our Hostel.

"Do you think we'll ever be as successful as Platou?" asked Woody.

"Probably not," I answered. "And we'll probably never be that tall or good-looking either." The following morning I replaced my suitcase with a small Norwegian rucksack. It was a beauty, with a tubular aluminum frame and light gray canvas trimmed with dark gray leather. I discovered that rucksacks were the popular means of carrying things in Europe. Every schoolchild used one to carry books. I was now one step closer to my goal of toothbrush and passport. The cheap cardboard suitcase, that served me well, was presented to a custodian at the Hostel. This middle-aged matron was so overjoyed she planted a kiss squarely on my lips.

On our last day in Oslo we visited Frogner Park to view the Vigeland sculptures. What an impressive display of one man's life work! There were nearly two hundred pieces consisting of six hundred full-size nude figures. Gustave Vigeland not only produced the sculptures single-handedly, but he designed the park and arranged every piece. The centerpiece was a monolith, which rose nearly fifty feet and contained over a hundred human figures struggling towards heaven. The monolith took fourteen years to complete, and was one of the most remarkable sights in Oslo.

"I'd like to meet some of Vigeland's models," commented Woody. "Have you ever seen such incredible bodies?"

"It sounds like you've seen too much architecture and not enough of the opposite sex. Maybe we can get you a date in Sweden."

"I'm ready," said Woody. "I've heard quite a bit about Swedish beauties."

That evening we boarded an overnight train to Stockholm. Another country, another adventure, and with a little luck, an attractive date for my love-starved traveling companion.

CHAPTER EIGHT

Sweden

Traveling on overnight trains was a great way to save the expense of hotels, but it didn't do much for a good night's rest. The train from Oslo to Stockholm was a case in point. Our third-class compartment was comfortable, but both Norwegian and Swedish customs officers awakened us several times during the night to check our passports. Conductors also randomly roused us to punch our tickets. One conductor, with an obviously defective memory, punched my ticket three times in the span of two hours. We purchased snacks before leaving Oslo, and were amazed at how inexpensive food was. Remarkably, a tube of caviar cost about twenty cents! That was cheaper than toothpaste, and Woody wondered why Norwegians didn't use caviar instead of Colgate.

We arrived in the morning during a miserably cold rainfall. I threw my rucksack on my back and hiked a short distance to the Stockholm Youth Hostel. What a wonderful place! The hostel was a converted three-masted sailing vessel from the nineteenth century that was permanently docked near the center of town. The interiors were paneled in teak, beautifully furnished, and had extraordinary porthole views. There were four bunks in each room, hot water, and even showers. Who could ask for anything more than an elegant yacht of one's own?

Because of the nasty weather, we spent that afternoon touring the nearby Stockholm City Hall, situated on the water not far from our floating hostel. This red brick, eclectic building was considered the masterpiece of architect Ragnar Östberg, who was awarded a gold medal for this structure twenty years earlier. It remained one of Stockholm's most popular national monuments.

We went touring the following day with two other American architectural students, who were also residents of our Hostel. Tim Sutherland and Carl Brody had just graduated from the University of Michigan and were exploring the architectural wonders of the world, as Woody and I were doing. The four of us met over breakfast and became friends almost immediately. Tim was blond, blue-eyed and could easily have passed for a native Swede, while Carl was tall, pleasant-looking, and seemed the more assertive of the two.

"Where are you off to today?" asked Carl.

"We're following Peter's personal list of important architecture," answered Woody. "If you haven't a better plan, why don't you tag along?"

"Have you included Asplund's Crematorium?" asked Tim.

"Of course." I said, "It's at the top of the list." That apparently convinced them.

During World War II, Sweden remained neutral, because as its Prime Minister declared, *We look on no one as an enemy, and we are determined to remain uninvolved in the conflicts of others*". Sweden sent humanitarian aid to Denmark and Finland, but they also supplied Germany with steel and other critical supplies. Winston Churchill saw the Swedish position of neutrality as cowardice. He claimed, *"Sweden ignored the greater moral issue and played both sides for profit"*. When we visited other Scandinavian countries we discovered that residual resentment toward Sweden was still widespread.

No European country had an easy time during the war, but Sweden didn't experience an occupation or suffer nearly as seriously as her neighbors. As a result, the country emerged from the war in relatively sound financial shape, permitting government leaders to invest in projects beneficial to the general population. These included some of the finest apartments, hospitals, and sanitariums the world had ever seen. We spent most of the day viewing these modern structures.

Finally, we came to Gunnar Asplund's masterpiece, the famous Crematorium. What an awesome monument! The elegant structure stood on rising ground with lawns, a pool, and thick foliage as background. A large, solitary cross was perfectly placed in the composition as an indication to the entrance. Rarely had architecture and landscaping blended so perfectly.

"So much better than the photos," said Tim. We all agreed.

By late afternoon we returned to the Hostel. It was time for me to telephone Henry Bergmann, a business associate of my uncle in Chicago. I didn't particularly want to call him, and I tried to discourage my uncle when he proposed the meeting, but he was insistent. The problem was this: I could not believe that my least favorite uncle, one of the most boring people on earth, knew anyone, anywhere, who was even remotely interesting. As it turned out, I was terribly mistaken.

"Delighted to hear from you," said Bergmann. "You uncle wrote and asked if I would look out for you. So here is what we've planned. Tomorrow you will come to our house for dinner, and tonight I will arrange for you to accompany my niece to the opera. I hope you like *Madame Butterfly*—that's the opera, not my niece," he chuckled. "Her name is Monika Eklund."

I was a bit overwhelmed by Bergmann's plan; it was far more than I expected. Then I thought: *What's the catch? Why the opera? What's wrong with the niece? Probably not much to look at—hasn't been out of the house in months—couldn't get a date if her life depended on it. My success rate on blind dates was close to zero. Why would this be different?*

I reluctantly called the number Bergmann gave me, and a pleasant voice answered.

"Hello," I began, "This is Peter Newman, an acquaintance of Henry Bergmann. I'm looking for Monika Eklund. I hope you speak English; I don't know a single word of Swedish."

I heard a delightful laugh as she answered, "I'm Monika, and I speak English well enough." She spoke with the barest trace of an accent. "I'm pleased to speak to you, Mr. Newman. My uncle tells me you are an architect traveling in Europe. But I don't know much more about you."

"Please, call me Peter," I said.

"All right, Peter. Did my uncle tell you what he's planned?"

"He mentioned *Madame Butterfly*."

"That's right; but first, I hope you can come here for an early meal."

She's throwing in a meal? God help me, she must look like Quasimodo!

I arrived at Monika Eklund's apartment at the appointed time with a small bunch of daisies I purchased along the way. When the door opened I was speechless. Standing before me was a stunning young woman. *Wait a minute, this can't be Monika. This is her roommate—or a friend—or maybe I have the wrong apartment.* Whoever she was, I could not take my eyes off her. She had dark hair, blue eyes, and she wore a short black dress that complimented her flawless figure. Around her throat was a silver chain that matched a band of the same design on her wrist.

"Are you Monika?" I asked with some trepidation.

"Yes, and you must be Peter. I'm so pleased to meet you."

"I can assure you, the pleasure is mine." But then my mind went blank; I couldn't think of another thing to say. After an awkward pause I held out the flowers and said, "These are for you."

"Oh how lovely," she said, "and how thoughtful. I love daisies."

I could not believe how misguided my negative fantasies had been. Even my least favorite uncle suddenly seemed less boring. We went into the living room where Monika had arranged a small feast of open-face sandwiches and pastries.

"I've chilled a bottle of champagne," she said. "Will you join me in a drink?"

"To new friends," she said as she lifted her glass. "*Skål!*" We ate and chatted for the next hour, and I learned that Monika was a first-year student at the Royal Medical School in Stockholm. She intended to become a pediatrician. "A difficult but satisfying career path," she said.

"Beautiful and bright," I commented, "and the best open-face sandwich maker I've ever met. I'm really impressed."

"Oh please, you're making me blush," she said. "What about you? Architect, fellowship student, good-looking American; you're not exactly *köttfärs,* as we say."

"Excuse me?"

"That means minced meat. But enough of this mutual admiration; we have an opera to see."

I had seen few operas in my life, but I did attend a production of *Madame Butterfly* two years before in San Francisco. As the curtain rose and the orchestra began to play I recalled that emotional experience. The Puccini opera is basically a tragedy, summarized as girl wins boy—girl loses boy—girl commits suicide. The girl, Cio-Cio San, is a fragile and unworldly teenager living in Nagasaki. Pinkerton, an American Naval Officer and classic cad, pursues and finally marries her. Almost immediately, Pinkerton must sail away. He returns three years later with an American wife, unaware that Cio-Cio San has borne his baby. Distraught with grief, Cho-Cho San commits hara-kiri. Like I said, the story is a classic tragedy; not the sort of thing that sends you tap dancing out of the theater.

The production of the Royal Swedish Opera Company could not have been better. The arias of love and loss, hope and despair, yearning and pain, were magnificently sung; and by the time Cio-Cio San lay dying, there was not a dry eye in the house. At several tense moments during the performance Monika reached for my hand, and as the curtain fell, tears ran down her cheeks.

"That was so sad," she said. "I hope that dreadful Pinkerton suffered a miserable life."

"I'm sure he did," I said. "But you know, not all Americans are like that."

"I'm sure *you're* not," she said.

When we arrived at Monika's apartment, she said, "Let me make you some coffee." We sat quietly sipping our drinks until she said, "I feel we've shared a special and intimate experience this evening. But now I must say goodnight; I have an early appointment tomorrow." She leaned towards me, put her hand on my face, and gently kissed me.

"Thank you for tonight," she said. "I really enjoyed being with you."

"And I with you," I answered. "But please, just one more kiss."

As we embraced I felt every curve of her body press against mine. Never before had I been kissed like that. It was warm and intimate and I knew I would never forget it.

When I returned to the hostel I found the gate to the pier locked. It was two hours after curfew, a fact I had completely forgotten. I walked back to the center of town and headed for the elegant Grand Hotel. It was after midnight, getting cold, and I figured I'd get some rest in the hotel lobby. Paying for a room was out of the question. I sank into a comfortable chair and almost immediately fell asleep. Moments later I was awakened by a hotel porter.

"I'm sorry, sir, you cannot sleep here. Can I help you?"

"I'm waiting for a friend." I said.

"Is your friend staying here?"

"He's arriving tonight, and I promised to meet him."

"May I have his name?"

Without hesitation I answered, "Marion Elwood." The porter left but returned a moment later and said, "I'm afraid no one by that name is registered here."

"Perhaps he's arriving without a reservation," I said.

"We're fully booked, sir. There is no room for your friend."

"Well, do you mind if I wait to give him the bad news?"

"Sorry sir, I'm afraid you must leave."

It was clear I would lose this argument. I arose and said, with just the right degree of bitterness, "When I see Mr. Elwood I will describe to him the callous treatment I received at the Grand Hotel. I doubt that he will ever stay here again. And, by the way, this is the last you will see of me as well. Good night, my good man, and thank you—for nothing!"

I felt better berating the poor employee, but it was a hollow victory; I had nowhere to go. I walked to a nearby park, lay down on a wooden bench, and attempted to sleep. It was useless; the temperature was close to freezing, and I was wearing my only lightweight tweed suit. Four hours later the gate to the Hostel was unlocked, and I fell into bed. Two hours later Woody awakened me.

"That must have been some date last night," he said.

"The date was wonderful, but I spent most of the night on a cold park bench."

"Well, that's too bad, but we've got to get going. Today we're visiting Skansen."

Skansen, located on its own small island and covering some seventy-five acres, was the world's largest outdoor museum. It contained a park, open-air zoo, aquarium, and a full replica of a mid-nineteenth century village. More than a hundred and fifty actual farmhouses, manor houses, and shops were relocated there. We spent the day marveling at the native architecture.

Early in the evening the hostel director knocked on our door to announce I had a guest. I went to the lounge and was surprised to see Monika, who looked absolutely stunning.

"What a wonderful surprise," I said. "I wasn't expecting you."

"I came to take you to my uncle's house for dinner. I hope you didn't forget."

"Not at all, but I didn't realize I would have an attractive escort. I'll get my coat." Woody returned with me to the lounge, and I introduced him to Monika.

"Delighted to meet you," he said. "Peter has spoken about you all day. You obviously impressed him, and now I can see why."

"I'm glad to know that," Monica answered. "I thought I was the only one who couldn't stop thinking about last night. Incidentally, Peter told me you were interested in meeting a Swedish girl. I spoke to my friend, Inga Olsson, this morning, and she is eager to meet an American architect. I think you two would get along well. Here is her number."

"Thanks," said Woody, "that's very nice of you. And, Peter, don't forget the curfew."

A bit later Monika asked about Woody's warning. "What did he mean about the curfew?"

"I forgot about it last night, and when I got back here, the hostel was closed."

"What did you do?"

Ignoring the embarrassing episode at the Grand Hotel, I said, "I ended up on a park bench."

"Oh, you poor dear! Why didn't you come back to my apartment?"

"I thought that might be presumptuous. We'd only known each other a few hours."

We arrived at Henry Bergmann's house and were greeted like long-lost relatives, though only one of us was. "Tell me about your uncle," said Henry. "Is he well?"

"Quite well, thank you, and he sends warmest regards to you." Henry and his wife, Olga, had no children, but they treated Monika like a daughter. The four of us enjoyed drinks and a delicious dinner their cook had prepared. The conversation was lively as we discussed last night's opera, Monika's classes at medical school, and world affairs. Henry asked about my uncle's dental supply business, the matter that initially brought the two of them together. I suddenly realized I knew nothing about that subject, because my uncle and his business held such little interest for me.

"I hear everything is going well," I said, "but, quite honestly, I don't know much about it."

Monika and I sat together, occasionally holding hands, and the evening could not have been more enjoyable. I realized that, were it not for my boring uncle, none of this would be happening. That, of course, made me feel guilty, but not guilty enough to ruin the evening.

When we got to Monika's apartment it was more than an hour past my hostel's curfew. Facing another sleepless night on a frigid park bench was a daunting prospect, but happily, my charming companion came to my rescue.

"You will stay here tonight," she said. "I cannot bear the idea of you freezing to death. I hope you don't mind the couch. Guests have told me it's really quite comfortable."

"Right now I wouldn't trade your couch for the presidential suite at the Grand Hotel."

Monika prepared the couch, fluffed the pillow, and said, "I'll be back to tuck you in."

As I lay there staring at the ceiling, the ghostly image of Deborah Wolfe spoke to me.

Holy moly, Peter, you are incorrigible! Honest to goodness, I think the center of all reason has settled in your crotch. I tried to ignore your flirtation with Anne Cleary. I understood when she seduced you at Bucklers Hard, but why did you compound the offense in Romsey? And that episode in Russell Square was shocking! What were you thinking? What if you had been caught? And now, my misguided friend, what are your intentions with Monika Eklund? Are you carrying on just to forget me? Is that what this is, a feeble attempt to erase me from your consciousness? Well, is it?

"No, no, not at all," I exclaimed aloud. "That's not it at all."

"Not what?" asked Monica, who suddenly appeared like a vision in a short nightgown.

"Oh, nothing," I answered. "It was just a fantasy conversation with an old friend."

"Are you all right?" she asked. "You seem unsettled."

"I'm fine; and I'm delighted to be here with you. Really, I'm okay."

"Good," she said, "because I've come to kiss you goodnight."

She turned down the light, sat on the edge of the couch, and we embraced.

"I'm glad you're here," she said. "So very glad." She pulled back the covers, lay down beside me and I suddenly stopped thinking about Deborah Wolfe. I was transported to another time and another place, a place very close to paradise.

I returned to the hostel moments after Woody arrived. "It looks like you had a nice evening," I said. "The smile is still on your face."

"Let me tell you about Inga Olsson," he said. "She is beautiful, bright, and best of all, she loves architects—especially American architects."

"That seems to be a common condition among Swedish women."

On our last full day in Stockholm we toured several modern residential projects. Much of the design was at a high level, but oddly, none of the architecture was outstanding. We returned to the Hostel, where I found a message from Henry Bergmann.

"I was going to call," I said, "to thank you for the wonderful dinner last night, and especially, for introducing me to your beautiful niece."

"My niece, in fact, is the reason I called," he said. "Since her parents died, she has become like a daughter to us, and we are concerned about well her being. You may not be aware, but Monika is engaged to a young man who is currently in Germany. I know she has feelings for you, but I do not wish to see her hurt. My question, therefore, is: What are your intentions?"

Intentions? What intentions? What's he talking about? My only intentions involved my fellowship and avoiding problems like the one I saw looming above me like a falling meteor.

"I like your niece, Henry, I like her very much; but I don't know if we have a future. I'm obliged to complete my travels; that comes first. Incidentally, she never mentioned being engaged."

"I don't know why she kept that from you. Could she have doubts? Is she unsure? This is becoming complicated. Perhaps I should just mind my own business."

I breathed a sigh of relief; Henry Bergmann had apparently solved his dilemma. Now, I wondered, how Monika would solve hers?

The following morning Woody and I caught a ship to Helsinki. Our new architect friends from Michigan, Tim Sutherland and Carl Brody, accompanied us. As we reached the dock I saw Monika Eklund, who had come to say goodbye. She ran to meet me, and we embraced.

"I wish you wouldn't go," she said. "I'm just getting to know you."

"I have no choice," I answered. "But if I did remain, it might get complicated. I spoke to your uncle yesterday, and he mentioned another person in your life—someone, he said, to whom you're engaged."

"There is someone else," she said, "someone I've known since we were children. But we're not actually engaged, I don't really love him, and worse yet—he's not you. Anyway, I don't plan to marry before completing medical school, and that's a long time from now."

"It's been wonderful to know you," I said. "I hope our paths cross again."

"Write to me," she said, "and tell me how you're doing. I'll answer every letter."

We held each other close and then we kissed. It was a kiss filled with love and regret and the sadness of separation. She looked as though she might cry, and I said, "Don't be sad. I want to remember you smiling your beautiful smile. It's something I'll never forget."

Our boat sailed into the Baltic Sea, and she remained on the dock until we could no longer see one another. I had no idea what was happening, but I suddenly felt a great loss.

CHAPTER NINE

Finland

Approaching Helsinki from the sea was an absolute thrill. It was a clear, cold morning, and the white stone buildings glistened in the sun. That morning also happened to be my twenty-fourth birthday. We were sitting in the ship's lounge, where we spent the night to avoid the expense of a private cabin. Woody, Carl, and Tim lifted their coffee mugs and proposed a toast. "To Peter," Woody began. "Congratulations on your special day, and may you always be surrounded by distinguished, handsome, and extraordinarily gifted architects." The others said, "Here, here! Distinguished, handsome, gifted. Right you are, Woody!"

"Thanks, fellows," I said a bit cynically. "Your modest words warm my heart."

After docking we walked to the nearby youth hostel. It was inexpensive, as usual, but more austere than previous ones. Nevertheless, it had adequate heating, which had recently become a matter of survival. According to the calendar, it was not quite autumn, but the temperature at night hovered around freezing.

Unlike Sweden, there were few English speakers among the Finns. Worse yet, their language was largely incomprehensible. The director of the hostel said, "The most analogous language is probably Hungarian." He might just as well have said Swahili. He also said to me, somewhat frivolously, "There are only two phrases you really should know, and they are *Minum nmeni on Petri*, and *Rakastan sinua*. The first phrase means, 'My name is Peter', and the second phrase means, 'I love you'. It is most effective if you say the two together—preferably to a woman."

Very funny, I thought, *but right now the last thing I need is another love in my life.*

While in Sweden we heard stories about the currency black market that operated in Finland, and one of our first goals was to locate that market. Controls established by most countries during the war years resulted in black markets nearly everywhere. Even in the U.S., after wartime rationing began, black market meat, sugar, and gasoline were available to those willing to pay the higher price and risk the legal penalties. Currency black markets operated in much the same way. All black markets were illegal, but they were universally popular.

The official rate of exchange in Finland was two hundred thirty Finnish marks to the dollar. In Stockholm we were offered three hundred, but within a half hour I found a young taxi driver who offered us three hundred fifty marks for one dollar! It felt like we had just robbed a bank.

"Are you going to Denmark?" asked the taxi driver. When I said we were, he suggested we see his uncle. "My uncle will sell you Danish kroner cheaper than you can get them anywhere, and you'll pay half of what they cost in Denmark. He also sells currency from other countries. And I won't even charge you for the ride."

"What do you think, Woody?"

"Why not?" he answered.

We drove to a seedy part of town, stopped in front of a shabby bar, and our driver led the way inside. "Watch your wallet," whispered Woody. Beyond the bar was a small room, and sitting at a desk in one corner was an elderly man. He wore a threadbare gray suit and a stained white shirt with no tie. His unkempt hair and full beard were completely white.

"This is Uncle Mikko," said the cab driver.

Uncle Mikko stared at us for a moment and then asked rather brusquely, but in perfect English, "What do you want?"

"We understand you sell black market currency here," I answered. He continued to stare.

"Black market? What are you talking about? Are you accusing me of something?"

I didn't know what to say. If Uncle Mikko sold black market money he must have known it was illegal. Why was he pretending to be insulted?

"Sorry, Mikko, but your nephew said you sell Danish kroner."

"He is *not* my nephew," exclaimed the old man.

"That's not the point," I said. "I don't care if you're related or not; can you help us?"

"Perhaps. But I take only dollars. If you don't have dollars, don't waste my time."

I wondered if all black market dealers were this rude. Uncle Mikko was downright hostile. In the end we received double the number of Danish kroner quoted earlier that morning at a nearby bank. Uncle Mikko then suggested we might need other currencies. We had no idea what the official rates of exchange were, but strangely, we trusted this disagreeable old Finn. We bought Deutschmarks, Austrian shillings, and Yugoslavian dinar; and Uncle Mikko assured us these were the best exchange rates this side of Beirut. *What if he's wrong?* I wondered. *What could we possibly do about it?*

When the transaction ended, Uncle Mikko arose and led us to the bar. "Now we drink," he said. He poured a tumbler of vodka for each of us and we clinked glasses. While he drained his drink in one large gulp, Woody and I took a sip and started coughing and wiping our eyes. It was the most powerful drink I ever had. You could have put that stuff in your gas tank. We shook hands with Uncle Mikko, and his so-called nephew drove us back to our hostel. It now felt as though we had more foreign currency than the National Bank of Finland.

That afternoon we began our tour of Finnish architecture. We visited the Helsinki Railway Station, Eliel Saarinen's most famous work and one of Finland's most celebrated monuments. Saarinen and his son, Eero, immigrated to the U.S. before the war, where they became two of the most renowned architects of the modern movement. The architectural tour continued for the next two days and included visits to the Olympic Stadium, as well as several modern schools, hospitals, and other public buildings.

Before leaving Helsinki, Woody decided that his belated birthday gift to me would be a visit to an authentic Finnish sauna.

"We could both use a scrubbing," he said, "and I hear that a sauna is quite an adventure." As it turned out, that was a monumental understatement.

We went to a public sauna recommended by the director of our hostel. After Woody paid the fee, we received locker keys and towels. We hung our clothes, wrapped the towel around us, and proceeded to the enclosed sauna room. The room consisted of rising tiers of wooden benches that surrounded a pile of heated rocks. Every so often an attendant threw cold water on the rocks, which produced clouds of superheated steam. As we entered the room we were blinded by the fog, shocked by the heat, and hit in the stomach by the lack of oxygen.

"Holy shit," exclaimed Woody. "I can't see and I can't breathe!" The attendant led us to a low-level wooden bench, where we sat gasping for breath.

"What have I gotten us into?" asked Woody.

I could barely answer; the heat was making me dizzy. Within five minutes perspiration was streaming from every pore, from toes to scalp.

I held my head as close to the floor as possible, but there was no more oxygen at floor level than there was a few feet higher. Ten minutes later the attendant encouraged us to move to a higher bench, one closer to the ceiling, where our heads were literally in the clouds. All the while, two older men, assumed to be natives, sat quietly with their eyes closed at the topmost bench opposite us.

"Do you think they're alive?" asked Woody.

"Hard to tell," I answered. "Try pinching one?"

"You first."

After a half hour my blood was at the boiling point. "I surrender," I said. "I've got to get out of here." I made a sign to the attendant, and he led me to the door. Woody staggered out behind me. It felt like we had just walked out of an oven and into a refrigerator. As we stood quietly regaining our breath, the female equivalent of a Japanese sumo wrestler approached. She was wearing a large apron, rubber boots, and had a colorful scarf tied around her head. She spoke no English but pointed to a badge indicating her name was Akka. Though we were nearly naked, there was little embarrassment. Akka was at least sixty years old, substantially overweight, and completely sexless. We followed her like two wilted sheep as she led us to a large swimming pool. With a gentle shove from Akka, we suddenly found ourselves plunged into ice water. Ice water! I had heard that Finns loved to roll around in the snow after their saunas, but I figured that was a myth. Boy, was I wrong!

"Holy shit!" shouted Woody. "I think I just heard my heart crack."

"This is not funny," I said. "This is definitely not funny!"

We paddled as quickly as possible to the edge of the pool, and the corpulent sadist helped us out. She continued to smile and speak to us in Finnish, not a single word of which we understood. She then led us to a wooden bench, where she indicated we should sit. Using a large brush and sponge, she scrubbed each of us more vigorously than we had ever been scrubbed before. She scoured every surface and every cavity until I thought my skin was permanently damaged. Since all dignity had vanished long before, we sat back unselfconsciously and tried to keep from whimpering. After the scrubbing, Akka picked up a common garden hose and washed away every trace of lather. By this time we were feeling like two wet noodles, but the treatment was not quite over. We were next led to the showers.

"No more ice water," shouted Woody. "Please, God, no more ice water!"

But the water was warm—warm and delicious—and I stood there for ten more minutes. We dried off, spent a few more marks and rented cots for the next few hours. We slept until it was dark and time for dinner. It would be another day before I fully regained my energy, but I had not been as sparkling clean or so thoroughly sanitized since I was one week old.

Woody and I took a bus to Turku the following morning to tour some early Alvar Aalto buildings. Aalto was the most prolific Finnish architect and a leading proponent of the International Style. While touring his Turun Sanomat newspaper plant, we were interviewed and photographed by the newspaper's staff. Our photo and an article appeared on the front page of the paper the next day, confirming—conclusively—that nothing even remotely noteworthy ever happened in Turku.

We intended to sail directly from Turku to Copenhagen, but that boat didn't sail for several days. Thus, we decided to go by way of an overnight boat to Stockholm. It would not only save time, but it would give me an opportunity to see Monika Eklund again. I called her when we arrived, and she was shocked to hear my voice.

"I thought I might never hear from you again," she said. "How long will you be here?"

"Not long, I'm afraid. We're leaving on the overnight train for Göteborg tonight."

"Tonight? That's no time at all. When can I see you?"

"How about now?"

"Yes, come to my place as soon as you can. I'll be waiting."

I arrived a half-hour later, and though we were apart for only a week it felt as though it had been months. We embraced and kissed and neither of us wanted the moment to end.

"Have you eaten?" she asked.

"I had coffee and a roll on the boat a couple of hours ago."

"Let me make you a proper breakfast," she said.

"I think I have to clean up first. I haven't bathed in a couple of days."

"Okay, clean up, and when you're through I'll give you a shave. You're beginning to resemble Karl Marx."

I showered and then Monika pulled out a straightedge razor and proceeded to shave me. I was a bit nervous at first, but her hand was steady and she manipulated the blade like a genuine swashbuckler. I was greatly impressed.

"Is there no end to your skills?"

"It's part of my medical training," she said. "And I love to feel your face."

"The feeling is mutual," I assured her.

When she finished she asked, "What do you prefer now, breakfast, a nap, or to make love?"

"Yes, yes, and yes. But let's start with your last idea first."

We took a long walk in the afternoon and had dinner at a small neighborhood restaurant.

"I must go now to meet my friend at the station. Our train leaves at ten o'clock."

"It seems we're always saying goodbye," she said.

"I didn't plan on returning to Stockholm," I said. "We couldn't get to Copenhagen directly, so we ended up here. I had no intention of disrupting your life."

"This is no disruption; I love seeing you. I just wish you'd stay long enough to give this relationship a chance."

"I'd love to. But, as we said before, I have my fellowship, you have your medical classes; you know the rest."

Monika walked with me to the Central Station. We greeted Woody at the station entrance. "You've got a little time," he said. "I'll meet you in our compartment in ten minutes."

We embraced for the last time and Monika said, "Write to me, and don't forget me."

"Of course I'll write, and I'll never forget you." She looked so beautiful and so sad.

"Thanks for today, I said. "It was one of the best days of my life." Then I turned and walked into the station. As I walked to my train I fantasized: *If I missed my train and stayed here another month would the Fellowship Committee ever know? And would a month be long enough?*

"Your friend is a real beauty," said Woody. "You're one lucky bastard."

"If I'm so lucky, what the hell am I doing in a crummy third-class compartment with you, instead of with Monika in her comfortable apartment?"

After an essentially sleepless night we arrived in Göteborg the following morning. We spent the day touring the charming city, as our train to Halsingborg didn't leave until midnight. By that time we were on another overnight train, exhausted, and becoming cranky.

"This is our third night without a bed," complained Woody. "When will this end?"

"Tomorrow, in Copenhagen," I answered. "Tomorrow we're getting a real hotel room with real beds and real mattresses."

We caught the early morning ferry from Halsingborg to Helsingør, and by mid-morning we arrived in Copenhagen. Along the way we passed Hamlet's castle, the site at which the character Marcellus says, *"Something is rotten in the state of Denmark."* If I had to guess, I'd say Marcellus was referring to the dozens of foul-smelling fishing boats surrounding us. But at last we were in Denmark, and we could hardly wait to explore the delightful capital.

CHAPTER TEN

Denmark

After three nights without a real bed Woody and I felt like two zombies. We treated ourselves to a first class hotel—one with plush beds with down comforters and private bath with a shower that spewed an unending supply of hot water. We felt like royalty. That night we slept for nearly twelve hours and awoke shortly before the chambermaid was tempted to call the coroner's office. Later that day we moved to a student hostel subsidized by a Danish shipping company. It was less attractive and less comfortable, but it cost a fraction of what we paid the previous night. As they say, no matter where in the world you are, you get what you pay for.

We began exploring the bustling capital city and realized at once that Copenhagen was special. To begin with, people were unusually cheerful and friendly, and most spoke English. As one native put it, "We learn English because we cannot assume the rest of the world will learn Danish." We marveled at the attractive boulevards, profusion of outdoor cafés, and the enormous number of bicycles. Bicycles clearly outnumbered cars; and—since they were noiseless—represented a greater threat to pedestrians. Nearly as prevalent were pastry shops; there seemed to be one on every corner. Danish pastry was legendary, and I was familiar with the American version; but these were much richer and more delicious than anything I'd ever tasted. The window displays were seductive, and several times during the day we stopped to sample another few delicacies.

That afternoon I called Jens Bøertmann, an architect friend of my professor Erik Nielsen.

"Nice to hear your voice," he said. "Erik wrote about you and suggested you might call. I know it's short notice, but if you're free tonight, please join us for dinner. Nothing fancy, but I think you'll find it agreeable. My wife is a very good cook."

I arrived at the Bøertmann apartment at seven o'clock and was warmly greeted. The apartment was compact but beautifully furnished. I recognized several distinguished teakwood and leather pieces designed by some of the most gifted Danish designers. I brought a bouquet of white asters and handed them to Jens' wife, Adriana.

"How lovely," she said, "but students should not spend their money so frivolously."

"I don't think celebrating beauty is ever frivolous," I answered.

"Spoken like a true architect," said Jens. "Tell me, how is my old friend, Erik?"

We spoke of our mutual acquaintance and within a few minutes I felt as though I had known this attractive Danish couple for years. During our discussion about architecture Jens described the difficulty in pursuing his career during the Nazi occupation. "But of course, everything was difficult then. Mostly, we focused on survival."

"Speaking of that," I said, "I read that not a single Danish Jew ended up in a death camp. How was that possible?"

"That is a remarkable story," Jens began. "The Nazis underestimated our determination to protect our citizens. You must understand that persecuting minorities was incompatible with Danish culture long before Hitler came along. The Germans did their best, but the reason for their failure is an inspiring story. It began during the occupation in

1943, when the Nazis ordered Jews to wear armbands, yellow bands with the Star of David. Our king had the habit of riding his horse each morning through the streets of Copenhagen. On the morning following the Nazi order, the King appeared as usual, but he wore a yellow armband. When the citizens saw that, they all put on yellow armbands, and the Germans couldn't possibly know who among us was Jewish. It was a most effective ploy. However, it angered the Nazis. They then decided to round up the Jews and deport them to Germany; which, as you know, meant concentration camps and certain death."

"What could you do about that?" I asked.

"We came up with a dramatic strategy," continued Jens. "The order to deport Jews was leaked to the Jewish community, and two days before the roundup, every Jew in Denmark—more than seven thousand people—simply disappeared. When I say disappeared, I mean every Dane took in a Jewish family and hid them—some in their basements, some in barns, some even in churches. As far as the Nazis were concerned, from one day to the next, Jews simply vanished, as if by magic.

Now here's the good part: The following evening every Jew was taken to the coast and transported across the Sound to Sweden. Since Sweden remained neutral during the war, it became a safe haven. It took two nights and several trips; and, in the process, every available fishing boat, ferry, yacht, and rowboat was used. It was a massive undertaking, and thousands of Danish Jews were transported the two miles from certain death to freedom. The plan was a brilliant success, and the Nazis didn't catch on until the exodus was completed."

"What an incredible story," I said. "It's almost unbelievable."

"But it did happen," said Adriana. "I know—I was one of those fortunate Jews. There was no other occupied country that defended their Jews. Not Poland, not Austria, not France—only here were Jews protected. Other countries gave up their Jews to the Nazis, and most perished."

"There is another little-known fact," said Jens. "When the war ended and the Danish Jews returned home, they found that their neighbors had cared for their houses, gardens, and even their pets. Not one single house was broken into."

"I doubt if that could happen anywhere else on earth," I said, "including America."

During our discussion Adriana served smoked herring appetizers with small glasses of aquavit. I had never before tasted this popular Danish liquor. It had a slight caraway flavor, which was delicious, but it was a powerful drink. By the time dinner was served I was a bit lightheaded, and my stomach was making embarrassing noises. The first course was lobster bisque—a delicious soup that appeared loaded with butter and cream. That, together with the several pounds of butter in the pastries I ate earlier, was beginning to produce an uncomfortable nausea. The condition degenerated until I was forced to leave the table.

"Excuse me," I said. "I don't feel very well." And then I sprinted to the bathroom. Once there, my entire digestive system erupted like an angry volcano. I threw up every morsel I had eaten since arriving in Denmark. The violent retching sounds reverberated through the thin walls of the small apartment, sounding—I was certain—like two gladiators fighting to the death in the bathroom. I could only guess what my hosts were thinking. It was the most profoundly embarrassing moment of my life, but I had no control over my predicament. After twenty more minutes of agony, I slowly emerged from the bathroom, pale and exhausted. Both Jens and Adriana were standing outside the door with concerned expressions.

"It was definitely *not* the lobster bisque," I said in a weak voice.

"Come lie down," said Adriana, as she led me to the couch. She applied a cold cloth to my head, and I began to feel better, but by no means normal.

"I don't know what to say. I assure you, this has never happened before. I think it had something to do with the pastries I ate today. I probably overdid it."

"What a pity," said Jens. "We planned to serve pastries for dessert." Then he laughed, and the terrible tension was broken. I remained on the couch for another half hour and then decided it was best to leave.

"I want to apologize for ruining your dinner, and thank you for understanding. If you happen to write professor Nielsen, you might just ignore what happened tonight."

"This will be our secret," said Jens. "Come, I'll drive you home."

Adriana gave me a hug and asked, "Are you sure you're alright? You're still very pale."

"I'll survive, but thanks for your concern. You've been wonderful."

It rained the next day, so we decided to attend a matinee performance of the Royal Danish Ballet. It was a thrilling performance. Our seats in the balcony cost the equivalent of twenty cents—cheaper than a movie back home. As rain continued the following morning, we went with our Michigan architect friends to tour the Carlsberg Brewery. We saw how beer was made and then were directed to the tasting room, where we sampled the various brews. The four of us consumed fourteen bottles of beer, after which we could barely stand up.

Every Dane we met complained about the foul weather we were having. "It's been like this for three months," said our hostel director. "Oh, except for one Tuesday in July; the sun actually appeared. We like to say that summer took place this year on a Tuesday."

When we arrived in Copenhagen I picked up a dozen letters at American Express. Most contained news of home from family and friends. But three were from my romantic partners in New York, England, and Sweden. I often thought about those fleeting affairs, and I wondered if there was anything I should do about them. The situation with Anne Cleary was uncomplicated. She had returned to Iowa and was looking for a job. Having spent a fantasy summer biking through England, her new life was a difficult adjustment. Anne yearned to have a life without responsibility, endless adventures, and exciting romantic encounters. She liked me; I'm sure of that, but only as a diversion, I think.

The situation with Deborah Wolfe and Monika Eklund was different. They were serious young women, focused on their careers, and I cared for them both. If I had to make a choice, it would have been impossible. If feasible, I would have chosen the bigamist's way out.

Deborah wrote about two small acting jobs she recently had, and how much she enjoyed living in New York. With the minor success came optimism, and the tone of her letter was cheerful.

All that's missing in my life is you, she wrote. *That would make everything perfect.*

Monika's boyfriend had returned from vacationing in Germany, and he was actively pursuing her. *Sadly*, she wrote, *I have no romantic feeling for him. He is a loyal friend, but he is not the one I want to be with. What I want is someone with whom I am comfortable, someone who makes me laugh, someone I cannot stop thinking about—You!*

Like I said—this was becoming a world-class predicament.

"I've made a date for us," said Woody. He dashed into our room with his usual enthusiasm.

"Oh no, Woody, I'm up to my eyeballs with romantic problems."

"This has nothing to do with romance," he said. "There's an organization called Meet the Danes that arranges for tourists to meet locals with similar interests. I've made a date for us to have dinner tomorrow night with two young architects."

Poul Hansen and Svend Mikkelsen were two delightful and charming hosts. The dinner was held at the house in which Svend lived with his parents. The parents were obviously successful, because the house was enormous, their cook prepared the dinner, and two other staff members served it. Poul and Svend were about our age, recent graduates of the Royal Danish Academy, and both spoke fluent English. They worked in the same large architectural office, and their attitudes about architecture and professional goals were similar to ours.

"I'm optimistic about my future," said Poul, "but if I stay at my current job I may never *have* a future. Our boss was trained under the Beaux Arts system, and he's still stuck in the past. He thinks every building should look like the Temple of Neptune."

"That's not entirely true," said Svend. "I'm working on a commercial building that's very Bauhaus. Unfortunately, you're doing additions to a classic bank."

"Every young architect thinks the older generation is too conventional," Woody said. "Even some of Frank Lloyd Wright's apprentices left Taliesen because they felt the old man couldn't get past the nineteenth century. And he's still one of the most creative architects alive."

"Dissatisfaction is certainly not uncommon among architects," I said. "For some, it's the driving force. Creative people want to change the world; it's part of their neurotic obsession to solve every problem on the horizon."

Svend had the last word: "I think we agree; most creative people are slightly wacky."

The next day Svend took the day off and drove us around Copenhagen to view several modern building we had been unable to see because of the relentless rain. That afternoon we drove to Helsingør where we had lunch along the Danish Riviera. I was amazed—as I had been the night before—at his enormous appetite. Most Danes, it seemed, ate and drank more than any other people on earth. Of course, food was plentiful and delicious, but it also appeared the Danes loved the social aspect of eating and drinking. A normal Danish meal could easily last two or three hours. Strangely, few Danes were overweight. In fact, as an ethnic group, they were every bit as attractive as other Scandinavians. When we finished lunch, Svend insisted on picking up the check.

"After all," he said, "I ate more than the two of you combined. But next year, when I come to the U.S., I hope you will reciprocate."

Our student hostel owned several bicycles that were available to us. Since the sun made a rare appearance the following day, Woody and I decided to bicycle around the city. Our hostel director gave us a rundown on the strict regulations, including hand signals, traffic lights, and rules of the road. We cycled along the coast to view the famous Little Mermaid statue, then to the picturesque Nyhavn area, and finally to Tivoli Gardens, where we stopped for lunch.

"I could see myself living here," said Woody. "This city has everything."

"No argument from me," I replied. "It's going to be tough to leave."

But leave we did—the following night. We caught an overnight boat for Aarhus and arrived early the next morning. We visited the modern City Hall, the new University, and the quaint old town. Late in the day we decided to save money by hitchhiking to Hamburg. Two rides and a couple of hours later we were in Horsens, only fifty kilometers from where we started; and at that point it began to rain. Actually, it was cold enough to snow. In the past couple of months when anything went wrong we would generally say: "It could be worse—It could be raining." Now we realized it couldn't be worse.

"Enough already!" exclaimed Woody. "Let's catch the next train."

We arrived in the small village of Padborg at midnight and decided to spend the night there. We located the only hotel in town and awakened the proprietor, who was annoyed at having to leave his warm bed for two scruffy-looking wanderers. The following morning we discovered that the German border was a five-minute walk from our hotel. Five minutes from Germany, but a million miles from our delightful adventures in Copenhagen.

CHAPTER ELEVEN

Germany

I knew there would be mixed emotions; a part of me dreaded being in Germany. Seven years earlier we were at war, and before that, my ethnic heritage marked me for death. What was I doing here, surrounded by people who would have sent me to a death camp without a second thought? Every German I saw looked like a character from a war movie. What about the director of the Hamburg youth hostel? Was he a former guard at Auschwitz? And the cleaning lady; could she have been a Nazi spy? After learning of the wartime atrocities I was suspicious of every German I saw. I even felt satisfaction when viewing the ruins in Hamburg caused by our Air Force. *Good show, boys!* But then I felt guilty for my reaction.

"They deserved it," said Woody. "The Luftwaffe did worse to London and Rotterdam."

"Yes, but we're architects; we believe in construction, not *destruction*."

The rains that plagued us in Denmark continued in Hamburg. Despite the weather, we took an extensive walking tour of the town. We had a satisfying dinner that evening at an attractive café that served sausages with sauerkraut, all washed down with a stein of local beer. It was a farewell dinner of sorts, because Woody was leaving the next morning to tour Belgium and Holland, two countries I would visit next spring. We planned to meet in Frankfurt after a couple of weeks.

"Are you sure you'll be okay without me?" I asked.

"I was wondering the same about you," he answered.

"Well," I said, "I might miss your cheerful personality, but I won't miss your top-sergeant enthusiasm or double-time marches through foreign cities." Woody often acted like he was leading men into battle. He frequently ran instead of walked, climbed steps two at a time, and at times seemed driven by a mysterious force beyond his control. It appeared he had something to prove. We got along so well and I had become so fond of him I hesitated to rock the boat. But now the subject had been broached.

"I've been meaning to ask, Woody, what's with all that macho stuff?"

He was quiet for a few moments, and then spoke slowly. "I suppose you could blame my parents," he said. "I always thought it weird that they named my older sister Petaluma, after a town in Sonoma County. Can you imagine? She hated her name and let them know it, but they apparently learned nothing. When I came along they named me Marion. Have you any idea what we went through as little kids? Especially me. Not only the boys, but also the girls made fun of me. Marion James Elwood. Why not James M. Elwood? No one would have paid attention to that."

"I don't recall anyone at school calling you Marion; it was either Jim or Woody."

"Yeah, but inside I felt like Marion. And I always thought I had to prove myself, be just a bit more masculine than any Mike or Bill or even Peter." His spirits seemed to be sinking.

"Well, just so you know, you don't have to prove anything to me. So relax."

"Thanks," he said. "I appreciate that."

We went to the Hamburg Central Station early the next morning and hugged goodbye. "See you in Frankfurt," Woody said. "Take care of yourself."

As he boarded his train for Brussels, I boarded mine for Cologne. I was on my own now, but it was not the same as in Bath. First of all, after nearly three months of travel I was considerably more confident. Besides, I knew we would meet again in Frankfurt.

The newly constructed youth hostel in Cologne was beautifully situated along the Rhine River. What a contrast with the hostel in Hamburg! That place was dark and depressing and looked more like a prisoner-of-war camp than a hostel. This place was bright, comfortable, and had every amenity. Oddly, the price of both hostels was forty pfennig a night—about ten cents! Since the sun made an unusual appearance, I immediately set out to tour the city. U.S. bombers devastated Cologne during the war, and about ninety percent of the city was leveled. There was a major reconstruction program in progress, but evidence of the massive destruction was everywhere. If you doubted the futility of war, a visit to Cologne would have convinced you. Just seeing injured people on crutches or in wheelchairs, many with missing limbs, was a sobering sight. I kept wondering why Germans so readily followed an obvious lunatic down that painful path to annihilation.

The biggest tourist attraction in town was the Cologne Cathedral, the largest Gothic church in Northern Europe. Our bombers did their best to avoid the Cathedral, but most of the stained glass was blown out and machine-gun holes pockmarked every wall.

I didn't particularly enjoy eating alone, but German food and drinks were delicious and reasonably priced. What a paradox that Germany—the loser—was faring so well, while England—the winner—still had rationing. It didn't seem quite right.

I went back to the hostel after dinner to write some letters. After an hour, I returned to the dormitory and discovered that my rucksack, containing everything I owned, was missing. At first I thought I had simply left it under the wrong bunk, but a quick search convinced me that the bag was gone. I had a desperate feeling as I raced to the director's office to report the loss.

"I think someone stole my bag," I said.

"Are you sure?" asked the director.

"All I know is my bag is gone!" My voice began to rise in concert with my blood pressure.

We returned to the dormitory and searched the room again. The bag was not there. The director made a phone call, and in five minutes two plainclothes detectives arrived. They searched the grounds and immediately discovered my camera beneath an open dormitory window.

"They didn't want to risk having an American camera," the director surmised, "especially one with an engraved serial number. Apparently, someone dropped your bag out the window, and an accomplice made off with it."

"Well, what are you going to do about it?" I shouted at the detectives.

"They don't speak English," said the director. *Oh, God, what a nightmare!*

The detectives were babbling in German, while I was becoming more frustrated by the minute. It seemed no one had the slightest idea what to do next. I felt an anxiety attack coming on. *My bag is gone; my clothes, my books, papers, letters, film, toilet articles, even my plastic raincoat. Why would someone steal a cheap plastic raincoat that was so filled with holes, it was mostly one big patchwork of scotch tape? I hope the miserable bastard gets caught in a hurricane!*

The director finally said, "The detectives suspect this may be an inside job. They're taking the employees to the police station for interrogation." *Waste of time,* I thought. *I'm never going to see my possessions again. It wouldn't even surprise me if the detectives were in on the scam—probably the director, too. They're all a bunch of anti-Semitic Nazi crooks!*

I felt a bit better the next morning, even though I barely slept. I kept thinking about my predicament and decided it could be worse, much worse. To begin with, I had the suit I was wearing in the writing room; and I had my wallet, which contained my passport and traveler's checks. In addition, I washed out some things before writing my letters, so I had a change of underwear hanging in the bathroom. The situation wasn't good, but it wasn't the end of the world either.

One of the detectives from the previous night came into the dormitory and said *"Guten Morgen,"* as he handed me a large envelope. The envelope contained my papers—my International Health Certificate, my official Fellowship Letter from the University, and several letters of introduction from Professor Mendelsohn. I was stunned, but thrilled beyond belief.

"Where did you find these?" I asked.

"In den Sträuchern," he said. I stared blankly, and then he led me to the window. Below were several uniformed policeman rummaging through the bushes. "They were in the bushes? *Danke, Danke,* you clever bastard! I take back every terrible thing I thought about you last night. You may be an ex-Nazi, you may have raped and pillaged during the war; but, by God, you're the finest person I've met in this miserable town."

I'm sure he didn't understand a single word I said, but he smiled as though he did.

My next visitor was the supervisor of the Youth Hostel Association of Western Germany.

"I want to offer condolences for the unfortunate events of last night," he said. "I have spoken with the local police, and later this morning I will take up the matter with the Lord Mayor." The Lord Mayor? My God, the "Cologne Catastrophe", as I now thought of it, was becoming a very big deal. Everyone's being so conciliatory, I think they're trying to avoid World War III.

I went out after breakfast and bought a toothbrush, razor, and a few other basic necessities. I also bought a kindergarten-sized pencil box to carry those items along with my change of underwear. I had finally achieved my goal—I was traveling lighter than Woody. In fact, I was carrying little more than Tarzan of the Apes, who wore only a loincloth and carried a knife, bow, and quiver of arrows. I returned to the hostel for lunch, since the director informed me that for the remainder of my stay all room and board charges would be waived. Terrific deal, but I would have gladly traded that benefit to see my Norwegian rucksack again.

The supervisor returned that evening and, with little fanfare, presented me with a check for five hundred Deutschmarks authorized by the city council of Cologne. I was in shock! This was more money than I needed to replace my losses and an incredibly generous gesture. I went to the bank the following morning, where I discovered the catch. Currency regulations prohibited buying traveler's checks with Deutschmarks or converting them into any other currency. Furthermore, the maximum amount one could take out of Germany was a hundred marks. I cashed my large check and decided I'd deal with the currency problem another time.

With little regret, I left Cologne for Bonn the next morning. It was a short bus ride, and by midday I was touring the important sights, including the thirteenth century Romanesque basilica and Ludwig van Beethoven's House. I got an inexpensive hotel room—*no more hostels for me*—enjoyed a good dinner, and slept more peacefully that night.

I intended to take a boat down the Rhine, but a series of unfortunate errors forced me to change my plans. First, I boarded the wrong train; next, I missed the stop in Koblenz; and finally, I ended up in Wiesbaden. Maybe Woody was right; I was having a lot of trouble getting along without him. The train paralleled the Rhine and was a beautiful experience; it just wasn't the boat ride I had planned. I had dinner in Wiesbaden and then took an overnight train to Nürnberg. My former college roommate, Billy Heston, had been working there as an architect since graduation. The agency he worked for designed commercial facilities such as markets, snack bars, and service stations for U.S. military personnel. Billy insisted that I visit when I reached Germany.

My train arrived early in the morning, at which time I called Billy.

"Happy to hear you voice, you old pain in the ass. Be there in ten minutes."

What a wonderful reunion we had, and how satisfying to finally see a friendly face.

"How long can you stay?" Billy wanted to know.

"About three days."

"Nonsense," he said, "I have a lot to show you. You'll stay a week."

"But I'm meeting Jim Elwood in Frankfurt."

"Woody? What's he doing here?"

"We've been traveling together for the last three months."

"Send him a note; tell him you'll be late. And give him my regards."

Billy's townhouse was located on a charming street at the outskirts of the city. He introduced his girlfriend, Caroline Murray, who worked as a receptionist in his office. She greeted me warmly and asked, "Is that pencil box your entire luggage?"

"Afraid so. My bag was stolen at the hostel in Cologne."

"Have you any idea how silly that looks?" asked Billy. "You know, we have access to a lot of stateside products. I'm sure we can replace most of what you need."

Caroline prepared a breakfast of bacon and eggs, gave me a copy of the Stars & Stripes, the Army newspaper that was delivered daily, and for a moment I felt I was back in America. After breakfast, Caroline showed me the attic guestroom.

"You have your own bedroom, bathroom, and sitting room up here, including a large closet that, apparently, you won't be needing. I hope you'll be comfortable."

"This is terrific. You may have trouble getting me out."

Later that morning Billy drove me to the Palace of Justice, where the architectural offices were located. About three-quarters of the staff in Billy's office were ex-Cal graduates. I recognized several familiar faces. John Lucas, who graduated three years earlier, ran the organization that included more than twenty architects.

"We're looking for a sharp designer," he said to me, "and Billy tells me you were the best in your class. Would you consider suspending your travels for a while and come work with us?"

"That's a tempting offer," I said, "but I'm committed to complete my fellowship obligation, and that won't end until next June."

"I admire your integrity," he said, "but think it over; and stay in touch. If we still need help next summer, you've got a job here." I was flattered and thrilled to be considered.

We next visited the Post Exchange and I found a beautiful nylon raincoat to replace the perforated plastic one that was stolen. I also picked up gloves, a sweater, and a few rolls of film.

"Will your pencil box accommodate all that stuff?" Billy asked sarcastically.

"I may have to buy a briefcase," I answered.

We attended a USO show the following night held at one of the local army bases. With the thousands of U.S. military personnel stationed nearby, it was a popular stop for the organization that entertained our troops throughout the war. The show lacked big Hollywood stars, but several New York musical performers presented numbers from current Broadway shows, such as *Pal Joey* and *Kiss Me Kate*. It was during the performance of *Why Can't You Behave?*—a song from the latter show—that I was struck by the appearance of the singer. She resembled Deborah Wolfe, my romantic partner from New York. As I continued to stare at her I finally realized it *was* Deborah! How could that be? I didn't know she was in Europe; why didn't she let me know? And I hadn't the faintest idea she could sing. I could hardly wait for the show to end.

"I have to see someone backstage," I said. "Don't wait for me, I'll find a way home."

I raced backstage and asked the stage manager where I could find Deborah. He pointed to a dressing room down the hall. I knocked and heard a voice say, "Come in." When I opened the door, she screamed, "Holy moly!" And then we embraced and remained locked in each other's arms.

Finally I said, "I can't believe you're here. I have a million questions."

"First, let me look at you," she said. "You've lost weight; but you look wonderful. I can't tell you how thrilled I am to see you. I thought we might never meet again."

"It would have been a lot easier if you had told me about this. What are you *doing* here?"

"It all happened so fast. I got this job only last week; then we were on a military plane to Germany, and I wasn't sure where you were or how to reach you. How did you find me?"

"An incredible coincidence. I'm visiting a friend who works in Nürnberg. Let's have a drink and I'll tell you everything, and you'll tell me where you learned to sing Cole Porter songs."

We spoke continuously for two hours, and then she asked, "Where are you staying?"

"I have a wonderful attic room at my friend's house. And you?"

"I'm staying at a hotel, but there are two others in my room. Can we go to your place?"

When we arrived, my hosts were asleep. "I love your room," she said. "Will your friends mind if I stay here?"

"Let's ask them in the morning. We have a lot of catching up to do."

We spent the night together, and it was every bit as exciting as our time in New York.

The following day was Columbus Day, a U.S. government holiday, and we all slept late. I introduced Deborah to Billy and Caroline, and they suggested the four of us go to Rothenburg, a charming medieval town about two hours from Nürnberg. It felt as though we were back in Berkeley, double dating and having a carefree time. It was a cold, crisp autumn day, and the yellow and red leaves were spectacular. We saw the sights, ate in a fine restaurant, and consumed several bottles of delicious Rhine wine. We got along wonderfully well, and the entire day was an unexpected gift. I wished our time together would never end, but two days later Deborah left for Wiesbaden. The company was doing another show that evening at an Air Corps base.

"I'm going to miss you," she said. "These past days have been like a honeymoon."

"Careful, Deborah, what would your father say?"

"I think he would love you," she said. "I know I do. Really, I do."

We kissed goodbye, and it was New York all over again. There was something about her that profoundly affected me. Was it love? I honestly wasn't sure. But it felt wonderful.

Billy used his influence at an Army base to convert my Deutschmarks into U.S. traveler's checks. What a relief! Later that day he drove me around the city and showed me the sights worth seeing, including the Frauenkirche and Hitler's famous podium at the Nazi Party rally grounds.

We drove to Frankfurt at the end of the week. Billy had business there, and Caroline came along for the ride. By the time we got to Würzburg it began to snow.

"Even this weather can't dampen my gratitude," I said. "I don't know how to thank you."

"Our pleasure," said Caroline. "It was great meeting you, *and* your girlfriend. By the way, is there any future there?"

"I don't know, I really don't know. But I can't stop thinking about her."

They dropped me off at the American Express office in Frankfurt, and as if by a miraculous coincidence, there was Woody, walking out the door.

"Woody!" I shouted. He turned and sprinted our way.

The four of us had lunch together, and for three hours the conversation never slowed.

"Sorry to end this wonderful reunion," said Billy, "but I have work to do."

We said our goodbyes, they drove off, and Woody and I began searching for a place to stay.

The trip from Frankfurt to Munich included several fascinating stops. We took an early train to Worms, a port city on the Rhine, to see the Romanesque Cathedral. Worms also had the remains of the Jewish community founded during the tenth century. The community was virtually destroyed during the famous Kristallnacht riots in 1938. Even the cemetery was desecrated. Continuing to Heidelberg, we toured the Cathedral, Castle, and the oldest University in Germany. Heidelberg was a bit of a tourist trap, but a quaint one. We left that same evening for Stuttgart.

"We've got to slow down," said Woody. "I'm beginning to forget what I saw this morning."

I had a letter of introduction to Richard Doecker, a professor of architecture and another old friend of Erich Mendelsohn. "Delighted you called," he said. "Unfortunately, I'm in a conference all day. However, my associate, Professor Glockner will be pleased to meet with you."

Glockner turned out to be an amiable young man with extensive architectural knowledge. We toured the school, viewed an exhibit of student work, and then he said, "You absolutely must see Weissenhof." The Weissenhof Housing Development of 1927 demonstrated the latest forms and techniques of modern design. Several leading architects of the modern movement, including Mies van der Rohe, Walter Gropius, and Le Corbusier, designed the thirty residential units that made up this historic collection. We spent three hours touring this amazing development.

We left that evening for Ulm to visit the finest and most impressive cathedral in Germany. Ulm was also the birthplace of Albert Einstein, a fact that was prominently emphasized on post cards and tourist literature. It was impossible, however, to ignore the hypocrisy. If Einstein hadn't fled to America, he would have perished along with nearly every other German Jew. That evening we boarded a train for Munich.

Since we next planned to visit Austria, one of our immediate goals was to obtain a Grey Card. This was required by the Russians to enter Vienna, a city currently divided into four sectors, but lying entirely within Austria's Russian zone. The partitioning of Austria by Americans, English, French, and Russians created enormous bureaucratic confusion, which was made worse by Russian paranoia. A cold war had replaced the hot one, and despite the camaraderie shared by Russia and the Allies after the defeat of Germany, there was now fear and distrust on both sides.

The American Consulate advised that Russian permission might take some time. But time is what we had plenty of. I was also waiting for a package from home that contained items unobtainable in Germany, such as nylon shirts. The package, sent by Pan Am Express, was supposed to take several days, but it was already a week overdue.

On our first day in Munich, I received a dozen letters, including one from the Chief of Police in Cologne. Great news! They caught the youth hostel thief and his accomplice! His name was Rudolph Schmitz, a teenage student, and his partner in crime was his girlfriend. They immediately sold most of my possessions, and my prized Bannister Fletcher history book was thoughtlessly tossed into the Rhine. I trust it provided architectural delight for curious fish. I hoped the pair would get a life sentence in Spandau Prison, but I suspected they would avoid serious punishment.

As the days drifted by, we continued to wait for our Grey Cards and my package from home. We spent leisurely autumn days exploring the attractive city of Munich. Much in the city was destroyed by the war, but it was not nearly as devastated as Cologne. Of interest was a visit to the famed Hofbräuhaus, an immense beer hall where Hitler was nearly assassinated. Beer was served in liter mugs and downed by locals at close to the speed of light. A small oom-pah band continuously played drinking songs, but their sound was nearly drowned out by the half-drunk patrons. The bar maids, most of whom were built like big-rig trucks, shoved their way through the crowd carrying three mugs in each hand. What a sight that was, and what a wonderful place to forget your troubles.

After more than a week, our Grey Cards were issued, and my package from home arrived. I also bought a new rucksack. It was clearly inferior to my Norwegian bag, but finally, I could throw away my pencil box. With no further reason to remain in Germany we boarded the midnight train to Innsbruck.

CHAPTER TWELVE

Austria

Austria was the birthplace of Adolph Hitler, a fact most Austrians preferred to ignore. Our landlady in Innsbruck explained that the lack of running water was caused by the recent war.

"Before Hitler," she said, "everything worked. Now, nothing works. Blame it on that dreadful German dictator."

"He may have been the German dictator," I cautiously pointed out, "but Hitler was actually Austrian."

"Nonsense!" she answered. "That's impossible! Austrians love art, music, and fine food; they have no interest in waging war." There was little point in confusing her with more facts, among which was another awkward truth: Anti-Semitism in Austria was clearly as pervasive as in Germany. There were few tears shed when Austria's Jews were shipped off to Hitler's death camps, and, in fact, many considered it a big favor.

The town of Innsbruck was set in a magnificent lush valley on the Inn River. It was surrounded by Tyrolean Alps that soared to lofty peaks already capped with snow. The town particularly appealed to ski enthusiasts who arrived each season following the first substantial snowfall. According to many, nearby ski resorts were among the finest in the world.

Other than its quaint setting, Innsbruck had little of architectural interest. Thus, after two days we proceeded to Salzburg. During our train ride we passed through some of the most glorious countryside I had ever seen. In a rare day of sunshine the intense autumn foliage sparkled against the backdrop of snow-capped mountains. It was one of those rides during which you hesitated to leave your seat for fear of missing one more spectacular sight. However, just prior to our arrival in Salzburg a black cloud appeared and remained above us for the next several days.

An old lady at the train station approached and asked, "Do you need a room for tonight?"

I was doubtful and shook my head, but Woody said, "Wait a minute, that's the way they rent rooms in a lot of places. Let's hear what she has to say."

She led us down several blocks, as a light rain continued to fall. Finally, we arrived at a charming house and found a clean, spacious room with two comfortable beds. We had already been told that the cost of the room was sixteen shillings, about sixty-five cents. Of course, that didn't include running water, a convenience that was not yet widely available in post-war Austria. Our pleasant landlady arrived each morning with two small bowls of steaming water with which to perform our rituals. After two days I became so expert I could brush my teeth, bathe, shave, and have enough hot water left over to prepare a cup of tea.

Salzburg was similar to Innsbruck in many respects. They were about the same size, both were situated on a river, and the architecture of the two cities was old, quaint, and of a consistent human scale. The city had great charm and an attractive setting, but little else. The people were polite, but most lacked any semblance of charm.

One evening we attended the premier performance of a new operetta by Oscar Straus called *Bozena*. It had a simple story that did not require knowledge of German, and the music was romantic and cheerful. The audience cheered at the finale, and they absolutely erupted when it was announced that Straus was in the audience. He arose and took a bow, and the cheering continued for another ten minutes.

"You'd think he was Frank Sinatra," said Woody.

We caught an early train to Linz the following morning. We visited the Cathedral, Rathaus, and a few other civic buildings. The most startling experience, however, was our first sighting of Russian troops. We began to cross a bridge over the Danube when a U.S. Army MP stopped us. "Where do you think you're going? Can't you read the sign?"

We suddenly noticed the large sign that stated: *Travel between the American and Soviet Zones is forbidden, unless prior permission is obtained from Soviet authorities in Vienna.*

"We just wanted to see a Baroque church on the other side," I said. "Are you saying we have to go to Vienna to get permission to cross a bridge in Linz?"

"You're lucky you don't have to go to Moscow," answered the soldier. "The Russians control everything on that side of the Danube. It's their sector, and they make the rules."

As we looked across the river we saw the red flag and Russian soldiers carrying rifles.

"Maybe we should skip the church," said Woody. "We're outnumbered and outgunned."

The afternoon train to Vienna stopped at the U.S.-Soviet demarcation line at Enns, which allowed Russian officers to verify our passports and Grey Cards. Heavily armed Russian soldiers boarded the train to examine our documents. One would have thought, by the size and firepower of the group, they were ready to quash a revolt. What an ominous presence; not one of them cracked a smile. Strangely, I felt little fear, even though their demeanor was clearly threatening. A

French student claimed his Grey Card was stolen. He pleaded his case to the Russians, but without success. He was promptly escorted off the train. "He's probably headed for Siberia," commented Woody.

After a half hour our train was permitted to enter the Soviet Zone. We arrived in Vienna and quickly found a comfortable room about a ten-minute walk from the center of town. The room was large, inexpensive, and had hot running water! It was also heated between the hours of six and seven in the evening. In post-war Austria, you couldn't really expect much more.

We spent most of the following day applying for permission to exit Vienna through the southern British sector. The special permission we sought required approval from the British, Americans, and Soviets, and it took three days to obtain. The red tape was astonishing!

We also had difficulty obtaining visas for Greece and Egypt, though the reasons were quite different. The officials at the Greek Consulate were simply slow-witted and incredibly inept. The Egyptian problem was more complicated; it related to the Arab-Israeli War. That war began in 1948, when the State of Israel was established, and though it ended with an armistice in 1949, the conflict was by no means resolved. The Arab nations suffered a humiliating defeat, and now—three years later—they were still upset. The visa application asked one to declare a religious preference. I was previously advised to check the box indicating "No Preference".

The Egyptian official was visibly unfriendly as he asked, "Newman, that's a Jewish name, is it not?" I was more than prepared for the question.

"Not necessarily," I answered. "Surely you've heard of John Henry Newman, the famous Roman Catholic Cardinal. Do you really believe he's Jewish? Then there's the great Confederate General from our civil war, Simon Ogilvy Newman, who was known to be a virulent anti-Semite. And everyone over the age of four knows of the eminent British scientist Sir Isaac Newman. He formulated the laws of gravitation. Even in Egypt they must have heard about the father of gravity!"

The officer eyed me quizzically and said, "You must come back tomorrow." Surprisingly, he never actually asked if I were Jewish.

We left the building and Woody said, "You really should work in a sideshow. That was a terrific sleight-of-hand performance."

"Anything for a visa," I said.

When we returned the following morning the same Egyptian official said, "I believe the British scientist you mentioned, Sir Isaac Newman, was actually Sir Isaac Newton. I know that's true, because I looked it up. Were you trying to mislead me?"

"Not at all," I said. "Your confusion is understandable. The family name for centuries was Newton, but when Sir Isaac's father died, his mother married an Anglican Bishop by the name of Barnabas Newman, and the young boy became Isaac Newman. He hated his stepfather, and when he left home, as a final affront to him, he changed his name back to Newton. So, I ask you, is it Newman or Newton? They're actually one and the same person."

The officer remained skeptical, and I could see that our visa was by no means assured. Finally, I pulled out the most potent weapon in my arsenal—my official letter from the university. The letter, written on university stationery and signed by Dean Warren Wilson, explained that I was a fellowship student, and it expressed appreciation for any favor that may be extended. The message was not nearly as important as the applied gold star with blue ribbons. The multi-pointed star was embossed with the official seal of the University of California, and it was mighty impressive.

I had been told that in most third-world countries there was nothing as significant to bureaucrats as gold seals applied to documents. The official took one look at my letter and his eyebrows arched upward as if to say, "Why didn't you say so in the first place?" Twenty minutes later we left the Egyptian Consulate with visas in hand.

As the somber weather continued so did our exploration of the exciting capital city. Some claimed that Vienna had lost her celebrated pre-war gaiety. Having been annexed by Germany in 1938, liberated by Russia in 1945, and under four-power rule since the war's end, no doubt it had changed. But the Vienna we observed was delightfully cosmopolitan with fine restaurants, attractive architecture, and citizens who spent endless hours in cafés, happily drinking and chatting.

We visited the Cathedral, National Gallery, Belvedere Palace, and spent a memorable afternoon at Schönbrunn Palace, the summer home of Austria's royal families. We also attended a concert by the Vienna Symphony and a performance of the operetta *Gypsy Baron*. Meals were invariably special events. One evening we ate at the Hofkeller, a charming restaurant created in an old wine cellar that was located two flights below the street. Aside from the wonderful food, the experience was highlighted by delightful zither music.

A high school friend, who was born in Vienna, requested that I call a distant relative of his by the name of Frederick Obermann. One morning, out of a sense of duty, I dialed his number.

"Delighted you called," he said. "Can you join us for lunch today?"

Obermann was a Professor of History at the University. He lived with his wife, Emma, and their lovely daughter, Astrid, in an attractive house in the suburbs. For the first hour we drank champagne and became acquainted. What a charming family! Finally, it was time to eat. Emma had prepared a spectacular meal of popular Austrian dishes:

Wiener schnitzel, Erdäpfel (potato and onion salad), and Apfelstrudel for dessert. We also had beer, wine, and after-dinner liqueurs. Two hours later I could barely stand up.

"This was one of the best meals I've ever had," I said, slightly slurring my words. "I cannot believe you eat and drink this way every day. If you did, you would all weigh a thousand pounds and have liver problems."

"We usually eat more modestly," said Emma, "but special guests call for special indulgences. I'm glad you enjoyed our local dishes."

Astrid was relatively quiet during our long meal, but while sipping our Kirschwasser she asked, "How long will you be in Vienna, Mr. Newman?"

"Three more days," I answered. "But, please call me Peter; Mr. Newman is my father."

"Alright, Peter. If you have time, I'd like to offer you a tour of our University."

"I'd like that," I said. *What a great idea—and a chance to get to know her.*

We made a date for the following day, and then it was time to leave.

I met Woody for dinner and he asked about my lunch with the Obermanns.

"Wonderful people, fabulous food, and their daughter? Well, what can I say?"

"Oh, no. I thought after all your recent problems you would be more careful. On the other hand, maybe you should write a guidebook for the rest of us."

"I don't get it," I said. "I went months in Berkeley without a girl ever looking at me. But since I've been in Europe, they're falling out of the trees and into my lap."

"Are you complaining?"

"Not at all; I'm just wondering how I can manage to stay in Europe forever."

The tour of the University was fascinating, and Astrid was a knowledgeable tour guide.

"I wish you were staying longer," she said. "I'd like to know more about you."

"That would be nice," I said, "but I've got to keep traveling. I hope we'll meet again, but it's goodbye for now. Many thanks for the wonderful tour."

She reached for my hand. "I want to kiss you goodbye," she said. I was unprepared for the passion of her embrace. It was a kiss I would remember for a long time. Then she said, "If I do not go now I will never leave." And then she was gone.

We were surprised to see Russian soldiers stationed in Vienna on almost every major street corner. For years we were told that Communists threatened our way of life. They were portrayed as evil and dangerous; and although we were not shooting at one another, we were engaged in a cold war in which neither side trusted the other. It was ironic, however, that without their grey uniforms and terrible haircuts Soviet soldiers could easily have passed for American college freshmen. They rarely spoke and never smiled, which Woody seemed to take as a personal challenge. One day he approached a young soldier and said, "Greetings, Mr. Ruski, how's it going?"

"What the hell are you doing?" I asked.

Ignoring me, Woody continued. "So, who'd you have in the World Series, the Yankees or Brooklyn? I gotta say, you look to me like a Dodger fan." The soldier appeared bewildered.

"And did you see Billy Martin's game-saving catch in Game Seven?" More silence. By this time the Soviet soldier was not only *not* smiling, he was frowning. "Let's go," I said. Just then the rifle came off his shoulder, and he undid the safety catch.

"Okay, Woody, he's obviously not a baseball fan. Let's get out of here—right now!"

I knew that Russians were totally isolated; they were not permitted to travel outside their country, nor were foreigners allowed to enter Russia. Frederick Obermann said, "When you cannot go, say, or do what you please, something must be terribly wrong with the system."

We checked out of our room the following morning and headed for the railway station and our train to Trieste. Between our room and the station, however, Woody decided to buy some postcards. He said he'd meet me at the train, but as the time for our departure passed, I knew something was wrong. Woody was never late. We discussed becoming separated long ago. "If that ever happens," I said, "here's what we do. Return to our hotel or where we were last together, and also leave a note at the American Express office."

I went back to our rented room, but he was not there. Then I went to the American Express office and left a note for him to meet me there at noon or at two-hour intervals after that. Then I went to a nearby café, ordered coffee, and began to wonder what in the world I would do next. I was on the verge of an anxiety attack. I figured it was too early to involve the police, but that would be my next step. I was running out of ideas as well as options.

That evening, after the American Express office closed, I returned to the Hofkeller where we had dinner the night before. I had not eaten all day and was becoming sick with worry. I also felt helpless and totally baffled by Woody's disappearance. *Had he been kidnapped? Was he in an accident? Is he still alive? Will I ever know?*

I kept going over the facts, as I became more and more agitated. Suddenly I yelled out, "Damn it, Woody, where the hell are you?"

As the echo of my outburst filled the room, patrons began to stare at this odd American student who appeared to be losing his mind before their very eyes. Then I heard a voice: "Here I am, Peter. I'm here!"

I raced towards the voice, and in a moment we were hugging in the middle of the restaurant.

"I can't believe it's really you," I said. "Where the hell have you been?"

"You're not going to believe this. The Soviets picked me up just after we separated. They apparently witnessed my conversation with the Russian soldier the other day, and they wanted to know what we spoke about. It was crazy—I don't speak a single word of Russian, but they figured something fishy was going on. We talked about the World Series—remember? And the doofus didn't understand a word I said. They kept me there all afternoon until I finally said I wanted to see someone from the U.S. Embassy. Then suddenly they said I was free to leave. What a bunch of paranoid bastards! I went back to our room, but you had checked us out. Then I went to AmEx, but they were closed. Finally, I figured you'd probably be having dinner at our favorite place."

"So here we are," I said. "I can't tell you how happy I am this day is over."

We left Vienna the next morning, and our unanticipated separation had so disturbed me I didn't let Woody out of my sight for the next few weeks.

CHAPTER THIRTEEN

Yugoslavia

"How is anyone supposed to know that going from Vienna to Trieste, not even three hundred miles, takes more than fifteen hours?" Woody asked. "I could do it in less time on a bicycle."

Expecting to reach our destination by noon, we actually arrived at midnight—an innocent mistake of a mere twelve hours. What we didn't realize was that our route followed treacherous mountain paths, an endless number of stops for passengers, and some of the most aggressive immigration and customs officials we had ever seen. Losing a day was disappointing, but a more serious concern was our lack of funds. We spent our last Austrian shilling earlier that morning and had no money for food. A fellow passenger heard our conversation and suggested we wait until reaching Graz.

"We should be there in another hour," he said, "and there'll be time to get off the train and buy some food. If you have an American dollar, you could practically buy the railway station."

Rather than the station, we bought a loaf of bread, some cheese, a few apples, and two bottles of white wine. We feasted for the next several hours. The ride was scenic and unusually varied as we traveled through mountain passes and valleys, along lakes, and over spectacular bridges. We even experienced a fierce snowstorm, reminding us that winter had almost arrived.

Our arrival in Trieste was a startling contrast. The night was almost balmy, and the sky was filled with stars and a full moon. If we had a place to sleep it would have been perfect, but it was a holiday and every available bed was occupied. As a last resort we located a U.S. Army hotel, where Woody presented his Air Corps reserve card. No rooms were available, but we were offered two oversized chairs in the lounge. After our endless train ride, the upholstered chairs looked to our weary eyes like pure feather down mattresses.

I awoke the next morning to a most remarkable sight; sunlight was streaming through the windows! We had not seen this joyful phenomenon in weeks. I shook Woody awake.

"You're not going to believe this," I said. "We're in sunny Italy—just like the travel posters promised. Let's get going; we can't afford to waste this glorious weather."

Our first stop was the American Express office, where we both picked up several letters, but more importantly, learned that we had a new president. General Dwight D. Eisenhower defeated Adlai Stevenson as decisively as he had beaten the German Army. It was an absolute landslide.

Five years earlier, as a merchant seaman, I had visited Trieste, but saw little, other than the results of the recent war. Half-sunk ships littered the harbor. We explored the castle, churches, marketplace, and also visited the busy waterfront with its picturesque fishing vessels and pleasure boats. Happily, the half-sunk ships were gone. The contrast with Germany and Austria was striking. The Italians spoke a melodious language, rather than the guttural sounds that had assaulted our ears the past few weeks. The architecture was also different, with light colored structures instead of the dark, oppressive stonework found in the north. That evening we enjoyed a wonderful pasta dinner along with a liter of vino di tavola.

"It would be nice to stay here a few days," said Woody.

"We'll be back in Italy in a couple of months," I said, "and then we can spend all the time and eat all the pasta we want."

The following night we took a train to Fiume, or Rijeka, as the Yugoslavs called it. The confusion of having two names for one city was nothing compared with the chaos of this area's history. As part of the Austro-Hungarian Empire, this area was originally known by the cumbersome name of Kingdom of the Serbs, Croats, and Slovenes. After World War I the area became a constitutional monarchy and was renamed Yugoslavia. During the recent war Axis forces invaded and dismembered the country. Communist Partisans led a wartime resistance movement, and when the war ended its founder, Marshall Josip Tito, became the Prime Minister. At first, it was a repressive communist state, but in the last few years Yugoslavia was known to be a freer and more open country. As we were soon to discover, that was an illusion.

So here was a complex group of countries with varied histories, ethnicities, and religions all held together by an iron-fisted leader. As visitors we were unaware of conflicts, because everyone seemed the same—a bit dour, unfriendly, and dreadfully poor. The war had devastated the country and revealed the enmity among neighboring groups. In fact, the very last European battle of World War II was fought between Yugoslav Partisans and a mixture of Croatians and Nazis. Oddly, the battle occurred two weeks after the suicide of Hitler and fall of Berlin.

Our train arrived quite late in Rijeka, where the weather was cold and blustery. The tourist office was closed, and there was no hotel in sight. However, an old woman approached and offered us a room for the night. We did not understand a single Slavic word she spoke, so it was not immediately clear what she was saying.

"I think she's looking for a handout," said Woody.

"No, I think she's selling something."

Then she began speaking Italian and German. I caught the words *stanza* and *schlafen*.

"I think she's offering us a place to sleep."

"Well, why the hell didn't she say so?" asked Woody.

"How much?" I asked. "*Quanto? Wie viel?*"

She picked up a twig and scratched a number in the dirt: 100.

"One hundred dinars is about thirty cents," I said. "What a deal!"

We walked for about ten minutes and finally arrived at a three-story dilapidated apartment building. The walls were marked by bullet holes, and the place looked ready for the wrecker's ball.

"It's only for the night," I said to my worried-looking companion.

"Let's hope we last that long," he said.

The room was certainly no palace, but it had two beds, appeared clean and tidy, and, not least of all, it was thirty cents! We were obliged to fill out endless governmental forms, courtesy of the Tito regime. While we were doing that, our sympathetic landlady prepared a plate of cheese and bread, which she served with freshly brewed tea. I was beginning to like this old lady.

Though the room was bare and primitive, we slept well and were up and out by five the next morning. We caught a ship heading for Split, and before the sun rose, we were steaming through the Adriatic Sea. The voyage took the entire day, during which we were never out of sight of land.

Shortly after leaving Rijeka we met an American passenger who introduced himself as Michael Figgs. He was director of the Yugoslavian Historical Society in New York. Figgs offered detailed information about the country, the people, and the Yugoslavian political system.

"As in other communist countries," Figgs began, "all means of production are owned by the people, but run by the government, which provides for the people's well-being. Everyone must work, and everyone must contribute. There's no private property here; everyone shares everything—at least that's the theory. Unfortunately, since the country has so little, there's not much to share. Most people lack basic necessities and, as you can see, luxuries simply don't exist. However, the situation is not all bad. Racial divisions and social classes have been eliminated, and workers are no longer exploited, as in capitalistic countries."

"Who makes these decisions?" asked Woody. "Who says I can't own my own house or become a beach bum if I want?"

"There's only one political party in Yugoslavia, and the party sets the policy. Their decisions are enforced by the police, or in extreme cases, by the army."

"That doesn't allow much free choice," I suggested.

"Communism is not about free choice," said Figgs, "it's about doing what's best for the majority of people."

"And who decides what's best?" I asked skeptically. "Some bureaucrat?"

"I didn't say the system was perfect," answered Figgs. "You know, all political systems have advantages and disadvantages."

"That may be," said Woody, "but if I choose not to work in the U.S., I won't be arrested."

We arrived in Split at about eight in the evening and got a nice room for about a dollar a night. The walled city of Split dated from Roman times, and one of its most interesting attractions was the ancient Palace of Diocletian, which we visited the following morning. Much of the original structure remained, and we found the ruins fascinating. The town had its charm, but the crushing poverty together with the dull weather made for a dismal visit.

We were scheduled to leave for Dubrovnik the next morning, but the government-run travel agency gave us erroneous information. We arrived at the dock at seven in the morning, only to discover our boat had left at six. When we complained the agent said, "You must have written down the wrong time. I distinctly said six." Some sympathy would have been welcome; but compassion, it seemed, was a rare commodity among Marxists.

We decided to spend our unanticipated free day visiting Trogir, a village originally settled by ancient Greeks. The one-hour bus trip was an adventure in itself. Our bus was a relic from 1930. When the vehicle was loaded—actually crammed full like a sardine can—the driver cranked the motor to life, and we were off. We left the last paved road ten minutes into the trip and for the next hour bounced along the rocky countryside like a canoe in the rapids. Upon our arrival Woody exclaimed, "Th-th-thank God it's over! I ca-ca-can't stop shaking!"

We discovered that Trogir residents were even more miserable than those in Split. As a group, they looked in worse shape than Dust Bowl migrants of the thirties. We speculated that those few with matching coats and trousers were government officials. Almost everyone else wore mismatched patched clothes, and the very worst-off had patches on top of patches.

Trogir had no main street, nor were any of the streets paved. Thus we wandered through mud and dust to view historic palaces, towers, and ancient fortifications. We also walked along the shopping street, but that was a sad misnomer. There was nothing to buy! One shop had a large display window, and at the center of this space were three, used, double edge razor blades. I'm not kidding; you had to look twice to even find them. Finally, there they were—three used razor blades!

"This must be the used razor blade shop," Woody joked, but it was more tragic than funny. I never imagined there could be such crushing poverty. What a relief to return that evening to the relative prosperity of cosmopolitan Split.

We left for Dubrovnik the next day on the early morning boat. A young student, Vladan Dragovic, attached himself to us and for the next eight hours related disturbing stories about conditions in Yugoslavia.

"I hope I can trust you," is how the conversation began. I was immediately suspicious. Why did he need our trust? "If you repeat any of this," he continued, "it could cause trouble. Communism in Yugoslavia is a miserable failure. If Ivan the Terrible ruled us it could not be worse. It's true the system has made everyone equal; but we are equally poor, equally cynical, and equally miserable. We have no freedom; we cannot speak openly, do as we like, or move about freely. We are like prisoners, and no one can complain. I could be arrested just for telling you this much."

"Do other people feel the way you do?" Woody asked.

"Yes; some say they will escape this country, even at the risk of death."

"Why are you telling us this?" I asked, still a bit skeptical.

"Perhaps you will return to America and tell people what life here is like. People should know what is happening in Yugoslavia. The party leaders who run our country have only one goal—maintaining power. Worst of all, most of the world believes Tito is a war hero; but actually, he is the most hated man in Yugoslavia."

I didn't know what to believe. Vladan spoke passionately, but we knew little about the situation. Everybody was dreadfully poor, that was obvious, but were they all as miserable and disillusioned? All I knew about communism is that many Americans feared it. After the war ended, Communism became our new enemy, and one of the nastiest names you could call a person was "Commie" or "Pinko". If the label stuck, you could lose your job and maybe your friends as well. An American wife-beater or bank robber had more respect than a member of the Communist Party.

We arrived in Dubrovnik late in the afternoon, and our new friend, Vladan, helped us get a room in a private house for less than a dollar a night. The room was sparse but comfortable, and it had a spectacular view of the Adriatic Sea.

"Come tonight to the Gradska Kafana," he suggested, "and you will see the best Dubrovnik has to offer—good food, good conversation, and many pretty girls."

Vladan's stories may have been distorted, but the promise of good food and pretty girls convinced us to give the place a try.

The Gradska Kafana was located along the Stradum, which was the popular promenade in the heart of the old town. Starting late in the afternoon the entire town of Dubrovnik could be found strolling and chatting along the length of the Stradum. When we arrived at the Gradska Kafana it was crowded to capacity. "Over here!" we heard our friend shout. He was sitting with several others, including three of the most attractive young women we had seen since leaving Scandinavia.

"These are my friends from the boat," Vladan explained to the group. "Woody and Peter are both architects from America."

Everyone spoke at once, as the lively group welcomed us. We soon learned that the café had been a historic meeting place for artists since the turn of the century. It was also a place where one could get a cup of coffee or glass of wine and spend endless hours in idle conversation.

"Doesn't Tito mind if you spend the day here, instead of working?" I asked.

"Even Tito can't change years of tradition," answered Karolina, the most attractive of the group. "People have met here for years. Besides, the eccentric habits of artists are rarely understood and most often ignored."

We drank and ate and the conversation continued long into the night. I learned that Karolina was a writer, who attempted for over a year to get a visa to visit England. Friends of hers at the British Consulate made the arrangements, but the government would not allow her to leave the country. She was refused a visa twice before, but she continued pursuing her goal.

Mikaela, who was a graphic artist, told the following story: "My mother owns a house not far from here, along the coast. When Tito came to power we were forced to accept a tenant because we had an empty room. The tenant is mentally unbalanced, and every day I am afraid to leave my mother alone with him. But we are not permitted to remove the tenant. Right now a friend is with my mother, but often she is alone. It is a dangerous situation, and there is nothing we can do."

Erik, an architect, said, "There is no freedom here, certainly not like in most other countries. You must design what you are told in the style dictated by the government. Don't you wonder why the new architecture here is so dreadful? There is no originality, no incentive to do good work. The government crushes all ambition. By the way, don't repeat this; I don't need any more trouble."

The following afternoon I asked Woody what he thought of those stories. We were splashing about in the Adriatic, my first swim since leaving the Nieuw Amsterdam months earlier. The water was cool, but the weather was warm and the skies clear.

"I don't think I'll settle here," he joked. "Too many rules. This place reminds me of the Building Department where all you hear is, 'Sorry, that's not allowed'". We continued visiting the sights of Dubrovnik and spent several evenings at the Gradska Kafana, which soon became our favorite bar, restaurant, and social club. On our last evening we attended a party at the British Consulate in honor of a British naval ship that had just arrived in port. The invitation came from Karolina's Consulate friends. She said, "I hope you can come. The food and drinks will be good, and everyone will be speaking English." Then she added, "Perhaps you will dance with me."

We ate and drank and danced until past midnight, at which time nearly every British sailor was drunk, and at least half of them unconscious.

"I thought sailors could hold their liquor," said Karolina.

"Not if they drink British martinis," I answered. "I've had two, and if you weren't holding me up, I'd probably be on the floor with the rest of them."

"Then, I better not let go of you," she said.

"You are much too kind, my dear." And then we whirled about the floor and I kissed her. She suddenly stopped dancing. "Why did you do that?" she asked.

"Because you are sweet and beautiful, and I am infatuated and drunk."

She held my face in her hands, and gave me a long kiss.

"Come home with me," she said. "I want you to spend your last night here with me."

Even if I were sober I could not have resisted. I told Woody I'd meet him at the train station the next morning. But he was so completely wrapped up in Mikaela's arms he had all he could do to nod in agreement.

"That was some party," Woody said the next morning. We were on an old train to Belgrade, and the ancient engine sounded as if it might give out before the daylong journey was over.

"I'm still a bit dizzy myself," I said. "But what a night!" And then I became lost in memory. We had a short layover during a snowstorm in Sarajevo, but by the time we reached Belgrade, the sky had cleared. Belgrade was a city of half a million, but that may have included the horses, which typically outnumbered the people in every Yugoslavian town. There was little of interest to see, and virtually nothing to do. It appeared the stores were having rummage sales, as most items were used goods. Also, here, as well as other places, there was an uncomfortable shortage of toilet paper. Had we not saved our paper napkins from restaurants, we might have suffered a genuine crisis.

The frigid weather, together with our unattractive, unheated room convinced us to leave for Greece as soon as possible. We purchased tickets on the Orient Express and the following morning bid our Marxist comrades a fond *dovidjenja*. We were off to Greece, where democracy was born nearly three thousand years earlier. It was bound to be a dramatic change from the communist state we were leaving.

CHAPTER FOURTEEN

Greece

The original Orient Express ran between Paris and Istanbul, and for years it had conjured up images of international luxury, mystery, and intrigue. Thus, we expected grand service, blazing speed, and perhaps an exotic adventure or two. Unfortunately, none of that happened. Our trip from Belgrade to Athens, a journey of over seven hundred miles, took thirty-six hours, during which we experienced boredom, frustration, and more than our share of discomfort. Our third-class car was filled with local peasants who squatted in the aisles, wailed native songs long into the night, and never stopped eating from bottomless baskets of malodorous food. Nevertheless, the long trip provided ample time to digest our recent experiences.

"I knew some communists in Berkeley," I said. "At least they believed they were; but I don't think any of them had the faintest idea what it was all about. They met across the hall in my rooming house, and all they did was drink vodka, sing folk songs, and practice free love. I think it was more about sex than politics."

"I don't think a classless system is possible," Woody said. "There will always be some who tell the others what to do. So a few rise to the top, and everybody else sinks to the bottom. Fascism, Communism, old-style monarchies—they're all the same. Democracy may be a terrible form of government, but as Churchill said, the others are worse."

We left our crowded coach after dark and moved forward to an empty first-class compartment, where we hoped for some uninterrupted sleep. But that idea was nipped in the bud. Before our shoes were off, a conductor asked to see our tickets. We were summarily kicked back to third class. We reached the Yugoslavian-Greek border around midnight, and since locals were not permitted to leave the country, the train became nearly empty. We were finally able to stretch out to sleep, but once again, bureaucratic interruptions made that difficult. First our luggage was searched; then our money was counted. Next, our passports were checked, as were our immigration papers. Finally, the conductor punched our tickets. The train moved slowly across the border, where Greek officials repeated the entire cycle. The border crossing took more than three hours! It was little consolation that those who spent a small fortune to occupy a sleeping compartment had no more sleep than we did. *Was this really the Orient Express?* I wondered.

We traveled the following day through rocky valleys, mountain passes, and endless tunnels, while a continuous rain fell. We arrived in Athens by early evening and went directly to the American School of Classical Studies, where—because of my fellowship—we had a reservation. Our adjoining rooms felt like a Greek branch of the Waldorf Astoria. Such luxury, not to mention privacy! Soft beds, hot water, showers, and all this for about a dollar a night.

"Do you think you'll be able to sleep without me in the room?" asked Woody.

"I might miss your snoring."

"I don't snore!" he protested. Of course—no one believes they snore.

That evening we had dinner in the school dining room and met several of the residents. They were almost all American archeology students and teachers. They were also—as a group—incredibly pedantic and totally humorless. The dinner conversation was entirely about their work. One student had just discovered a small oil lamp, another recently unearthed an ancient coin, and there was a thirty-minute debate about a small bit of marble molding that defied identification. The conversations were interesting for the first fifteen minutes, but then I noticed Woody yawning.

"How much fun are you having?" I whispered.

"The Vomiting Venus was fun," he answered. "This is painful."

Sitting next to me was a young student named Edgar Potter. "Where do you go in Athens for entertainment?" I asked.

"What do you mean?" He looked confused.

"You know, drinking, dancing, movies—having fun."

"Having fun for us is starting a new dig," he said. "Exploring archaeological sites, identifying new artifacts, solving ancient mysteries. That's how archaeologists amuse themselves."

"Does anyone at the school date girls?" Woody asked. "Is that permitted?"

"I suppose it is," answered Potter, "but, as you can see, there aren't many girls here."

"How about Greek girls?"

"Greek girls?" he asked. "Are girls all that architects think about?"

"Pretty much," said Woody. "You know, as a group, architects are remarkably oversexed." Edgar Potter had no response for that.

After a wonderful night's sleep, we returned to the dining hall moments before they stopped serving breakfast. And what a breakfast! Eggs, bacon, toast, and American coffee. It felt like we were at a coffee shop back in the States.

As we left the School the skies cleared and a brilliant sun appeared. We headed for the most famous sight in Athens and one of the greatest monuments of Western Civilization—the Acropolis. On this natural hill was built, over two thousand years earlier, the most important structures from the Hellenic Period of Greek civilization. Foremost among these was the Parthenon, a temple of such refined elegance that it served for centuries as a model of absolute architectural perfection.

"I remember this from school," said Woody, "but I never expected to be so moved."

Woody was right, no plan or photograph could possibly convey the emotional power of walking among these marvelous monuments. We spent the entire day viewing the various temples and realized that, up to that moment, it was the most significant architectural experience of our trip.

That evening we decided to find a restaurant that served Greek specialties. Although the food at the school was quite good, it was almost exclusively American style. Edgar Potter had said, "All Greek restaurants are the same, so find any old *estiatorio* and you'll be okay." The trouble was, what did that look like in Greek?

"I'll bet that's it," I said pointing to a sign that said *ΕΣΤΙΑΤΟΡΙΟ*.

Sure enough, it was a restaurant; but how would we translate the menu? The proprietor, who spoke English, came to our rescue. "Let me suggest our specialties," he said. "Feta cheese salad, baked lamb with yoghurt, and for dessert, almond pie."

We began with a powerful glass of ouzo, which made us both a bit dizzy. Then we spent more than an hour consuming the house specialties. The flavors were unusual, but pleasant. Less than two hours later my stomach was contorted into a Gordian knot. Desperate for help, I visited the director of the school, who gave me a strong dose of medicine.

"Eating in Athens can be treacherous," he said. "It looks like a touch of Plato's Plague."

"What's that?" I asked.

"The usual traveler's complaint," he answered. "Abdominal cramps, diarrhea, nausea. It comes from unfriendly bacteria, and it's common in less developed countries. You may have heard of "Montezuma's Revenge" in Mexico. Well, there's also "Delhi Belly" in India and "Mummy Tummy" in Egypt. Here it's "Plato's Plague", but it's all the same, and it's no fun. However, it's not fatal, and you should be better by tomorrow. Just be careful what you eat."

I did feel better the next day, but I had little appetite. Woody was apparently unaffected.

"You must have a cast iron stomach," I said.

"Pretty much," he answered. "But you might have noticed, I skipped the salad. In my opinion, vegetables are not particularly good for you." I figured every nutritionist in the world would be shocked by that news.

I picked up a dozen letters at American Express and spent the rest of the day at a sidewalk café quietly sipping tea and reading my mail. Among the usual letters from family and friends were one each from Deborah Wolfe and Monika Ecklund. Those exciting romantic encounters seemed so long ago, but their words brought to mind memorable experiences.

I felt well enough the following day to resume our sightseeing program. There were so many ancient monuments to see, one hardly knew where to begin. We visited the Temple of Zeus and Tower of the Winds, as well as the National Archaeological Museum, which housed sculptural masterpieces from the classic Hellenic period. What a time that Golden Age must have been! I knew that the Greek civilization influenced our way of life, but I had no idea that our philosophy, government, mathematics, art, literature, and principles of beauty were still affected to this day by Grecian standards. That was some of what we learned during our short stay in Athens.

We spent the following day trying to plan the next leg of our journey. What a battle that was! We consulted schedules, studied maps, and compared prices, but no one travel agency in the entire city of Athens had all the information we needed. For example, if you wanted to go to Egypt, which we did, and you wanted to fly there, you had to find the one agency that dealt with flights to Egypt. If you wanted to take a boat to Egypt, there was a different agency for that. And if you wanted to go to anywhere else, let's say Tel Aviv, you had to find the particular agency that had information about Israel. There was no agency that could even tell us which agency dealt with which country.

Further complicating our planning was the restriction that did not permit anyone with a passport stamp from Israel to enter an Arab country. We finally found a flight to Cairo on the Egyptian Airline at a student rate, which was half the normal rate. But just as we were about to purchase the tickets, the agent said, "Of course you realize this is a round trip fare. You must return to Athens within the month."

"That's impossible," I said. "We plan to visit Israel, and we won't be able to return to Egypt with an Israeli stamp in our passport. How do you expect us to catch a flight back here from Cairo?" We obviously needed a new plan.

"Here's a thought," said Woody. "Forget Egypt for now; let's go to Turkey. We'll see the mosques and minarets, and once we're there we can figure out our next move."

I hadn't considered traveling as far as Turkey—that was practically Asia; but it certainly sounded appealing. We booked passage the following day on an Italian ship sailing from Piraeus to Istanbul in four days. What a relief it was to finally have a plan.

We took a bus the next day to Delphi, which was about a hundred miles northwest of Athens. The bus was ancient, the road was little more than a mule path, and the driver raced over steep mountain roads like a former Indy 500 driver. After four harrowing hours we arrived in Delphi and found a room at one of the two hotels in town. The room cost sixteen thousand drachmas, which sounded hideously expensive, but amounted to just over a dollar.

Delphi was a small town perched precariously on the side of a mountain. It was a great archaeological center and major site for the worship of the god Apollo. It was also the site of the most famous oracle in ancient Greece. People would come to the Oracle of Delphi to consult on matters from public policy to personal affairs. We arose early to visit the ruins. We climbed quite a distance and saw the ancient theater, stadium, and Temple of Apollo—all wonderful examples of classic architecture. We also visited the famous Oracle.

"Now's your chance," I said to Woody. "If there's anything on your mind, ask the Oracle."

"This may not be original," he said, "but I've got to know—will I find true love in the next year?" This was the first hint that my peripatetic friend was thinking of settling down.

Just then a brilliant flash of lightening lit up the sky. A deafening explosion of thunder followed; and then came a torrential downpour.

"Does that answer your question?" I asked.

"Yeah, but what does it mean?"

"That's got to be a yes," I said, as we raced down the hill towards our hotel. By the time we reached shelter we were drenched. We couldn't change clothes, because everything we owned was in Athens—everything, that is, except our raincoats. Those we had left in the hotel room. Looking like two wet sponges, we caught the bus to Athens and returned to the school a soggy mess.

"Now that the Oracle has promised you true love," I said, "you better get that suit pressed. Otherwise Miss Right will take one look and walk right on by."

On the morning of our departure we said goodbye to the archaeology students, thanked the helpful director, and caught an early bus to Piraeus. The port of Athens and our ship to Istanbul was located about ten kilometers south of the city, which translated into an easy thirty-minute bus ride. Once there, however, the fun and games began.

"Where do we get our passports stamped?" we asked at the dock.

"The Passport Agency is in that direction," answered the official pointing up the road.

"How far?"

"Not far."

"How long does it take to get there?"

"Not long."

"And the Currency Control Bureau?"

"That's four blocks from the Passport Agency."

"Four blocks east or west?"

"Yes."

"I'm not even going to ask about the Customs Office," I said to Woody. "I might turn into an ugly American and strangle this guy."

The obvious lack of any system in modern-day Greece was frustrating and difficult to understand. The ruins surrounding these people were a constant reminder of one of the greatest civilizations that ever existed. Ancient Greece was the absolute model of logic and rational thought. Where did all that common sense go? Why were we forced to visit three obscurely located and widely separated offices in Piraeus to gather enough official documents to board our ship? Did they forget every lesson from two thousand years ago?

We allowed the entire morning to accomplish the requisites of our departure; nevertheless, we boarded our ship just moments before the anchor was raised. With great relief we sailed into the Aegean Sea and headed for Turkey. In another thirty hours we would be in a different country, with different people of a different culture speaking a different language. It was a thrilling thought, and I knew then, despite the endless frustrations, I would never lose enthusiasm for my true love of travel.

CHAPTER FIFTEEN

Turkey

The *Barletta* was a relatively small ship, but it was tidy and comfortable. We shared a cabin with two young Italians who spoke no English, but with a few *buon giornos* and appropriate gestures, we got along fine. Most of the crew, including the cooks, were also Italian; and shortly after leaving Piraeus they prepared a three-course lunch that was the finest food we had eaten since our stopover in Trieste a few weeks before.

"Isn't this simply marvelous food?" asked our tablemate at lunch. He introduced himself as Adolph Altshuler, a retired stockbroker from San Francisco. Altshuler was slender, bald, wore horn-rimmed glasses, and was fashionably dressed. He appeared to be in his late forties.

"You seem rather young to be retired," I said.

"Do you call sixty-two young?" he asked.

"Sixty-two? You look fifteen years younger," I said. "What's your secret?"

"Mostly luck," he said, "but it also doesn't hurt to stay active and remain curious."

Over coffee in the lounge, we continued our conversation and learned that Altshuler's wife and only child died five years earlier in a tragic auto accident. "That horrible event changed everything," he said. "In a matter of moments my family was gone and I was completely alone. I suffered through a terrible depression for more than a year.

Finally, I decided a year of self-pity was enough; it was time to move on. I quit my job and decided to travel—something I had always wanted to do. Traveling seemed to help, and I've been at it ever since."

"Do you ever miss your work?" I asked.

"Sometimes. I was pretty good at what I did, and I made a lot of money. But after the accident I realized that making more money didn't change anything. I needed some time off."

"That's a touching story, Mr. Altshuler," said Woody.

"Please—the name is Adolph. I know Hitler didn't do people like me any favor, but I'm okay with Adolph. You know, my parents gave me that name before the war. I always thought, not so bad, really; they could have named me Attila." Then he chuckled at his own little joke.

We awoke the next morning to find ourselves sailing through the Dardanelles Strait, which connected the Aegean Sea to the Sea of Marmara. I went on deck and found Adolph leaning on the rail and staring at land that was visible on both sides of this narrow strip of water.

"Good morning," he said. "Did you sleep well?"

"I did until one of my Italian roommates began fighting World War II again. I guess he was having a nightmare. He seemed to be back in Sicily during the Allied invasion."

By early afternoon the city of Istanbul was clearly visible on the horizon. An hour later, as we entered the harbor, we marveled at the mosques and minarets that made up the unique skyline. Approaching Istanbul from the sea was one of the most exotic views one could imagine. It resembled an illustration out of the Arabian Nights. After docking we proceeded through Immigration and Customs. An inspector stopped me to examine my metal watchband. It was gold-plated, and he wanted to know more about it.

"It's just a simple band," I said. "Not even real gold. You can buy one for about a dollar."

Nevertheless, he recorded its existence in my passport, fearing, perhaps, that I would sell it while in Turkey. On the other hand, he completely ignored my foreign currency that was normally recorded in passports and which amounted to considerably more than a dollar.

We found a small hotel while walking towards the center of town. It seemed a bit dilapidated, but at a cost of two-and-a-half liras, we couldn't complain. The official rate of exchange was just under three liras to the dollar, but later that day we located the black market and got more than four. Thus, our room cost about sixty cents a night. Unfortunately, it wasn't worth much more. The room was small, but it accommodated two beds with sagging mattresses and furnishings that appeared to be Salvation Army castoffs. The bathroom was down the hall, and it contained a tub with rust stains. The toilet was in its own compartment, and it was there I came upon my first "Turkish John". I had heard of this diabolical Middle Eastern invention, but to see it and use it was an experience I will never forget.

The Turkish John consisted of a flat porcelain platform, about two-feet square, that was attached to the floor. At its center was a small opening, and on either side of the opening were textured footpads. The footpads were raised an inch or so above the level of the hole. To use this unpleasant device, one had to place his feet—or I suppose *her* feet—on the platforms, squat in a most uncomfortable position, and hope the experience would end before losing your balance. Finally, there was a water tank located high on the wall behind the device. To flush, one pulled a chain attached to the water tank, and this action released a Niagara-sized torrent of water guaranteed to soak your shoes unless you leaped off the foul contraption with the agility of an acrobat. Subsequently, when the need arose, I sought out more modern public toilets elsewhere in the city. I believe to this day the Turkish John is the most disgusting receptacle for elimination that ever existed. I would gladly take a hike in the woods and risk a charging grizzly to avoid it.

Plumbing was only the tip of the iceberg, with regard to exotic Turkish life; everything in this part of the world seemed more foreign than anything we previously experienced. This historic area, known as Byzantium, was the ancient capital of the Byzantine Empire. When the Roman Emperor Constantine made it the capital of the Eastern Empire, he renamed the city Constantinople. Following its fall to the Ottoman Turks in the fourteenth century, it was finally renamed Istanbul. Evidence of previous empires was everywhere, making the city a living, historical museum.

Istanbul was divided into three principal parts. Our hotel was located in the European section. Across the water to the southwest was the real Istanbul, the Old City. And the third part, across the Bosporus, was Asia Minor. That was the spot where Europe and Asia met. Most of the historic monuments, as well as other interesting sights, were located in the Old City, so that's where we headed.

The greatest monument ever built in Istanbul was Hagia Sophia, considered the masterpiece of Byzantine architecture and one of the most extraordinary structures ever built. The Roman Emperor Justinian set out to build the largest cathedral the world had ever seen. It remained that for nearly a thousand years. The Ottoman Turks later converted it to a mosque. Hagia Sophia combined the artistry of Greece, the engineering genius of Rome, and the color and mysticism of the East.

We were completely stunned by the size, scope, and power of the church's interior space.

The main dome was immense—more than a hundred feet in diameter—and it floated a hundred and eighty feet above the floor! We spent the entire morning studying the mosaics and frescoes, and marveling at this incredible feat of engineering. One cannot visit such a unique monument and remain unaffected. We had a late lunch and sat nearly silent as the impressions of our visit sank in.

"I'm glad you talked me into Turkey," I said. "I'll never forget this."

"Believe me," said Woody, "I had no idea what we were in for."

We visited the Blue Mosque that afternoon and found details similar to Hagia Sophia, but not the same level of perfection. However, unlike Hagia Sophia, the Blue Mosque was still used for worship, and that was a new experience We were obliged to remove our shoes before entering, and Woody's concern was that someone would take off with them and leave in their place a pair of cheap, worn-out sandals. Glancing at his shoes I suggested, "That might be doing you a favor."

The entire floor of the Mosque was covered with classic Oriental rugs. As we watched, many devout visitors performed their rituals, which consisted of executing gymnastic-like maneuvers that ended with their heads on the floor bowed to the east. In addition to the movements there was constant chanting and wailing going on, which sounded less like prayer and more like the endless moaning of people who just lost their fortunes at the race track.

The following day was Thanksgiving, which meant absolutely nothing in this part of the world. We spent most of the day at the famous Grand Bazaar. What an experience that was! The enclosed area covered over fifty streets and contained nearly a thousand shops. There were several impressive entrances, and the ornate arched walkways were richly decorated with mosaics and glazed tiles. As we entered this crowded area exotic sights and sounds overwhelmed us. It was like being in the middle of a three-ring circus. People were shouting at each other as they bargained over jewelry, leather goods, pottery, tapestries, water pipes, and foods like yoghurt, spices, and tea. There were also many restaurants, each of which filled the air with exotic aromas. The crowd consisted of all classes, from wealthy business people to beggars and thieves, and strangely, they all seemed to be having a wonderful time.

"What a scene!" said Woody. "Like Times Square on New Year's Eve, only more so."

"Just keep a hand on your wallet," I advised.

The general rule for shoppers at the Grand Bazaar was never accept the first price offered. Shop owners considered business a game in which patrons were obliged to bargain for the lowest possible price. Thus, one allowed considerable time to negotiate, bluff, protest, shout, and eventually throw up one's hands. Sometimes one just walked away in disgust, only to return a moment later to resume the game. Since prices were not displayed, one had no idea what anything cost or how little a shop owner would accept. It was clear, however, that the most aggressive shoppers bought at the lowest price. But who knew what it did to their digestive system?

Woody and I wandered the colorfully tiled streets for several hours, as we watched people purchasing everything from gold rings to colorful rugs. It was uniquely entertaining. We were offered all manner of products and services, including black market money and escort services that promised to satisfy any sexual fantasy one could imagine.

"I have a pretty good imagination," said my friend. "What do you think they have in mind?"

Suddenly, and without warning, I saw Woody turn quickly and catch the wrist of a small boy who had his hand in his rear pocket.

"What the hell!" shouted Woody. "What do you think you're doing, you little shit-head?" The boy tried to run, but Woody's grip was like a vise. "No you don't," he yelled. "Show me what's in your hand!"

The boy, who was perhaps ten years old, opened his hand to reveal the key to our room.

"What?" shouted Woody, "You risked getting your arm broken for a key to our lousy room? It's not worth it, kid; the room's a dump."

The child was almost in tears by now, and a small group had gathered to see what the fuss was about. A shopkeeper from a jewelry booth across the street approached and said, "I know this child; he is the son of a friend. If you allow me, I will return him to his parents."

"What if had stolen my wallet? asked Woody. "What would we do then?"

"But it was only a key," said the shopkeeper.

"Today it's a key," said Woody; "tomorrow it could be a gold watch from *your* shop."

"I will impress that message upon him *and* his parents," said the shopkeeper. "What more would you have me do?"

"Let it go," I said to Woody. "We don't want this little crook to end up in jail. Let his parents handle it. You've made your point, and he looks like he's suffered enough."

The boy handed over the key, and Woody said, "I don't ever want to see you again, kid. The next time you put your hand in my pocket, you're going to lose a couple of fingers. Now go home and read the Ten Commandments. Maybe you'll learn something about morality." The child probably didn't understand a word Woody said, but he seemed contrite and relieved that his criminal venture had not ended more seriously.

Our new friend, Adolph Altshuler insisted that we be his guests at a holiday dinner. He was staying at the elegant Palace Hotel located next to the famous Topkapi Palace, former home of the Ottoman Sultans. Adolph seemed thrilled to be sharing Thanksgiving with fellow Americans.

"I've been working on this dinner all day," he said. "Strange as it sounds, Turkey is not the easiest bird to find in Turkey. It would have been easier to arrange a dinner with pigeons. But I spoke with the hotel chef, and he's been very cooperative. A word of warning: our Thanksgiving dinner, will not be typical." What an understatement that turned out to be!

We entered the ornate dining room and were seated at a comfortable table overlooking the adjacent Palace. We were sipping cocktails when Adolph said, "I have something to say. You know, I haven't celebrated Thanksgiving since my family's death, but this holiday has always meant a lot to me." Tears suddenly appeared in his eyes. There was a long pause as he regained his composure. "I thought I was over that," he said, "but apparently not." After another long pause he said, "I'm thankful for so much; being with you two, my good health, and the means to enjoy this dinner."

"We also are thankful," I said, "especially for our unexpected meeting."

"That goes double for me," said Woody. "You're a generous host, Adolph."

The first course was a delicious bowl of lentil soup served with a dollop of yoghurt and toasted strips of pita bread. Then came a salad of fresh spinach, zucchini, and green peppers. Finally slices of roast turkey arrived. A mixture of baked eggplant, chickpeas, and rice accompanied the turkey—apparently the chef's version of dressing. The dinner ended with baklava and small cups of Turkish coffee. There were no cranberries, sweet potatoes, string beans, or pumpkin pie, but our Thanksgiving dinner at the Palace Hotel was one of the most memorable meals I ever had.

As we sat around the table sipping coffee our friend Adolph Altshuler kept repeating, "Turkey in Turkey—who would believe that?" It was the identical message I received on holiday cards in subsequent years.

Do you remember that wonderful Thanksgiving when we had turkey in Turkey? Who would believe that?

In the following days we visited Roman and Byzantine ruins and generally wandered about Istanbul absorbing the city's exotic flavor. We noticed a few indications of wealth, but the vast majority was noticeably impoverished. Many wore rags, in the literal sense of the word, and some were without shoes. Transportation appeared to be from another century, as sad-looking horses and human pack animals did the majority of work. One brave fellow we saw carried a small piano on his back. Another was dwarfed by a tall grandfather's clock that he carried over one shoulder. "Maybe we should tell him," said Woody, recalling the age-old joke, "they have wrist watches now." Women were no longer veiled, as the government outlawed that practice years earlier. But some wore scarves pulled across their mouths in a veil-like fashion. Apparently, old habits died slowly.

At the end of the week we began to plan the next leg of our journey. It was a typically frustrating experience. We obtained a visa to visit Lebanon, as that would be our next stop; and after Lebanon we planned a trip to Syria. However, when the Syrian official saw the Lebanese visa, he refused to issue a transit visa. There was no reason, no explanation, and definitely no visa.

Woody got out his map and within ten minutes we came up with a dramatic change of plan: we would fly to Cairo. We figured we'd deal with the other countries after that. As the Turkish Airline accepted payment in local currency, we used black market money, and the flight turned out to be an incredible bargain. The night before our flight we checked into a decent hotel so we could finally have modern plumbing, a good dinner, and a bed that didn't feel like a hammock from an eighteenth-century sailing ship.

The airline bus picked us up early the following morning and drove us to the airport, where our DC-3 was parked. Fog in Ankara delayed our departure, but then we were off, sailing high over snow-capped mountains. We went through customs and passport control during our stop in Ankara, and by early afternoon our plane headed for Beirut. We arrived after sunset, and the captain informed us that we would spend the night there.

"Why?" I asked. "Why not continue to Cairo?"

"Sorry," said the captain, "we do not fly after dark." More peculiar rules.

A Turkish Airline bus drove us to downtown Beirut, put us up at a first class hotel, bought us a wonderful dinner, and practically tucked us into a cozy bed. Just before turning out the light Woody said, "I feel a bit guilty using black market money to pay for this fabulous trip, but I don't think the guilt will keep me awake." I, on the other hand, remained awake for some time thinking; *tomorrow we'll be in the land of the ancient pyramids. God, this is exciting!* I eventually fell asleep and dreamed about pharaohs, high priests, and nubile handmaidens.

CHAPTER SIXTEEN

Egypt

"Egypt, mysterious land of the Pharaohs, was the oldest civilization the world has known!" That was how Professor Baumeister began his initial lecture during our first year of school. "Just think," he said, "Egypt was a great society a thousand years before Moses led the Israelites out of bondage. A thousand years!" he repeated. "And the reason we study Egyptian structures today is because those imposing temples and eternal tombs were forerunners of our architectural tradition. So pay close attention. One day you may visit the Valley of the Nile and view for yourself these amazing monuments—monuments that were built to last forever. And when you do, you will realize the thrill of what I am about to tell you."

I recalled those memorable words as we stepped off the plane at the Cairo airport. We were greeted by a blast of hot air, which was the first really warm weather I experienced since being in New York five months earlier. Passports were checked and custom officials counted our money. Then they reviewed an odd list of "Seriously Prohibited" items, confirming that we did not carry pistols, pornography, or parrots. "The three nasty Ps," Woody noted. I imagined that anyone getting off a plane in Cairo with a six-shooter on his hip, a stash of French postcards in his pocket, and a colorful parrot on his shoulder would be arrested and convicted in less time than Polly could beg for a cracker.

The airline bus dropped us off downtown, and a knowledgeable employee suggested a modest hotel in the heart of the city. The cost of the room was thirty-five piasters per night, about eighty cents. We quickly settled into our room and decided at once to visit Egypt's greatest architectural monuments—the ancient pyramids. I'm sure everyone on earth knows what the pyramids look like, but it was impossible to anticipate the emotional impact of seeing them in person. Professor Baumeister was right; it was an unforgettable thrill. There they were, the oldest and sole survivor of the Seven Ancient Wonders of the World! It took your breath away. These massive piles of masonry, created from immense blocks of limestone, rose five hundred feet above the sandy base of the Giza plateau. Built forty-five hundred years ago, the pyramids were the tallest man-made structures in the world for nearly four thousand years and, clearly, the oldest structures we would ever see. We spent the afternoon in Giza and watched a spectacular sunset turn these massive monuments crimson then violet then black.

"We've got to go back," said Woody. "A half day is not nearly enough time." So the following morning we left the hotel at sunrise and returned to the west bank of the Nile. As on our previous visit, a determined swarm of young "guides" immediately surrounded us. They offered post cards, camel rides, tours, and anything else a tourist might desire. One of the most popular souvenirs they promoted was "authentic" mummy wrappings.

"Where did you get these?" I asked a young boy.

"From a tomb in the Valley of the Kings," he replied.

"You mean you found a four thousand year old tomb, broke into the royal chamber, opened the coffin, and unwrapped the mummified body?"

"Yes," came the deadpan reply. "This is real, and it's worth a lot of money. But I sell it to you for only two Egyptian pounds."

"That's only five dollars," said Woody. "What a bargain!"

"If they were real," I said. "But they look to me like strips torn from an old linen curtain and soaked in a pot of Turkish coffee."

"Oh no," cried the boy, "these came from a real pharaoh."

The persistence of the guides was unbelievable; nothing could deter them. A simple "no thank you" was completely ignored, and an emphatic "*Yalla imshi!*" (Get out of here—right now!) was treated as an invitation to continue the harangue. Woody insisted to one young man that we didn't speak English, whereupon the young man continued his spiel in French, German, and Italian. There was absolutely no way to discourage or even slow down this super-salesman.

We decided to visit Khufu's burial chamber, which was located at the center of the great pyramid. Access was through a low, narrow passageway that was less than four feet high and seemed endless in length. It was one of the most claustrophobic experiences of my life. Just before panic overwhelmed me we reached the Grand Gallery and the spacious burial chamber beyond. The chamber was faced with pink granite slabs, and in the center of this large space was an empty stone sarcophagus. It appeared as though the pharaoh had just stepped out for a breath of air, but that moment was several hundred years earlier when grave robbers broke into the pyramid.

"He wasn't very tall," said Woody. "I wonder if I'd fit in that thing." Since we were alone, Woody impetuously climbed into the pharaoh's stone tomb.

"What the hell are you doing?" I shouted. But before he could answer I heard someone approach from the narrow passageway. "Stay where you are!" I whispered.

An elderly woman entered the burial chamber. "*Bon jour, monsieur,*" she said. I nodded and then positioned myself between her and the tomb. As she approached the tomb I moved to block her view. "*Pardon, monsieur,"* she said. Pretending I didn't understand I continued to block her from reaching the sarcophagus. Finally she walked swiftly around me, and at that precise moment Woody sat up in the tomb and uttered a blood-curdling shriek.

The elderly woman turned white, screamed, *"Mon Dieu!"* and fled the chamber. Woody leaped out of the sarcophagus and we followed the frantic victim down the claustrophobic passageway. When we reached the entrance we saw that the woman had collapsed and was being assisted by a guard. He was fanning her with a palm leaf.

"What happened up there?" asked the guard.

"I have no idea," I answered. "She just suddenly screamed and ran. That's all I know."

"She said the pharaoh rose up in his tomb and shouted something."

"Well obviously, that's impossible. She must have been hallucinating."

We sat at the nearby snack bar having a drink, and I said to Woody, "You know, you nearly gave both of us a heart attack. What were you thinking?"

"Sorry, Peter, but I couldn't think of any other way to get out of there."

After a while Woody looked up at the enormous pyramid and said, "You know, I've always wanted to climb that damn thing. Care to join me?""

A young guide overheard our conversation. He approached, introduced himself as Sameer and said, "You will need a guide to climb the pyramid."

"Thanks," I said, "but we'd prefer to be on our own. Anyway, why should we believe you?"

"This is a government rule," insisted the earnest young man. "I would not lie to you; it is for your own safety. Would you even know where to begin your climb?"

We looked up at this massive mound of masonry and Woody said, "He's right; I have no idea where to begin. Every side looks the same—impossible. I'm afraid we need help."

"Have you climbed this before?" I asked.

"Hundreds of times," Sameer answered.

"Hundreds of times? How old are you?"

"I will be fourteen in two weeks."

"I notice you have no shoes."

"Mountain goats have no shoes either," replied our young philosopher.

"Okay, Sameer, you've got a job."

"You can call me Sam," he said smiling.

Sam walked about fifty feet from the corner where we stood and asked, "Are you ready?" He found the remote steps and began moving slowly from one stone to the next, weaving a convoluted path generally along the northeast corner of the pyramid. Wherever he went there seemed to be small steps cut into the massive blocks of stone. However, there were no handrails or anything to hold onto. We were about a quarter of the way up when Sam paused to rest. I glanced down for the first time and felt a wave of panic.

Holy shit! This is crazy! Absolutely suicidal! Could it be as dangerous as it seems? Why on earth is this even permitted?

Another fleeting glance downward convinced me; it *was* as dangerous as it seemed, and incredibly, it *was* permitted. This adventure now looked utterly reckless.

"Shall we continue?" asked Sam. I looked at Woody. He appeared worried but said nothing.

"Why not?" I answered, but I could think of a hundred reasons why not.

When seen from the valley floor the height of Khufu was deceptive; there was nothing in the desert to give it scale. But from our current position—the equivalent height of a thirteen-story building—people on the ground appeared to be specks. We continued up the pyramid's corner, block by block, where any misstep could result in a fatal plunge. I concentrated on every move and every step as we plodded on.

"You know," said Sam, "sometimes people climb to the top of the pyramid only to throw themselves off. It is a popular way for Egyptians to commit suicide."

Why did he have to bring that up? Didn't we look frightened enough? Or did he suspect we'd fling ourselves off the top, bounce to our death, and he wouldn't be paid?

"Well, that's not our plan," I answered. "So let's be extra careful."

Eventually we reached the summit and found ourselves nearly five hundred feet above the desert floor. Having just climbed the equivalent of a fifty-story building we were physically and emotionally exhausted. We lay down on the stone platform and breathed a sigh of relief. The top of the pyramid was flattened into an area about thirty feet square, and every inch of the surface was covered with initials and names carved into the sandstone by previous visitors. Some carried dates from two centuries earlier.

"Look," said our young guide. "Over there is Sakkara." Sure enough, we could see the Step Pyramid of King Djoser, which was some fifteen miles away. "And across the Nile is Cairo." It appeared that all of Egypt was visible from our lofty vantage point. We remained atop Khufu for nearly three hours as we watched the birds above and the ant-like tourists below. During that time we were joined by half a dozen adventurous tourists, none of whom spoke English. The sun was moving lower when Sam suggested we begin our climb down. "It is difficult to climb during the day and nearly impossible in the dark."

Climbing down the pyramid was far more difficult than going up, because looking at the ground reminded you how far you had to fall. Despite our knowledgeable guide we realized we were pretty much on our own. He led the way, but he was powerless to prevent an inadvertent misstep. And a misstep seemed easily possible with nothing to hold onto. Thus, by the time we reached the ground we were dripping with perspiration and emotionally drained.

"We deserve a medal," said Woody.

"I'd settle for a cold shower and good dinner," I replied.

Before leaving Giza we visited the famous Sphinx, which sat a short distance from the pyramids and represented the oldest and largest monumental sculpture in existence. This reclining lion with a human head was about seventy feet high and as long as a football field. It was at least as old as the pyramids and, as an ancient work of art, equally impressive.

The following morning I called Ali Malek, an architectural classmate from Berkeley.

"Welcome to Cairo, Peter. I didn't believe you'd actually make it here."

"I only came because I knew how disappointed you'd be if I didn't."

"You will come to dinner tonight. Tia will cook something special."

"I'm traveling with Jim Elwood. Do you remember him from school?"

"Of course, bring him along."

Ali lived in Heliopolis, an elegant suburb of Cairo, in a home that, by any measure, would be considered a mansion. I realized that most foreign students at Berkeley either had money or affluent sponsors, but I had no idea that Ali was genuinely wealthy. We entered a large gated courtyard and were admitted to the house by a butler. Ali and his wife Tia greeted us in the entry hall as if we were long-lost relatives. There were hugs, kisses, and expressions of delight at our being together. Ali and I were cordial at school but hardly what you'd call best friends. Nevertheless, he acted as though we were the closest of fraternity brothers. The butler served drinks, and a maid passed a tray of hors d'oeuvres. Dinner was served in the dining room at a table that could have seated at least twenty more people.

"I know I promised that Tia would cook something special," said Ali, "but that's before I knew she was in a meeting all day. So we had the cook whip up a few Egyptian specialties. I hope you won't be disappointed."

No one could have been disappointed by that dinner. The main course was a spicy lamb dish served with lentils and rice. This was followed by a cold spinach and onion salad. Dessert consisted of an Egyptian orange cake with a chocolate glaze. "It is a local specialty," said Tia. Coffee was served in the living room, which resembled a room out of Vienna's Schönbrunn Palace. In fact, the entire house seemed fit for royalty. Before dinner I visited the bathroom, where it took several minutes to locate the toilet. The room was an oval about twenty-five feet long, and near the center was an ornate tub that could easily accommodate four adults. The toilet compartment was located in its own large space behind one of the several doors. Behind other doors were a bidet compartment, a shower compartment, a small sauna facility, and another small compartment for brushing teeth and nothing more. I wondered if this were really the guest bathroom.

"I've got to ask you, Ali, what's with the bathroom? I've never seen such an elaborate room. If you added a hot-plate, a family of four could live there very happily."

Tia laughed. "I suppose you've noticed," she said, "we're not in Berkeley any more. You see, our families bought this house for us when we got married. It's certainly more than we need, but they expect we will fill it with grandchildren."

Ali and Tia picked us up the following day and drove us to Medieval Cairo, the old Islamic section of the city. Cairo, the largest city in Africa, was often described as crowded, dusty, and exotic. We experienced all that and more. Traffic was chaotic; signals were mostly ignored, and donkey carts competed for space with the latest foreign automobiles.

After a typical Egyptian lunch we visited the Citadel, several mosques, and a lively bazaar, where one could purchase anything from live chickens to gold bracelets. The next day Ali drove us to Memphis and Sakkara.

"Are you sure it's no problem taking off time from work?" I asked.

"It's my father's architectural firm," he answered. "It's not a problem. Anyway, I love showing tourists my home town—especially when the tourists are architects."

Toward the end of the week we made plans to visit the monuments of Upper Egypt.

"Before you leave Cairo," said Ali, "you must come with us to Alexandria. It's only a couple of hours north, and the city has a beautiful setting right on the Mediterranean."

Alexandria, founded by Alexander the Great, was the country's capital for a thousand years. "We can visit some museums," said Ali, "see the Catacombs, or tour religious buildings. But I suggest we drive around and get the feeling of the place. Later we'll have a nice lunch along the Mediterranean and then it will be time to get you back to Cairo."

"Good plan," Woody and I agreed. We were exhausted from sightseeing and welcomed an effortless day of being pampered tourists. The restaurant Tia suggested was called *Maison Pharaon*, and its waterside setting was spectacular.

"One of their specialties here is roast pigeon," said Tia. "I heartily recommend it."

We sat beneath an umbrella on the outdoor terrace sipping our aperitifs and watching the harbor traffic. The sun was bright, the weather comfortable, and we savored this peaceful moment. Our lunch arrived and the pigeon on my plate looked delicious. I unfolded my napkin and was putting it on my lap when a blur of mottled fur flashed before my eyes. In less than a second a large cat had leaped across the table, snatched the pigeon from my plate, and was gone in an instant. It happened so incredibly fast I was unable to utter a sound. So there I sat, stunned, plate empty, and feeling more like a pigeon than the pigeon that got away.

"What happened?" the waiter wanted to know.

"Your cat just left with my pigeon," I said, "and he didn't leave a tip for you."

After we all had a good laugh, my pigeon was replaced and we enjoyed a memorable lunch. We drove back to the Cairo station where our overnight train to Luxor waited. We said goodbye and raced to board our third-class car, which was already moving when we reached the platform. Another close call, but it was nothing compared to the excitement that lay ahead.

CHAPTER SEVENTEEN

Upper Egypt

The train ride from Cairo to Luxor was possibly the most dreadful experience one could purchase for the mere cost of a third-class ticket. Our car bounced about as though the tracks were uneven, or perhaps one of the ancient wheels wasn't quite round. The car was grimy when we boarded, and the general filth increased as we proceeded south. The turbaned and draped natives showed little respect for their surroundings as they discarded wrappings, peelings, and bits of food on the floor. Natural functions proceeded as if we were all one big forgiving family. If someone had to spit, he spat; if an infant required nursing, he was nursed; but, thank God, most used the toilet compartment at the end of the car. This compartment consisted of a disgusting Turkish John arrangement that had added grab bars, in recognition of the train's erratic movements.

Several times during the endless trip those who felt the need to pray did so by unrolling a small prayer rug in the aisle, falling to their knees towards Mecca, and wailing away until the mood passed. How anyone could determine the direction of Mecca, as the train snaked its way through the desert, was a mystery. Needless to say, none of these conditions was conducive to getting much rest—let alone sleep.

Another disagreeable problem was the dust—actually very fine particles of sand. Regardless of the class you rode or how much you paid, at the end of the trip you were covered with dust. Having been warned, we wore our most expendable clothes. Nevertheless, by journey's end my dark hair was beige and every pore was clogged with desert sand. Most fellow travelers wrapped themselves in robes and escaped the worst of it. When Woody unpacked his small aluminum case that night he took out his toilet kit and removed his toothbrush from its metallic container. The container was filled with fine sand. Unbelievably, the sand had penetrated not only his case, but his toilet kit, and toothbrush container as well! If the trip had lasted much longer we might very well have been buried alive while sitting quietly in our third-class seats.

We reached Luxor by early morning and left the station with two American archaeologists we met during the trip. "We're staying at the University of Chicago's Dig House," said one of them. "Maybe there's room for a couple of architects."

For seventy piasters, less than two dollars, we got a clean room and three meals a day.

Since a guide was an absolute necessity, we decided to save money by sharing a guide and touring with the American archaeologists. We went first to the Great Temple of Ammon at Karnak, which was a vast area composed of several temples. The structures, carvings, and hieroglyphics were remarkable and impressive. The temperature climbed to the high nineties by midday, so we took a three-hour lunch break and remained inside. Late in the afternoon we toured the Temple of Ammon, the colossus of Ramses, and obelisk of Queen Hatshepsut. I found it difficult to fully appreciate the incredible age of these monuments. Some of these structures were four thousand years old when the Mayflower set sail for America! Yet their power remained beyond description.

Ancient Egyptians constructed temples for the living on the east bank of the Nile, while tombs for the dead were built on the west side of the river. Thus, the following morning we took a boat across the Nile to Thebes. Once ashore we were still a few miles from the road leading to the tombs in the Valley of the Kings. Our choice was an hour's walk under the punishing sun or a half hour donkey ride for the equivalent of fifteen cents. We opted for the donkeys. When we reached the road there were several pre-war vintage taxis waiting to take tourists to the archaeological sites.

We visited a number of tombs including those of King Tut, Rameses, and Amenophis. The tombs were cut deep into the mountain rock and consisted of chambers connected by passageways and intended solely for the sarcophagus containing the mummified pharaoh. The chambers were decorated with hieroglyphics and wall paintings intended to aid the pharaoh in his journey through the afterlife. It was in the tomb of Amenophis that Woody suddenly felt an odd queasiness.

"Something's wrong," he said. "I don't feel very well. Oh, God, I'm nauseous!" And then he bolted out of the burial chamber and raced up the passageway to the entrance. Before reaching the outside, however, he threw up violently in the passageway. I followed several steps behind and arrived as he continued retching and gagging as though he were about to die.

"What's wrong?" I asked. "You're absolutely white."

"Must be something I ate. Let's get out of here; I don't want to explain this horrible mess."

I half carried Woody up the entrance ramp, and we both sat down under a tree some distance from the tomb entrance. "How embarrassing!" he said. "I haven't thrown up since I was a freshman at Berkeley. And that was after a Friday night beer party."

"It's not you," I said. "We're completely surrounded by hostile bacteria."

We found a small café and sat quietly while Woody had some hot tea and toast. Two hours later he felt well enough to resume our sightseeing. We visited the sepulchral temple of Queen Hapshepsut and the Ramesseum. The sheer number of monuments and the consistency of their quality were remarkable. We realized this was one of the most extraordinary experiences we would ever have, and something we would remember for the rest of our lives.

That night had to be memorable for Luxor's mosquito population, as each insect returned home with a large sample of pure Newman blood. We left the room window open because of the uncomfortable heat and ignored the mosquito nets because neither of us was accustomed to using such a device. Woody miraculously escaped unharmed, but every part of my exposed body was covered with bites. If I had slept two hours longer I would surely have needed a transfusion. It was intensely uncomfortable, and the itching persisted for days. And then I wondered: why didn't Noah think to exclude from his Ark treacherous insects like mosquitoes? People worldwide would be so much happier.

The next morning we traveled to Edfu, site of the temple of Horus, the most completely preserved structure from the Ptolemaic period. We walked through the massive pylon into the great court and beyond that into the famous hypostyle hall. I imagined how people over two thousand years ago must have felt surrounded by this powerful architecture. Among them, must have been Cleopatra—yes, that Cleopatra—the one who famously romanced Mark Anthony. This incredible temple was completed during her reign. I recalled the story about Cleopatra committing suicide after Anthony's death by allowing a poisonous asp to bite her. What an odd feeling to know that we were literally walking in the footsteps of that legendary queen.

Late that afternoon we continued by train to Aswan, where we discovered that the Grand Hotel was the only lodging fit for human habitation. The next cheapest hotel was so disgusting we felt we had no choice but to spend more than twice the amount we spent in Luxor. However, we were able to shower, have a good dinner, and finally sleep safely beneath mosquito nets.

We continued to visit the rock-cut tombs the next morning and reached the Aswan Dam by afternoon. This remarkably modern development was in stark contrast with the ancient ruins and backward lives of most natives. The dam controlled the flow of the Nile for over four hundred miles and also supplied power to the Nile Valley.

At every tourist destination we found more guides and salespeople who were eager to part tourists from their money. Each seemed to have an array of authentic, one-of-a-kind, ancient artifacts that he was willing to sell for a modest sum. "How could you pass up such a bargain?" one would ask. "This treasure belongs in a museum; there is no other like it!" Except, of course, for the several dozen similar treasures being hawked by his compatriots.

Before dinner that night I sensed something amiss in my digestive system. I skipped dinner and two hours later suffered a violent attack of dysentery. Emergency trips to the bathroom continued at hourly intervals throughout the night and most of the next day. I had rarely felt so weak and miserable. "I can't even think about sightseeing," I said. "For one thing, I can't be more than ten feet away from a toilet."

"I'm not exactly a hundred percent myself," Woody answered. "Why don't we call it quits and go back to Cairo?"

And that's what we did, except this time I traded in my third-class return ticket for a second-class private sleeper compartment. We boarded the train in separate cars, and after our tickets were punched Woody moved through several cars to my compartment.

"Nice to see you again, but I've got to say, you look just awful."

"I've been thinking," I said, "Egypt, mysterious land of the Pharaohs" should really be renamed. I think it should be "Egypt, mysterious land of the loose bowels."

"Not bad," said Woody, "for a guy who's borderline delirious. I think I'll stick around and keep an eye on you."

"Why don't you crawl into the upper bunk," I suggested. "If the conductor comes by I'll tell him that's my laundry up there."

At eight the next morning, fifteen hours after leaving Aswan, we arrived in Cairo. We returned to our old hotel where I remained in bed the entire day. I called my friend Ali Malek, and he suggested some medicine that I took that afternoon. I felt well enough by dinnertime to have a bowl of soup—my first food in more than two days.

Ali called the next morning to inquire about my condition. When I reported a sudden improvement he suggested we go that evening to a local nightspot where we could see some authentic Egyptian dancing. The floorshow began after dinner and was as exotic a performance as I had ever seen. The native melodies and sinuous motions of beautifully costumed dancers were like something out of the Arabian Nights. It was thrilling to watch. Several other acts followed the dancing, but sadly, most of them were the kind that killed vaudeville.

We thanked our hosts and said goodbye; the next morning we were flying to Beirut.

When we reached the airport checkpoint, carrying a dozen government forms, the Immigration Officer quickly leafed through the forms and asked, "Where are your exit visas?"

"Exit visas? What's that? Nobody mentioned exit visas."

The officer said "Sorry, you cannot leave Egypt without an exit visa." And then he promptly ripped up every one of our forms.

"What the hell are you doing?" asked Woody.

The officer retreated to his office without a reply. We were in a state of shock. There were difficulties entering certain countries, but never before was there a problem leaving a country. The matter was serious; if we missed our plane there would not be another for a week. We demanded to see someone in authority; we simply had to plead our case.

By this time Woody was nearly apoplectic. "How dare these bureaucratic bastards keep us here against our will?" Just then another uniformed officer approached. "I understand you want to leave our country without an exit visa," he said.

"We've never heard of an exit visa," I said as calmly as possible. "Perhaps this regulation can be modified; our plane leaves in thirty minutes."

The officer said, "I'll see what I can do." He picked up a phone and began speaking rapidly in Arabic. As our departure time approached the conversation became more rapid, louder, and then quite suddenly he slammed down the phone. *Oh no, it's over. We're stuck in Cairo for another week. Will we ever get out of here?*

The officer was unsmiling as he said, "You may leave now."

"Excuse me," said Woody. "Did you say we could leave now?"

"Yes; please hurry before the Director of Immigration changes his mind."

I could see that Woody wanted an explanation. He needed to know the logic behind an exit visa, to begin with, and the sudden change in regulations as it applied to us. But I didn't care; all I wanted was to board our plane and get the hell out of Egypt.

"Forget it," I said. "We have to leave right now."

We raced to the Customs Office, where, before the exit visa problem arose, we expected trouble. We were taking half a dozen rolls of exposed film out of the country, and to the Egyptians that was as serious as smuggling opium.

"Anything to declare?" asked the Customs Officer.

"No," we answered in unison. Without hesitation he motioned for us to continue. Our last hurdle was the Currency Control Office. They knew how much money we brought into the country, and they knew how long we were in Egypt. But because our money was exchanged illegally, on the black market, it appeared we had been living on literally pennies a day. However, the Currency Control Officer failed to verify any of this information as he waved us through the last checkpoint.

We boarded our DC-3 moments before the cabin door closed and breathed a sigh of relief that could be heard all the way to Beirut, where we were now headed. Another crisis overcome, another exotic destination on the horizon, and who could possibly guess what unexpected adventures lay ahead?

CHAPTER EIGHTEEN

The Middle East

Woody continued grumbling about Egyptian bureaucracy for the first thirty minutes into our flight.

"The nerve of those people," he said. "How is anyone supposed to know that leaving a country is tougher than entering it in the first place? If you ask me, an exit visa is just another way to screw the unsuspecting tourist."

"Actually," said the passenger sitting across from us, "there are reasons for exit visas." He was a well-dressed large man, and he spoke with a strong Middle Eastern accent "Forgive my interruption, but you should know that exit visas can identify criminals who are leaving a country to avoid arrest. Exit visas also help identify illegal aliens. So you must understand, there are serious purposes for exit visas."

"Do you work for the government?" Woody asked.

"Why, yes. How did you know?"

Our plane arrived in Beirut late in the morning, and we were soon checked into a modest hotel near the central part of town. Beirut was beautifully set along the Mediterranean, and since the weather was pleasant we strolled along the seashore. Many of the city's buildings appeared European, as the country was under French rule since the First World War. However, it seemed a bit backward and chaotic. Although the bible described Lebanon as "the land of milk and honey", I doubt if you would risk drinking the milk or spreading that honey on your English muffin.

I had an invitation to visit the American University, the largest American school outside the U.S. We wandered through the beautiful campus and toured the architecture department. The work appeared uninspired, but I suspect most Americans were there to explore the exotic Middle East, rather than learn to be architects.

Lebanon had a transportation system unlike anything we had seen before. Most people walked, used bicycles, or rode horses and donkeys. There was an occasional bus, and though we noticed some rail tracks, we never actually saw a streetcar or train. The few automobiles we saw were all late American models. If you wished to travel any distance you would go to the center of town, where private cars gathered. Drivers shouted out specific destinations, and when their cars were fully loaded they departed. Since there were no schedules, one might wait five minutes or perhaps a few hours. But as no one seemed to be in a hurry it didn't much matter. Upon reaching the highway, however, it was a different story. Everyone drove as though it were the final lap of a Formula One Grand Prix event.

After several days of touring Beirut we traveled by car to Baalbeck, site of some of the finest Roman ruins in existence. The weather was warm and sunny, and the ride through mountains and countryside was beautiful. Many of the two thousand-year-old Roman temples were remarkably preserved, and we spent the entire day walking among these architectural ghosts from the past.

The next day we headed for the famous Cedars of Lebanon. We had a thrilling ride though the mountains and reached our destination as the sun was setting. We found a comfortable three-room hotel where we spent the chilly night. We were at an elevation of six thousand feet, the temperature was well below freezing, and several inches of snow covered the ground.

The owners of the small hotel served a forgettable dinner, and then we were ready for bed. Imagine our surprise and delight to discover hot water bottles under the covers! That age-old device made it possible for us to survive the frigid night.

The Cedars of Lebanon were about four thousand years old. The vast forests that covered much of the area had been reduced in size since the time of the ancient Egyptians, who prized the wood for shipbuilding. Assyrians, Babylonians, and Persians later exploited the timber; and even King Solomon used Lebanese cedar to construct the first temple in Jerusalem. Some of the trees we saw were a hundred feet tall, with trunks forty feet around. They were immense! Lebanon apparently had little else of distinction, because this magnificent tree became the symbol of the country. Cedars were prominently displayed on flags, postage stamps, and commercial products.

That afternoon we borrowed skis from the hotel proprietor, climbed the hill behind the hotel, and enjoyed a pleasant time in the snow. There was not enough snow for serious skiing, but since we were not serious skiers it hardly mattered. The next morning we returned to Beirut and took advantage of Lebanon's open currency market, one of the most unregulated in the world. I purchased Italian, French, and Spanish money, and the saving over the official rates was substantial. I was now carrying six kinds of currency, and my concern was spending the right money in the right place. Woody also bought Italian money as well as some Israeli pounds, which in later days actually saved us from starvation.

We hired another car the following day for our journey to Syria and Jordan. What a day that was! I could swear it lasted a week. Our nerve-shattering driver made former drivers look like amateurs, as he made it to the Syrian border in thirty minutes. Then the bureaucratic fun began. We were prepared with passports, entry visas, exit visas, immigration forms, custom declaration forms, and currency forms. However, the border officer wanted to know more.

"How long were you in Lebanon? What did you do there? How long will you be in Syria? What are your plans after leaving Syria?"

"That's none of their damn business," said Woody.

"Just tell them our destination is Jordan; but whatever you do, don't mention Israel. That's what I think this is about."

The border crossing took more than two hours, and we didn't reach Damascus until noon. It was a cloudy and cold day, which did little to enhance the city's charm. Our stomach problems in Egypt had made us wary of native food. In Beirut we survived by patronizing French cafés, but in Damascus the only available food was native Syrian dishes, much of which defied identification. I mean, you really couldn't tell what kind of animal, vegetable, or mineral was sitting on your plate. But, it was noon and we were starved.

We selected a nearby restaurant and Woody joked, "Botulism, ptomaine, or salmonella? Take your pick." We had no idea what we ate, but it was delicious. And, happily, there were few unpleasant consequences, unless you count the excess gas that developed over the next two hours.

We toured the prominent Mosque of Umayyad, which was one of the oldest and largest mosques in the world. It was originally built as an Early Christian basilica dedicated to John the Baptist. After the Arabs conquered Damascus it was converted to a Muslim mosque. In the basilica's central space was an ancient stone tomb that allegedly contained the body of John the Baptist; but since the tomb was sealed shut, who knows? We also visited the native bazaars, or *souks*, as they were called. They were similar to those we saw in Turkey and Egypt, complete with the frenetic chaos of a three-ring circus.

Woody and I separated so that we could wander through the bazaar independently. At one point I stopped to take a picture of two native women carrying large water jugs on their heads. They were dressed in colorful robes and veils and stood in front of an open shop. It was an exotic scene. Suddenly, a short bulldog of a man appeared waving and shouting frantically. I turned to see at whom he was ranting and soon discovered it was I! As he approached he grabbed the camera strap around my neck, all the while spouting in Arabic. Clearly, he did not want me to take the picture, but I had no idea why. A crowd began to gather, and the small, noisy man still had a grip on my camera strap. Finally, I had enough.

"Get your goddam hands off my camera, you miserable midget!"

I'm sure he didn't understand a word, but he couldn't possibly mistake my tone of voice. An old man in the growing crowd said to me in English, "The policeman wants you to go with him." *What? This is a cop? Where's the uniform? Where's the badge? And what kind of policeman is four-and-a-half feet tall?* Anyway, I was glad I hadn't punched him. I thought Woody would notice the commotion and come to my rescue, but he was nowhere in sight. The miniature cop finally took his hands off my camera, and I followed him to the station. I was officially under arrest. We went into the chief's office and Arabic began to fly about the room like a swarm of mosquitoes. The chief was slightly taller than the short cop but weighed about twice as much. He wore an elaborate uniform, had a bushy moustache, and sported the worst toupee I ever saw. It looked like a dead animal was lying on his head. He finally turned to me and asked, in perfect English, "What were you photographing in the souk?"

"Two lovely Syrian women with clay water jugs on their heads."

"Let me explain something to you, young man. Many Syrians don't care to be photographed. They believe a camera steals their immortal soul. It is like an evil eye that causes injury or bad luck to the person at whom it is directed. Do you understand what I am telling you?"

"I know what you're saying," I replied, "but that's nonsense."

"Who are you to say what is nonsense in Syria?"

"I mean no disrespect, but the idea of an evil eye is medieval superstition."

Just then the office door opened and Woody was led in.

"Peter!" he shouted. "What the hell's going on?"

"Do you know this man?" the chief asked me.

"Yes, sir; he is my friend. Where have you been?" I asked with obvious frustration.

"I noticed the crowd down the street," he said, "but I had no idea it was *you*."

"Gentlemen," said the chief, "I have no more time for this. You may now leave."

"But I'd like to know . . ." I began.

"No! No more discussion!" shouted the chief. "If you do not leave now I will lock up the both of you!" So the highlight of my short visit to Syria turned out to be the twenty-minute period during which I was arrested, lectured to, and suddenly exonerated. Hardly your typical stopover.

We left Damascus late that afternoon and headed for Jordan, where another festival of red tape awaited us. We produced our passports and filled out several additional forms. "You know," I said, "we don't want to emigrate; we're just passing through." The guard didn't understand a word I said, so the sarcasm flew right over his head. Then an officer appeared. He looked like a relative of the one in Damascus: short, thick moustache, and wearing an elaborate uniform that appeared two sizes too small. And then I began to wonder: what is it about uniforms that turn perfectly ordinary people into hostile tyrants? Every border crossing, it seemed, had a handful of sadistic officials who believed their mission on earth was to cause anguish and misery.

The Jordanian officer said in English, "Come with me." We rose and the officer said to Woody, "Not you, just him."

When we entered his private office, the officer asked, "Where are you going?"

"Jerusalem," I answered. It would be Christmas in another four days.

"And what will you do there?" he asked.

"Be a tourist; see the sights. Why the questions?"

"Your name is Newman. There is a chain of German department stores originally owned by a prominent Jewish family named Newman. Do you know these people?"

"I wish I did. But what has that to do with me? I'm American, not German, and, as you can see by my visa application, I did not state a religious preference." I could see where this was going. It was like the Egyptian Consulate in Vienna all over again. Anyone named Newman was suspected of being an Israeli freedom fighter, sworn to destroy Arabs, and likely carrying grenades in his shorts. I then launched into my history of famous non-Jewish Newmans, including the famous British scientist, Sir Isaac Newman, which seemed to greatly impress the little bigot.

"Furthermore," I said, "if I *were* related to the wealthy German Newmans, do you think I would cross a border in the middle of the night wearing this shabby, crumpled suit? Don't you think the Newmans have more dignity than that?"

"I assume, then," said the officer, "you do not plan to visit Israel."

At that point I felt it necessary to resort to my official university letter, the one used in Vienna some weeks earlier to obtain visas to Egypt. I whipped out the letter with the golden multi-pointed star and thrust it towards the officer. "Kindly read this letter," I said. The officer stared at the embossed seal of the university and suddenly became more amiable. "I was unaware that you were on official business," he said. "Please forgive this misunderstanding."

I could not get over the abrupt change in the officer's attitude or the power of a golden seal attached to a letter. I began to suspect that, with that letter, I could literally get away with murder in just about any third-world country.

"Yes, your honor, my client admits to strangling the Director of Immigration, but there are mitigating circumstances. To wit, he possesses a letter containing a gold star with the embossed seal of the University of California. Thus, we rest our case."

The judge's verdict echoes through the courtroom: "Case dismissed!"

After an uncomfortable night at a dreadful hotel in Amman, our journey to Jerusalem continued the following day. We viewed the Dead Sea and River Jordan before reaching our destination, which was the American School of Oriental Studies. Because of my fellowship, a room was reserved for us. What an oasis that turned out to be! And what a delight to have comfortable beds, modern plumbing, and be surrounded by rational, English-speaking American students.

The city of Jerusalem was one of the holiest and most intriguing spots on earth, sacred to Christians, Jews, and Muslims alike. The city was divided by a desolate, heavily mined no-man's land separating the Israeli and Arab sectors. Despite the shaky truce that existed, shots were periodically fired from one side to the other. It was a particularly dangerous place to be.

In the following days we toured many of the historic, biblical sites, including the Mount of Olives, Garden of Gethsemane, Church of the Holy Sepulcher, and Dome of the Rock. Each site was fascinating, but I wondered if the biblical accounts actually occurred as written. I mean, after all, it was two thousand years ago. Maybe the author had a rich imagination or possibly a bad memory. Nonetheless, biblical stories were generally regarded as absolute fact.

On Christmas Eve we joined our fellow students and went by car to Bethlehem. We first stopped at Shepherd's Field, where a sunset service and traditional caroling took place. The evening was clear and chilly. At the conclusion of the service, the moon and evening star became visible, just as it might have appeared two thousand years earlier. It almost seemed divinely inspired. We then had a shepherd's dinner consisting of lamb roasted on an open fire, native flat bread, and wine. It was meant to simulate the dinner ancient shepherds might have had.

"This has been incredibly emotional, wouldn't you agree?" The attractive woman standing next to me was Laura Ross, who was also a guest at the American School. We met two days earlier and I was immediately attracted to her. Laura lived in Rome, worked at the American Embassy there, and was spending her holiday in Jerusalem. She had a vivacious personality and a particularly appealing smile.

"I'm not terribly spiritual," I said, "but I have to agree. I always thought biblical stories were fairytales, but now I see them as history; that is, except for the occasional miracle."

"I know what you mean," she said. "I still don't believe someone can walk on water."

"Well, maybe with a little more wine . . ."

The banter continued until it was time to leave for Bethlehem. "Mind if I ride with you?" asked Laura. I was pleased to spend more time with her. We climbed into one of the school cars and were off. The trip of six miles took an hour, as the narrow road was clogged with pilgrims. Once there, we headed for the Church of the Nativity, which was built directly over the spot where Jesus was born. We descended a spiral stairway and eventually reached the Grotto of the Nativity, where the manger supposedly lay. The precise spot was marked on the stone floor with an elaborate inlaid silver cross.

"Are they sure it wasn't a few inches to the right or left?" asked Laura facetiously.

"Spoken like a true skeptic," I said. "Are you looking to be struck by lightening?"

We returned to Manger Square, which had turned into a *souk* of sorts. Arabs were hawking religious objects from holy water to "genuine" centuries-old scrolls. There were also scores of indigents begging for *baksheesh*, or handouts. It was a chaotic scene. Adjacent to the Square was a fifteenth-century Roman Catholic Church at which a special midnight mass was being held. As residents of the school we received tickets, which were as valuable as fifty-yard-line Super Bowl seats. We decided to attend this rare event, since we had no idea when we'd come this way again. The mass was in progress as we entered, and every seat was occupied. We stood at the rear of the church and watched the proceedings with fascination. The organ was playing loudly as the priest and his entourage walked down the aisle. The priest was dressed in his finest robes and was carrying a baby Jesus doll. No kidding, an actual toy doll!

"My God," I said, "that looks exactly like an old *Betsy Wetsy* my cousin used to have" Laura began to giggle, and several disapproving looks were aimed in our direction.

"Stop that," I said, "you'll get us into trouble."

"Sorry, but that's the funniest thing I ever saw." She seemed unable to control the giggling.

"Come on," I finally said, "we've got to get out of here."

We stood in Manger Square and, in time, Laura stopped laughing. "I can't help it, that scene just struck my funny bone. By the way, Peter, I have a confession to make."

"I think you'll have to go back to the church for that."

"No, not that kind; I just think you should know—I'm Jewish."

"Well, *mazel tov*; so am I! What are we doing here? We're on the wrong side of the barbed wire." We laughed and hugged and began to feel giddy. "Merry Christmas" Laura shouted to no one in particular. Several voices responded. Then we kissed. It was sudden and it was passionate. Finally Laura said, "Let's go home. You know, I've a room to myself, and it *is* Christmas Eve. So if you want to celebrate that famous Jewish baby, well . . ."

We did celebrate, and it was almost a religious experience. After all, it *was* the Holy Land!

I saw Woody the next morning as he staggered into the lounge. "What a Christmas Eve! These theology students really know how to party. What did you do?"

"Laura Ross and I spent some time together; and, I've got to say, she's terrific!"

"Oh no, Peter, not again. I thought you were ready to join a monastery."

"Not quite yet, my friend."

Christmas dinner at the School was served at noon, and it included everything from roast turkey to flaming plum pudding. I can't imagine where they found those ingredients in this primitive country, but it was beautifully prepared and as delicious as any holiday dinner I'd had. After dinner we exchanged gifts, having selected names at random the previous day. Gifts were limited to twenty-five piasters, about sixty cents. I received a pair of cufflinks, which was about as useful to me as an electric can opener. Laura gave me a holiday card thanking me for making this Christmas so special. She also promised to be my personal guide when I reached Rome. Suddenly, I couldn't wait to be in Italy.

Throughout my wanderings in the Holy Land I hoped I might discover the true spirit of religious faith. What I found instead was intolerance, suspicion, and commercialized voodoo. All religions urged one to love thy neighbor; but here in the holiest spot on earth I found bickering, bigotry, and an actual war, where people were being killed in the name of God. Worse yet, everyone's God was allegedly the only true God. I never witnessed such incredible hypocrisy. Sadly, it marked the beginning of the end of any appeal organized religion might have had for me.

Two days later we left the American School and literally walked to Israel. The American Consulate arranged for our passage by negotiating with Arabs and Jews, who had not spoken to each other since the 1948 war. We arrived, passes in hand, at the Mandelbaum Gate, the only crossing point between Jordan and Israel. This narrow no man's land was a few blocks long and consisted of concrete tank traps, barbed wire entanglements, and the ruins of buildings that once stood there. I never felt as isolated, vulnerable, and fearful as I did during that short walk between the two warring countries. Woody said nothing but later confessed that his greatest fear was being shot by one side or the other, and never knowing which side or why.

We reached the Israeli side of Jerusalem, underwent immigration, customs, and currency controls, and were now officially in a different country, but still in the same city. How weird was *that*? A helpful United Nations officer gave us a ride to the YMCA, where we got a wonderful room for less than two pounds. It was Saturday, the Sabbath, and the entire city was a ghost town. Everything was closed for the day, including currency exchanges and restaurants.

"How will we survive until tomorrow?" I asked.

"We'll tap a few black market pounds from my shoe bank," said Woody, "and then we'll find a hotel with a restaurant. There has to be one of those." He took off his left shoe and removed money that had been in his sock since Beirut. Our first meal in Israel was expensive and the food genuinely poor. You could blame the rationing, I suppose, but clearly, the person in the kitchen knew less about cooking than my aunt Ethel, whose dreadful cooking was a family legend. Sadly, in the short time we spent in Israel I was convinced that Aunt Ethel had prepared every single meal.

We caught an early train to Tel Aviv the next morning, and found the contrast with the surrounding Arab states even more extreme. The people, language, architecture, and attitudes were incredibly different. Israeli cities appeared cosmopolitan and quite European, whereas the Arab states appeared to be stuck in the eighteenth century. My professor, Erich Mendelsohn, had given me a letter of introduction to Aaron Ben Sira, a young Israeli architect. He greeted us at his office, and we chatted for two hours. Ben Sira gave us useful information about Israel, the new architecture, and the perpetual problems of being surrounded on all sides by enemies.

"Arabs are determined to push us into the sea," he said, "but this new state will endure. Many of us came here because we had no other place to go. Few countries would accept Jewish refugees during the war, including your country. So here we are and here we will stay. We intend to survive as we have for thousands of years. You know, we outlasted the ancient Egyptians, Greeks, and Romans, and we will outlast the Arabs as well."

Ben Sira was passionate, which I found to be the prevailing spirit of this new Jewish homeland. What I originally believed to be arrogance I now saw as intense determination.

"What of the Palestinian refugees in Jordan?" I asked."They claim to be displaced, and they are living in large camps under terrible conditions."

"We sympathize with the refugees," answered Ben Sira, "but no Arab state will take them. Lebanon, Syria, Jordan, Egypt, even Saudi Arabia has plenty of room for them, but these countries prefer to keep them in camps, perpetuate their suffering, and use them as political pawns."

We took a bus to the port city of Haifa two days later. The city dated from biblical times and was set on beautiful Haifa Bay along the Mediterranean. Aside from being the major gateway for Jewish immigration, Haifa was home to the historic Technion, Israel's equivalent of MIT. We had a tour through their architectural department and were impressed by the quality of design work. As there was little more of interest, we booked passage to Naples the following day.

The Italian passenger ship, the Grimani, was due to sail the afternoon of the last day of the year. What a way to celebrate the New Year! We would sail through the Mediterranean for nearly five days; and at the end of that time we would be in Italy, a country I had longed to visit for years. The great composer Giuseppe Verdi once said, "You may have the universe if I may have Italy." I needed to know what was behind that quote.

CHAPTER NINETEEN

Rome

We sailed into the Mediterranean on the last day of the year, and two hours later land was out of sight. That evening a rather sedate New Year's Eve party was held in the first class lounge to which all passengers were invited. A trio of piano, violin, and drums played American dance tunes, and some passengers attempted to dance on the unsteady floor. Just before midnight the crew passed out silly hats and noisemakers, and the countdown began. At the stroke of midnight the ship's horn tooted, everybody yelled "Happy New Year" in several languages, and people kissed. The sedate party suddenly turned into a Hieronymus Bosch orgy scene. Woody and I happily participated by hugging and kissing a number of desirable women. However, as in every crowd, someone eventually spoils the fun. An aristocratic Italian gentleman approached Woody and his attractive partner, whose lips were firmly locked.

"That, sir, is my wife!" he said angrily.

"You are one lucky bastard," said Woody. "She kisses like a Hoover vacuum cleaner!"

Somewhat later several raucous crewmembers entered the bar playing an accordion and singing Italian drinking songs. By three o'clock the party was over, and everyone was asleep.

We made a brief stop at Cyprus the following day, and two days later arrived in Piraeus, the port near Athens. Most passengers were happy to have a break in the voyage, as our erratic weather had made many of them ill.

I was fortunate to survive the few days of cold rain and rough seas, but the day before arriving in Naples I awoke with a terrible headache and upset stomach. I remained in bed the entire day, but my condition worsened. Woody contacted the ship's doctor, but the person who showed up appeared more like a character from an operetta.

"Dottore Carlo De Luca," he said in his thick accent. "At your service."

De Luca was short, bald, and considerably overweight. He was dressed like an Italian naval officer, but his uniform appeared to be stolen from some backstage wardrobe. Enveloping the doctor was the unmistakable aroma of garlic that grew more intense with every word he spoke.

"Now, what is the problem?" he asked.

"Nausea, headache, weakness," I answered. "I also think I have a fever."

De Luca opened his bag and removed the tools of his trade. He took my temperature, listened to my heartbeat, and shined a small flashlight in each eye. "You have influenza," he proclaimed.

"Are you sure?"

"I am rarely wrong," he answered.

"What should I do about it?" I asked.

"Stay in bed, drink hot tea, and stop smoking immediately."

"But I don't smoke."

"You see, you're on the road to recovery already."

Our ship docked in Naples the following afternoon, my fever continued, and I felt worse than the day before. I was so weak I could barely walk down the gangway. We took a taxi to an inexpensive hotel, and I fell into bed. We caught a train to Rome the next morning and went immediately to the American Academy, where, because of my fellowship, a room was reserved for me. Unfortunately, Woody was not permitted to stay at the Academy, but the director arranged a room for him at the *pensione* next door. The day was dreary—rain, freezing temperature, and everything shut down for a religious holiday. It seemed prudent to spend the day in bed. I spent the following day in bed as well, and finally, I began to feel better.

We began serious sightseeing during the next two days and visited the Coliseum, Roman Forum, Pantheon, St. Peters, and a half dozen lesser churches. I was still weak and had little appetite, but the thrill of viewing Rome's historic monuments helped me ignore the physical problems. The cold weather continued, and there were even snow flurries one afternoon. When I returned to the Academy, I found an invitation from the director to a cocktail party that evening. I was so exhausted, however, I went straight to bed.

I saw the director the next morning and he said, "We missed you last evening, and you missed a wonderful party."

"Sorry I couldn't attend, but I wasn't feeling well."

"If you'll forgive my saying, you still don't look very well. Perhaps you should see a friend of mine at Salvator Mundi. It's a hospital just around the corner from here."

The director's friend, Doctor Nicolas Romano, spoke perfect English, as he had trained and lived in New York for several years. "Sorry to break it to you, my friend; you have hepatitis. It's rarely fatal, but you have to check in right now. You should also plan to stay a few weeks."

"That's impossible," I said. "I have obligations to the University; I have to continue my travels. Besides, I can't afford to stay in a hospital. Isn't there an alternative?"

"Afraid not; you need treatment, and you need it now! Come look in the mirror. Look at your eyes. Do you see how the whites are turning yellow? You're jaundiced!" The doctor's voice became stern. "If you don't check in right now you'll be taking a serious and unnecessary risk!"

So that's how I ended up spending four weeks at the Salvator Mundi International Hospital in Rome. After the first few days of painful shots, mysterious medications, and continuous bed rest I definitely felt better. And within a week, under the skilled supervision of Doctor Nick and the care of a sisterhood of strict but compassionate nuns, I felt much like the old me. In fact, I was ready to discharge myself and return to exploring the sights of Rome.

"Not so fast," said Doctor Nick. "You may feel like the old you, but your liver says otherwise. You must remain here while we continue the medication and maintain your diet." The diet was ultra bland—yogurt, oatmeal, clear broth, mashed potatoes; actually, it was pretty much baby food. Meats and fats were not allowed, and alcohol was strictly prohibited. I doubt that one could have maintained that diet anywhere in Rome outside of Salvator Mundi.

Woody was incredibly solicitous during my first week of medical confinement. He visited every day, picked up my mail, and was genuinely sympathetic. He even—unbeknown to me—wrote a letter to my family assuring them I was in good hands and getting excellent treatment. His first visit was memorable. "Jesus Christ," he said, "have you looked in a mirror lately? You look like a walking Sunkist lemon."

"Thanks for noticing," I said. "You should see me pee—pure cadmium orange!"

Woody came one day with Alvin Jacobs, an American artist he met a year earlier when they sailed to Europe aboard the Ile de France. Alvin studied painting in Paris for six months and was now living and painting in Rome. I liked Alvin immediately; he was bright, charming, and looked exactly as an artist should—long hair, horn rimmed glasses, and a knitted turtleneck sweater. "You chose a great place to be sick," he said. "This is the finest hospital in Europe."

"You know, I didn't actually choose this place: I just happened to become sick here."

"Anyway," he continued, "Ingrid Bergman had her twins here a few weeks ago. And Errol Flynn was cured of hepatitis about a month ago. This is a swinging place!"

"Good to know, but I'm not quite ready to swing."

"Since you'll be tied up for a few weeks," said Woody, "Alvin and I decided to visit Sicily next week. We ought to be back by the time you're ready to break out of here."

My hospital days settled into a predictable routine. After breakfast I received vitamin shots, ate a bland lunch, and spent afternoons reading the Rome Daily American. I also read books from the hospital library, wrote letters, and was examined by Doctor Nick each afternoon. I was usually exhausted by late afternoon and fell asleep just after my tasteless dinner. Each Sunday, like clockwork, Sister Agnes insisted I attend holy mass in the hospital chapel, and each Sunday I informed her I was not Christian. Apparently, it mattered little to Sister Agnes. Though my predicament was frustrating, I soon realized how lucky I was to be at Salvator Mundi. By the second week my yellow complexion had faded. Since my appearance was more normal I decided to call Laura Ross, my amorous companion from Christmas Eve in Bethlehem.

"I thought you had forgotten about me," she said. "Where have you been?"

"Most recently at Salvator Mundi."

"The hospital? What's wrong?"

"I've had hepatitis, but I'm fine now. Just can't eat meat, drink wine, or go dancing."

"You poor dear. I'm going to come right over and bring you a pepperoni pizza."

"Can't have pepperoni or anything with olive oil, either."

"I'll think of something. See you later." Laura arrived late in the day with a large container of lemon Jell-O and said "No one ever died from eating Jell-O."

We embraced and I asked, "Where in Rome did you find Jell-O, and in my favorite color?"

"My parents send me stuff all the time. They must think I'm starving. God, you look terrible. I can't imagine what you've been through."

"Yeah, it's been hell. You never should have abandoned me in Jordan."

"I've missed you," she said. "I keep thinking about our special Christmas Eve.

"Me too. Best Christmas Eve ever."

"Before we relive those magical moments I have to ask you, is hepatitis contagious?"

"Here's what Doctor Nick says: Kissing, okay; fondling, okay; anything more, *not* okay."

"Well, this is going to be a challenge," she said.

Just then there was a knock on the door and Sister Agnes entered. "I'm sorry, Mr. Newman, I did not know you had a guest."

"Sister Agnes," I said, "I'd like you to meet Laura Ross, a friend I met in Jerusalem. Laura, Sister Agnes is the one who saved my life. She is a genuine angel." The two women exchanged greetings, and Sister Agnes said, "I hope you do not plan to stay long, Miss Ross. Mr. Newman needs rest and should not be encouraged to do anything that might elevate his heart rate." Sister Agnes always seemed to know what everyone was thinking.

"I understand completely," said Laura. "We both have an interest in his well being."

Sister Agnes said goodbye and left the room. "Well, my sick friend, it appears our devious plan faces serious obstacles."

"Well, we could always have a Jell-O party."

She approached my bed, laid down next to me, and we kissed. "How's the heart rate?"

"Hardly elevated," I answered. "Let's try that again."

Laura remained for another half hour and then left with a promise to return the next day.

Suddenly, I felt healthier than ever. I began to think that non-medical treatments ranked right up there with the most modern medicines.

I had the least expensive accommodations at Salvator Mundi, a room with four beds; but after two weeks of being alone I was assigned a roommate. Johnny Testa was an American soldier with a Brooklyn accent who fought in the recent war. He was at Salvator Mundi to receive a new prosthetic leg. Johnny was a cheerful character, who said when introducing himself, "Testa, like in testicle. It's Italian." Except for the missing left leg Johnny was in excellent health, so he used the hospital as a hotel and was gone most days hopping happily into town on crutches. When he was there, however, Johnny was a one-man vaudeville show. He told fascinating war stories, sang Italian arias, and amused me with jokes and card tricks. Johnny also dispensed advice based upon personal prejudices; for example, "Two glasses of wine are better than one shot of whiskey; it enriches the blood." Unfortunately, I was on the wagon, so who knows?

Upon Johnny's arrival my relative privacy disappeared. When Laura was able to visit in the evening Johnny was generally in the room, so our time alone became more difficult.

"If you want," suggested Johnny, "I could stay with friends a couple of nights a week."

"I couldn't ask you to do that," I said.

"You didn't ask, I just offered."

So our romantic encounters continued unabated. Our only concern was the possible interruption by Sister Agnes or other staff members. Our solution was to place a chair against the door, and if we heard the chair move, Laura would leap into Johnny's bed and pretend to be asleep. That happened only twice, but talk about elevating the heart rate!

Before leaving Jerusalem I had purchased several yards of genuine Scottish Harris Tweed at an absolute bargain price. My intent was to have a sport coat tailored for me when I reached Italy. In the past half year my only suit had taken a terrible beating; buttons, pockets, and lining were patched so many times the coat was composed mostly of thread. And you could practically read the Rome Daily American through the seat of my pants. My well-informed roommate happened to know the "Greatest Tailor in Italy" who would convert this splendid fabric into a stylish sport coat.

Giuseppe Del Sarto appeared one afternoon to apply for the job. He was old, very short, and could not have weighed more than eighty pounds. There was no hair on his head, but he sported a bushy white moustache. "*Buon giorno*," he said quite cheerfully. "How may I help you?"

I unwrapped my Scottish tweed and presented it to Del Sarto. "I would like you make this into a fashionable and comfortable sport coat."

Del Sarto ran his hand over the material and said, "Fine fabric!" He looked upward as though awaiting divine inspiration, and after a long pause, said, "Yes, I can do this job. I will charge you the special price of twenty thousand lire." That was about thirty-two dollars.

"Sorry, Signore Del Sarto, I cannot afford your services at that price."

"Then how about fifteen thousand?" In an instant he had sliced the price of his services by twenty-five percent.

My roommate, Johnny Testa, began speaking to Del Sarto in Italian, and there ensued a vigorous conversation punctuated with hand gestures, raised voices, and much posturing. Finally there was a silence that lasted a full minute. Del Sarto said, "My good friend, I will do this job for ten thousand lire—not one centesimo less—and I will include a pair of grey flannel pants."

"It's a deal," I said.

Del Sarto whipped out a tape measure and proceeded to take measurements. Then he asked, "Narrow lapels or wide lapels?"

"Somewhere in between," I answered.

"One rear vent, two rear vents, or no rear vent?"

"What would you suggest?" I asked the Greatest Tailor in Italy.

"Leave it to me," he answered, "I shall return next week."

When Del Sarto left I asked Johnny about their conversation. "What did you say that saved me five thousand lire and got him to throw in a pair of pants?"

"I told him you were in the hospital with a terminal illness, and you needed a new outfit for your funeral. I also told him to hurry; you didn't have much time."

"But Johnny, you know that's not true."

"Take it easy, Peter, Del Sarto is making plenty on this job."

Giuseppi Del Sarto returned the following week with a tacked together model of my jacket. It had no sleeves, but that, he said, was not a problem. He wanted to be certain the body dimensions were accurate. The coat fit perfectly, and I admired—once again—the rich fabric I had chosen. The only problem I noted was that the lining seemed thick. "The coat is a bit heavy," I said.

"Do not worry. When it is complete it will be perfect. I guarantee it."

After one more fitting and two more weeks of work the coat was finished. It was a brilliant piece of tailoring, but the lining seemed heavier than ever. When I mentioned that, Del Sarto assured me it would be appropriate for the weather we were having. I tried on the coat with the new flannel pants and admired the reflection in my mirror.

"Terrific fit," said Johnny. "I told you, he's the Greatest Tailor in Italy!"

"But what about the lining?" I asked. "It feels like a bulletproof vest."

"I should mention," said Johnny, "Del Sarto has done some work for the Mafia. I think he threw in some extra protection . . . but at least he didn't charge for it."

"Nice to know," I said. "At least I'll be ready when the shooting starts." So now I had a beautiful, solidly built new outfit; but still, no place to go.

It was a sunny day in mid-February when I was discharged from Salvator Mundi. I was thrilled to be transformed from patient to tourist, and I practically danced out the hospital door. Doctor Nick claimed I was fortunate to be cured so quickly. "Many hepatitis patients are going into their seventh or eighth week," he said. I was not surprised; my mother always claimed I spent little time fighting diseases. I had measles for two days, whooping cough for one day, and mumps for six hours. I went back to my old room at the American Academy, and the following afternoon Woody returned from southern Italy. We spent the entire evening catching up on each other's activities.

"How was it traveling with Alvin Jacobs?" I asked.

"He's an interesting guy and very easy-going. And he really knows his art history. He mentioned visiting Spain during Holy Week. Since you're also going to Spain, and I'll be on my way home, why don't you hook up with him?"

"Good idea. I'll speak to him about that."

During the next several days we continued our exploration of Rome. We generally visited three or four churches before lunch each day. Each had incredible frescoes, paintings, mosaics, or sculptures; and each was a superb example of the richness and beauty of its period. We also toured Vatican City, several museums, and spent a fascinating day in Pompeii, just south of Naples. What an experience that was! Pompeii was a thriving Roman city that was buried by ash in 79 AD when Mount Vesuvius unexpectedly erupted. It was in an amazing state of preservation, as though it were abandoned a few weeks earlier. We visited houses, shops, temples, and—not least of all—the *Lupanare*, the oldest known brothel in the world. Inside were wall paintings and frescoes depicting an immense range of erotic and explicit sexual activities and positions. It was enough to convince us that, during the intervening two thousand years, absolutely nothing had changed!

Alvin Jacobs had a wide range of friends and acquaintances in Rome, and he generously invited us to art shows, performances, and parties. Our social life exploded. It seems there was a not-to-be-missed event every night. Laura accompanied me on several occasions, and in return, she invited me to several Embassy parties. My social life could not have been more satisfying. Of course, eating a fat-free diet continued to be a challenge, and drinking was still taboo. The only acceptable excuse for turning down a drink was "*mal di fegato*". That meant, "I have a liver problem," to which everyone nodded in sympathetic understanding.

"I wish we didn't have to leave Rome," said Woody. "Our life has become a wonderful fantasy. But we really have to move on; there's so much more of Italy to see."

Our last night in Rome was memorable; Woody, Laura, Alvin and I had dinner and then went to the apartment of mutual friends to say goodbye. We walked into handfuls of confetti and colorful streamers. It was a surprise going away party! Being the last day of *Carnivale* throughout Italy everyone was in costume. Costumes were also provided for us. There was food, music, and endless bottles of wine. Covering the walls were expert caricatures drawn by Alvin depicting Woody and me in imaginative costumes in various countries. We laughed and danced and finally kissed our Roman friends goodbye.

I went home with Laura for a special goodbye, and made plans to meet Woody at the train station in the morning. I also arranged to meet Alvin along the French Riviera the following month. We would stay in touch and travel to Spain together. I felt particularly good about my life. I survived a month-long illness, made several good friends, and was walking through the streets of Rome with an attractive and affectionate companion. Eternal Rome had been one of the most extraordinary highlights of my fellowship year and a perfect blend of my three true loves. Could anything top that?

CHAPTER TWENTY

Italy

We were sitting in our third-class train compartment, heading for the hill towns of Umbria, and Woody said, "I loved Rome. I think it was our best city yet."

"I agree; Rome was special. Even my month at Salvator Mundi was memorable."

"And your attractive friend, Laura Ross," he continued, "what a great addition to your list of true loves! That list must be getting pretty long by now. Let's see, Monika Eklund in Stockholm; Deborah Wolfe, the American actress in Nürnberg, the Obermann daughter, Astrid, in Vienna; Karolina what's-her-name in Dubrovnik; and finally Laura. Did I leave anyone out?"

"Yes, but that was before we started traveling together."

"Oh yes, Anne Cleary, that sexpot who seduced you in London."

"So what's your point? The list sounds like a rap sheet. These weren't crimes, you know."

"I'm not so sure; breaking a heart should be at least a misdemeanor."

"You're exaggerating; no hearts were broken. Besides, we had great times, and there's nothing to feel guilty about."

Woody had struck a nerve. I did feel guilty, and I think I knew why. How could anyone claim to have so many true loves? Was it arrogant, indiscriminate, or just unrealistic?

We spent the next few days exploring the hill towns of Orvieto, Perugia, and Assisi. Each town was built into rocky hillsides hundreds of years before, and they now appeared to be growing out of the landscape like mature organisms. It didn't take long before I was exhausted from the endless hours of hiking over cobblestone streets, and I realized that after a lengthy hospital stay it would take more time before my energy returned.

Assisi, birthplace of St. Francis, was the most charming of the hill towns. Built high in the Umbrian hills this medieval town consisted of winding streets and attractive stone buildings. The day was sunny and warm as we climbed to the ramparts of the ancient fortress with our picnic lunch. We sat there a few hours and enjoyed the sunshine, food, and fine view. Among Assisi's notable structures was the Basilica of Saint Francis, which comprised a monastery, two churches, and some of Giotto's greatest frescoes. The town was rich with art and architecture, and it was dark by the time we returned to our hotel.

We continued to Siena the following morning. After finding a modest *pensione*, we headed for the center of town to visit the *duomo*, which was one of the greatest examples of Italian Romanesque architecture. The structure was built with alternating stripes of black and white marble, presenting an odd zebra-like appearance. Nearby was the Piazza del Campo, the town square, which was filled with bars and cafés and was the center of a rich civic life.

Siena was fascinating, not only the sights and the people, but also the food was as delicious as any in Italy. Every meal was memorable; the simplest plate of pasta was a gourmet treat, and the Tuscan wines were delicious. Unfortunately, I was limited to one glass a day in order to protect my recuperating liver. As in Rome, there was the marvelous aroma of roasted coffee that pervaded nearly every neighborhood. Even today, the scent of freshly roasted coffee evokes images of Italy.

As for the people, it was difficult to believe that a few years ago we were enemies on the battlefield. The Italians we met were in no way belligerent or even confrontational. They seemed far more interested in art, music, and romance. The Italians had a love of life that seemed rare in the dispirited post-war world.

Our next destination was the famous city of Florence. The weather turned warm, and our bus ride through the Tuscan countryside was a beautiful excursion. The landscaped hills, vineyards, and quaint villages were like stunning pastoral paintings. We arrived in the early afternoon and stopped at the tourist office to inquire about a hotel room. Inside the office was a poster announcing an afternoon concert featuring the music of George Gershwin, one of my favorite composers.

"Can you get us tickets for that concert?" I asked the office manager.

"Yes, I have some here," she replied, "but you must hurry. The concert begins in thirty minutes."

We dropped our bags, grabbed the tickets, and rushed across several blocks to the theater. What remarkable luck! The orchestra was the New York Philharmonic led by Artur Rodzinski. They were touring Europe and were in Florence for only this one Sunday concert. We heard *Rhapsody in Blue, An American in Paris*, and a medley of other Gershwin masterpieces. It was a marvelous treat, and those melodic themes ran through my head for the next several weeks.

Florence was so filled with incredible art and architecture we had to organize a plan to avoid missing any important sight during our two weeks there. Our first stop was the Florence cathedral, Santa Maria del Fiore, and within moments we bumped into our friend from Rome, Alvin Jacobs.

"What on earth are you doing here?" exclaimed Woody.

"Waiting for you," he answered. "I asked myself, where would two architects begin their tour of Florence? Probably some magnificent gothic cathedral, I thought. And if the cathedral sported a famous dome by Brunelleschi, well of course, that's where they'll be!"

"Amazing," said Woody. "But why didn't you mention this last week?"

"It was spur of the moment; by the time I decided, you were gone. I'd wanted to visit Florence for some time and thought it might be fun to do it together. I figured you'd explain the architecture, and I'd help you out with the paintings and sculpture." Alvin moved to our hotel, and we began touring the Florentine sights together. How can I describe the incredible treasures of that city? There were so many masterpieces of art, architecture and sculpture the entire city seemed to be one heavenly museum. The Italian Renaissance began in Florence; and geniuses like Michelangelo, Leonardo da Vinci, and dozens of others worked in this area.

I once heard that certain works of art could arouse such deep emotions they could bring tears to your eyes. I always wondered how that was possible. Then I saw Botticelli's *Venus* and Michelangelo's *David* and I understood the power of great art. Florence was replete with such experiences: Fra Filippo Lippi's *Madonna*, Donatello's *David*, and Ghiberti's *Gates of Paradise* at the Florence Baptistery, these were some of the masterpieces that made our visit so memorable.

Early one morning we took a day trip to Pisa, home of the world-famous leaning tower. Everyone on earth knows what the tower looks like, but just as with the Great Pyramids, seeing it was a genuine shock to the senses. The tilt was so conspicuous, so severe, it appeared to be defying gravity. It was a strange sensation. As remarkable as the tower was, more stunning yet were the cathedral and baptistery, which comprised the entire architectural composition.

By this time, I figured, we must have seen at least a hundred or more Italian churches. Amazingly, that was a fraction of the religious buildings in that country. Rome alone had over two thousand churches! Could there possibly be a country with more churches than Italy?

We spent most of our waking hours seeing the sights, but we also spent time observing the Italian way of life. It was slower than our frenetic pace and included long midday periods of rest. At one o'clock each afternoon most activities came to a halt. Shops reopened at four and remained open until eight o'clock. Dinner was usually eaten after the shops closed. The ambiance in restaurants was also relaxed. The American custom of fast food and rapid service never caught on in Italy. When one called a waiter, he would immediately answer, "*Subito!*", which translates as "Right away!", but right away could be ten minutes later.

There were, however, two activities during which Italians exhibited a more dynamic pace. Conversations were rapid and energetic. It often appeared like a physical workout in which arms flailed away as if in mortal combat. Just before one or the other seemed ready to pull out a dagger they smiled, shook hands, and said, "*Ciao*". The other high-octane activity was driving. Putting a windshield in front of an Italian was like waving a red flag before a bull. Drivers were aggressive in the extreme as they propelled their miniature autos or noisy Vespas with little regard for life—theirs or anyone else's. Pedestrians were in perpetual danger as drivers often used sidewalks to avoid crowded streets. One was never safe, except within a building, and sometimes not even then, as we once saw a Vespa drive right through the front door of a restaurant.

As for the food, Florentine cooking was consistently wonderful, and an amazing bargain. Our favorite place became *Il Piccolo Cucina*, a small restaurant that had, according to its name, an even smaller kitchen. For three-hundred-fifty lire, about fifty-five cents, we would get a green salad, a large plate of pasta with meat sauce, a quarter liter of table wine, and fresh fruit for dessert. We also found a place that made pizzas for less than twenty-five cents. If it weren't for the many miles of walking each day I would have quickly outgrown my new bulletproof sport coat.

After a most stimulating and satisfying two weeks we decided to leave Florence. I could have remained there another month or two, but Woody was forced to return home before his last dollar was spent. That meant he had to leave Europe by the middle of March. We had two weeks to go and all of northern Italy to explore. Alvin Jacobs returned to Rome, and we caught an early morning train to Bologna. The trip took us over the Apennine Mountains, which ran the length of the Italian peninsula. We passed through endless tunnels and over snow-covered summits before reaching Bologna. It was not a particularly interesting town, but it provided a convenient stop on the way to Ravenna, the center of great Byzantine mosaics.

Eventually we reached Venice, the most amazing and fascinating city in all of Italy, if not the world. As you may know, Venice is a large peninsula interlaced by more than a hundred and fifty canals. There were no streets; consequently, no autos, buses, or streetcars. Instead, there were boats—thousands of boats—not only beautiful gondolas propelled by professional gondoliers, but motorboats for carrying passengers and freight. There were also police boats, ambulance boats, and even water-going hearses.

Pedestrians were relegated to narrow sidewalks that ran alongside most canals and to the many bridges that crossed over them. The real problem in Venice, however, was finding one's way. It was the most bewildering city I ever visited. No two canals, it seemed, were parallel or perpendicular; and the Grand Canal, the city's major artery, snaked across the city in a perfect "S" shape. During our week in Venice I was consistently disoriented and frequently lost.

We found a room close to St. Mark's Square that was run by a sisterhood of nuns. The place was austere but scrupulously clean; and the price was less than a dollar a night. When Woody inquired about an available room a severe-looking nun replied, "We do have a room, but first you must understand our house rules. We do not allow visitors of the opposite sex in the room, nor do we permit alcohol of any kind. And the front door is locked at eleven o'clock every evening."

Woody turned to me and asked, "Think you can handle the restrictions?"

"I don't intend to fall in love, get drunk, or stay out late, if that's what you mean. In fact, I'd be willing to sign a statement to that effect."

"That won't be necessary," replied the humorless nun, whose name was Sister Sara.

Our landladies may have been strict, but they could not have been more amiable. They gave us directions to popular sights, recommended local restaurants, and often furnished us with snacks. One evening Sister Sara brought two small glasses of Campari accompanied by a plate of biscotti.

"We appreciate this," I said. "But what about the house rule concerning alcohol?"

"Campari is an aperitif," she answered, "and therefore, an exception."

St. Mark's Square was the focus of tourists and natives alike. At one end of the *piazza* was the famous Byzantine basilica of San Marco. Adjacent were the Doges Palace and soaring Campanile, and surrounding the vast open space were stately arcades. We spent much time relaxing at the cafes and feeding the pigeons that filled the piazza. We also visited several other churches, palazzos, and galleries. Venice was overflowing with great art, but it was the city itself that was the most fascinating attraction. It was as unique and unreal as a fairy tale.

The week passed quickly, and early one morning we began our accelerated tour of northern Italian cities. Each town was like the delicious bite of a sweet apple. And each day of sightseeing ended with a tasty plate of pasta, which invariably cost a hundred lire, about sixteen cents. The pasta shapes were wildly varied, and most were homemade. The choice of sauce was always *al burro* or *al sugo*, butter or tomato, and the heap of noodles was always topped with freshly grated Parmesan cheese. It was a treat of which we never tired.

Finally we arrived in Milan, Italy's second largest city. Despite its industrial character there were a number of artistic treasures. The *duomo* was an immense, richly decorated work of Gothic art. Referring to the scores of sculpted figures on the exterior, the structure was once described as "petrified fireworks". At the Church of S. Maria della Grazie was "The Last Supper", Leonardo da Vinci's celebrated fresco. The building that housed the painting was severely damaged during the war, and three of the building's walls were totally destroyed. The fourth wall, containing Leonardo's masterpiece, miraculously survived. I had often seen reproductions of this painting, but viewing it in person was an entirely new experience.

Milan was also home to La Scala, one of the world's most famous opera houses. Woody and I attended a performance of Puccini's "Tosca". The dramatic opera was famous for its story of torture, murder, and suicide, but we found the theater's architecture to be nearly as dramatic.

After several days of continuous sightseeing we caught a train for Turin. Much of the new architecture in Italy's northern cities, especially Turin, was the result of the extensive damage caused by Allied bombers during the war. Few areas remained unscathed, and though the destruction was not as intense as in Germany, large areas of debris remained.

"God this is awful," said Woody viewing the blocks of rubble. "I hope the fascists have learned something from all this. It was such a waste, such a tragedy!"

Turin was the last city in which Woody and I were together. After eight months of continuous travel, marvelous adventures, and genuine camaraderie we were parting company. The following morning Woody would leave for Paris and ultimately a transatlantic liner to New York. And I would travel to Marseilles to meet Alvin Jacobs before touring Spain. For the last week or two Woody appeared ready to return home. He often spoke of hamburgers and milkshakes and the relief of not having to search for a room every night. He also spoke of settling down.

"I'm cured," he said. "The wanderlust has passed. I'm ready to settle in one place for a while. I want to fall in love, get married, and live a conventional life."

"Nonsense," I said. "There's nothing even remotely conventional about you. You'll be a rebel for the rest of your life; that's just the way you are."

"Maybe in my work," he said, "but I need a structured life. The way I feel now, I'll probably marry the first woman I see when I get off that ship in New York." Little did he realize how prophetic those words were.

We sat in an attractive *trattoria* that final night in Turin, finishing the last plate of pasta we would enjoy for a very long time. We were also sipping the last of a liter of *vino da tavola rosso*.

"You're going to remember this meal," I said, "and one day you'll dream about this food."

"This meal and your company," he said. "This has been one hell of a ride, and bumping into you in London was probably my luckiest accident."

"Lucky for us both," I said. "Do you realize what we've done? The amazing sights we've seen? The number of predicaments we've gotten in and out of? It's been a wonderful journey, and I'll always be grateful to you for making it such a pleasure."

"Stop it, you're going to make me cry. Anyway, you have all of Spain and France to look forward to and the company of our pal, Alvin. He's a great guy, and you should really hit it off."

We walked to the railway station the following morning. We hugged, wished each other good luck, and boarded our respective trains. As we pulled away from the station I felt a genuine sadness. I would not see Woody again for another half year. We would meet again in the Bay Area, and our lives would be different. But our memories would remain unchanged—memories of eight wonderful months that so dramatically shaped our lives.

CHAPTER TWENTY-ONE

The Riviera

The arrival of spring—according to the calendar—was a week away, but it actually appeared the moment I crossed from Italy into France. The sun appeared, and fruit trees and flowers were suddenly in bloom everywhere. The border crossing was relatively easy, as no one inspected my bag or inquired about money. However, one inspector asked if I carried any film. I replied, "*cinq rouleaux*", which meant five rolls. However, I pronounced "*cinq*" like "*cent*", which meant one hundred rolls, whereupon the inspector started jumping up and down. The matter was quickly resolved, and thus, my first encounter with the French language was a near calamity.

The one semester of French I had in school failed to warn that knowing the word but mispronouncing it left you no better off than not knowing the word to begin with. I found that in most cases if I pronounced the first few letters of a word and let the rest of it more or less fade away, somewhat through the nose, I had a fifty-fifty chance of being understood. Armed, therefore, with a kindergartener's vocabulary, I arrived in Nice on an absolutely beautiful evening. I quickly found a hotel a block from the beach. My room cost five hundred francs—a bit more than a dollar.

As I went to dinner that night I noticed a few older tourist types in the hotel lounge as well as several attractive women. I assumed there was a fashion conference in town, because the young women were particularly well dressed. After my long train ride and wonderful dinner I slept that night as if drugged. Nevertheless, I became aware during the early morning hours of an unusual amount of traffic in the hotel corridor. I spoke to the manager in the morning and he said, "Many guests arrived late from a nearby party. I hope they didn't disturb you."

"Not at all," I replied. "I slept wonderfully well."

I went into the breakfast room and had a powerful cup of coffee and the most delicate, flaky croissant one could imagine. What a way to start the day! Moments later a pretty young woman sat down at the next table and wished me a *bon jour*. "*Bon jour* to you," I replied. She said something in French, and I said, "Is there any chance you speak English? My French is almost nonexistent."

"Of course," she answered. "I asked if I might join you for breakfast."

"I would be delighted."

"My name is Michelle, Michelle Garnier," she said as she sat down.

"Peter Newman," I answered. "Pleased to meet you, Michelle." I could not imagine what she was doing there, but I hoped she would never leave. Michelle was extremely attractive, with delicate features and an engaging smile. She looked to be in her mid-twenties. Her dark hair was cropped short, and she wore a black turtleneck sweater with a tight gray skirt.

"Are you staying at the hotel?" I asked.

"Yes, I stay here from time to time. And you? Are you a tourist?"

"Yes," I answered. "I arrived in Nice just last night."

"Perhaps I can help you," she said. "I know Nice very well. I know the best sights to see and the most romantic things to do." The last part was said with a coy smile.

"How did you know that travel and romance were two of my true loves?" I asked.

"I just had a feeling about you. Possibly we can do business."

"What sort of business are we talking about?"

"Anything that pleases you," she said.

"Anything?" I asked. I could not believe this conversation.

"Yes," she replied, "anything at all." I began to wonder if I were possibly on the verge of a monumental sexual encounter. And then came the pail of cold water.

"I think you will find my fee reasonable."

Fee? Like in money? What was she saying? Oh, God, how dense could I possibly be? What a fool to think she was attracted to me! She sells her services, you idiot. Michelle is a prostitute!

Now I understood the women in the lounge and the late night traffic in the corridor; my hotel was a brothel! Randomly and innocently I had stumbled into a whorehouse! What luck!

"I think there's been a terrible misunderstanding, Michelle. You are charming and attractive, but I am not a wealthy tourist. I'm just a struggling student. I could not possibly afford to pay for your services, though I suspect they would be well worth the fee."

"*Quel dommage*, what a pity," she said. "I find you attractive, too. But business is business."

"I quite understand," I said. "But perhaps we can be friends."

"Why not?" she said. "But I must go now." She rose, kissed me on the cheek, and with a casual *au revoir* she was gone. It was my first day in Nice, and I had already made a friend.

I wandered towards the shore and was shocked to discover that the fabulous beach I heard so much about was nothing more than a ten-foot-wide strip of small, uncomfortable pebbles. Having been raised in Southern California, I expected—at the very least—sand.

How could they even call this a beach? The weather was clear, but not quite warm enough for swimming. Nevertheless, a few hardy souls were splashing about in the water. I sat on the pebbles and enjoyed the sun and delicious aroma of the Mediterranean. I bought a sandwich for lunch and remained on the beach reading my book for nearly the entire afternoon. Eventually, I fell asleep.

Suddenly, I heard a pleasant voice, "So, is this your idea of sightseeing?" It was Michelle looking very appealing in a large straw hat and white bathing suit.

"Just so you know, I've been traveling for more than eight months. I'm exhausted and tired of sightseeing. I refuse to feel guilty about spending an afternoon at the beach."

"Sorry," she said, "I was just making a small joke. May I join you?" She sat down on a blanket, opened her large bag, and pulled out a bottle of wine. She also had two wine glasses.

"Do you always travel with a portable bar?" I asked.

"No, I was hoping to find you on the beach. Do you care for a drink?"

"Please don't tell me there is a fee for this."

"That remark was not necessary," she said. She seemed offended.

"I apologize; that was sarcastic, and I'm sorry."

We sat quietly enjoying the wine as the sun moved lower in the sky.

"Now I must work on my tan." And with that she unselfconsciously removed the top of her suit. She lay back on the blanket, closed her eyes, and appeared to nap. I, on the other hand, continued to gawk at her sensuous body like I was back at the Uffizi staring at Botticelli's Venus. This, however, was infinitely more arousing. As the sun fell below the horizon Michelle put on a sweater and said, "Let's go, it's getting cold."

When we reached the hotel she suggested we finish the bottle of wine in her room. I was excited, but a bit apprehensive. At what point, I wondered, did a pleasant afternoon at the beach turn into *strictly business*? She must have noticed my reticence. "I do not have an appointment this evening," she said. "So I thought we might spend some time together—as friends."

My new friend and I finished the wine and I suggested we have dinner. I went to my room to change clothes, and when I returned she was ready to go. As we left the hotel the other women in the lounge smiled at me. "They must think I'm your new boyfriend."

"Well, I suppose you are."

We went to a neighborhood bistro, a place I discovered earlier and knew I could afford.

"We could go Dutch treat, as you Americans say. I can afford to pay my way."

"I wouldn't dream of that," I said. "Allow me to be chivalrous."

"Well then, my treat will come later." I could hardly imagine what she had in mind for dessert. After a delicious dinner we strolled back to our hotel. I was curious to know why this gorgeous woman became a prostitute, but I was reluctant to ask. I feared she would take the question as criticism. So I said, "Tell me about your childhood."

"Not much to tell. I became an orphan during the war, and a strict uncle raised me. I could not wait to be out of his house. When I was seventeen a kind man offered to support me. All I had to do, he said, was be nice to him, and—as I discovered—to many of his friends as well. Little did I realize how he was using me. I left him after two months and decided I would work on my own terms. If I do not like a man I will not be with him. I am a prostitute, yes, but I have principles."

"I am so sorry," I said. "That is a sad story."

"Not so sad, really. I have survived very well, and now I have money of my own."

"But you should be with someone who loves you and takes care of you."

"That is a romantic notion. I'm not sure I believe in love."

"Well, that's even more cynical."

When we arrived at our hotel she said, "I prefer that we go to your room. You are not a client. I would like to think you are wooing me."

After closing the door to my room I said, "I would like to woo you, but I'm a bit intimidated. You are very experienced, and I am not sure what to do next."

"Do not think of that. Pretend I am your girlfriend. We just met; we like each other very much. Do what comes naturally."

Then I kissed her. It was tender and passionate and we embraced for a long time.

"I don't have to pretend," I said. "I like you very much. I'm sorry you don't believe in love, because I could so easily love you."

We sat on the bed and she said, "Let me take care of you." She dimmed the light and then began to unbutton my shirt. I tried to help, but she said, "No, I will do everything. Just relax." She removed my clothes, and then removed hers. Finally, she lay on top of me. The rest of the evening was an incredible fantasy come true. We made love in ways I had never experienced. Michelle was passionate and gentle and extraordinarily lovable. It was an evening I would never forget.

We did not see each another for the next two days. Michelle had *appointments*, as she put it, and I tried not to think about that. I toured the popular sights of Nice, but was disappointed that there was so little of architectural interest. One morning I took a short bus ride to Vence, site of Henri Matisse's famous Chapel of the Rosary. This famous structure was designed and constructed over a period of four years by the modernist artist, who lived nearby. The decorative murals and stained glass were some of the finest work he ever produced.

Finally, it was time to continue my travels. I planned to meet Alvin Jacobs in Marseilles the following day. I saw Michelle in the breakfast room of our hotel and told her I would be leaving the following morning. "Then we must spend this evening together," she said, and suddenly, I could not wait for the day to end.

During dinner that night I said, "I wish I could stay in Nice a while longer but it would probably interfere with your life."

"You have your obligations," she said, "and I have mine."

"But you can't do this forever."

"No, but soon I no longer will. A client of mine, an older gentleman who lives in Paris, wants to marry me. He is wealthy and says he is very much in love with me."

"Do you love him?"

"That is not terribly important. He is kind, and he will take care of me."

"I hope you're right, but I can't help being concerned about you."

"Please don't worry; let's enjoy our time together." And that's what we did. We made love until the early morning, and then it was time to leave for the train station.

"I won't forget you," I said. "You have made my visit to Nice very special."

"And I will never forget how close I came to believing in love. For that, I thank you."

We kissed goodbye, and, somewhat sadly, I walked to the station.

Four hours later I was in Marseille. I arrived at the American Express office at noon, and there was Alvin Jacobs, just as we planned. He was smiling broadly and looking every bit like the starving artist he actually was. I suddenly felt elated. We went to a nearby bistro and didn't stop talking throughout our two-hour lunch.

The following morning we traveled to the suburbs to visit the recently completed Unite d'Habitation, which was one of Le Corbusier's most anticipated projects. This remarkable twelve-story concrete apartment block was published in every architectural journal and had become quite famous. As the comfortable weather continued we strolled through the old harbor area of Marseille and watched fishermen sell their fresh catches right off their boats.

Our journey to the Spanish border took us through several southern French cities. The first of these was Arles, where we viewed amazing Roman ruins. One of the most famous residents of Arles was Vincent Van Gogh, who also happened to be one of Alvin's favorite artists. Thus, much of our time was spent tracking down cafes, churches, and other subjects found in Van Gogh's paintings. We next traveled to the walled city of Avignon and then to Nîmes, where more Roman ruins were on display. We viewed the well-preserved Amphitheater; the Pont du Gard, a monumental aqueduct; and Maison Carrée, which was the best-preserved Roman temple in the entire world—including Rome!

Our final night in southern France was spent in the small town of Perpignan, very close to the Spanish border. The Spanish State Railway system, an organization that marched to its own demented drummer, made it impossible to enter Spain at any other point from this part of France.

"I'm afraid everything we've heard about Spanish trains is true," said Alvin.

"I hope not," I answered. "Woody never stopped talking about his horrendous experiences in Spain. He was absolutely convinced that you could walk faster than most trains traveled at top speed. He was also sure that Spanish trains had square wheels."

"Well, I guess we'll find out tomorrow, won't we."

I fell asleep at once and dreamed about being on a slow train. Sitting next to me in our compartment was a Spanish peasant girl who resembled Michelle Garnier. *There's no question about it*, I thought, *I'm going to love Spain.*

CHAPTER TWENTY-TWO

Spain

After the marriage of Ferdinand and Isabella, during the fifteenth century, Spain became a unified nation and the most powerful kingdom in the world. At the end of the sixteenth century, however, a downward spiral began. The formerly invincible Spanish Armada was defeated by England, and things very quickly went from bad to worse. The decline continued for centuries and was still going on the very day Alvin Jacobs and I crossed the Spanish border.

We were obliged to change trains at the border because, as incredible as it sounds, the gauge of Spanish tracks differed from those in every other country. Imagine that! Train tracks throughout Europe were one width, but Spanish tracks were considerably narrower.

"Do you suppose they're trying keep out foreign trains?" Alvin suggested.

"Maybe," I replied, "but more likely they haven't the faintest idea what's going on in the rest of the world. And I suspect they don't care."

Our trip to Barcelona, a distance of eighty miles, took four hours. Everything we heard about Spanish trains proved to be true; transportation was a relic from another century. We were offered a number of rooms at the Barcelona station and soon found a *pension* for forty pesetas. At the black market rate of exchange obtained in Beirut, that was about eighty-five cents for a room—including all meals! Clearly, Spain was the least expensive country in Europe.

The elementary Spanish I learned in school came back quickly, but it took a while to adjust to the Spanish pace of life. It seemed relaxed in the extreme, as if every single Spaniard was on tranquilizers. Meals, for example, were served later than probably anywhere else on earth. Breakfast was not available before nine o'clock, lunch was served at two in the afternoon, and that was followed by a two-hour siesta period. Shops reopened at four and remained open until eight o'clock in the evening. Dinner was available between nine and eleven at night, but it was considered unfashionable to dine before ten. This took a bit of getting used to. For the first week we were in Spain my stomach growled long before meals were available. It also generally growled after downing mysterious food that was often swimming in olive oil. Spanish cooking had much in common with their transportation system; both were disagreeable relics from primitive times past.

Barcelona, the second largest city in Spain, had wide streets and spacious plazas. The city also had fine museums, lovely gardens, and interesting architecture, including several examples by the architect Antonio Gaudi. We studied Gaudi's work in school, and it was a thrill to visit his Church of the Sagrada Familia. Among the museums, Alvin favored those featuring Catalan painters, and they became my favorites as well.

While strolling through the city we noticed colorful posters advertising weekly bullfights.

"We really should see one of those," suggested Alvin. "Hemingway wrote about them, and friends in Rome insisted this was a not-to-be-missed event."

The following Sunday we purchased tickets for the Plaza de Toros. The pageantry began as we settled into our seats. It was a thrilling scene! While musicians played the rousing *paso doble*, a colorful parade of participants entered the ring and took their positions. A trumpet call announced the appearance of the first bull, and the crowd became hushed in anticipation. A monstrous black animal, weighing well over a thousand pounds, came charging into the arena. He galloped across the field of battle and made a spectacular leap over the fence into the front-row crowd.

"Holy shit!" cried Alvin. "That's not supposed to happen." Patrons ran for their lives as members of the bullfighting team guided the bull back into the arena. It was immediately apparent this bull was not about to go quietly. Out came the *picadors* on their padded horses. Their purpose was to weaken the animal by stabbing his neck muscles with their lances. But the bull had other ideas. He charged the first picador, lodged his horns beneath the horse's padding, and threw horse and rider to the ground. The crowd gasped in horror as the horse lay mortally wounded and the rider fled for his life.

"I don't think that's supposed to happen either," I said. "What the hell's going on?" Meanwhile, the bull continued to snort, paw at the ground, and remain obstinate. Next came the *banderilleros*, whose job it was to place two barbed sticks into the bull's shoulders to further weaken the animal. During the first pass one banderillo stuck in the bull's shoulder, but the other flew into the air as the bull hooked the right arm of the banderillero. The poor guy raced to a protective wall spurting blood all the way. As the murmur of the crowd grew louder I suddenly began to root for the bull, who seemed very much in control of the situation.

Finally the *matador* appeared in his glorious suit of lights. He carried a small red cape and a dangerous looking sword. He taunted the bull, and when the bull charged, the matador made a deft move and escaped harm. The crowd cried "*Ole, ole!*" Several more passes produced a variety of skillful moves and more cheers that grew in intensity. The crowd seemed thrilled that the matador had finally taken control of the fight.

"Do you think the bull's got a chance?" I asked.

"Forget it," Alvin replied. "The odds are totally stacked against the poor bastard."

Just then the bull charged close to the matador, hooked the surprised fighter in the groin, and threw him over his head. The matador landed in an unconscious heap some fifteen feet away. The crowd let loose a collective shudder as team members attempted to distract the bull. But the bull was not to be put off. He continued to attack the matador with his horns and—for good measure—stomp the motionless body with his hoofs. Clearly, this was one furious bull. He probably figured, "If I'm ending up in a meatloaf, I'm taking this guy with me."

When a matador is incapacitated it is the obligation of others to complete the fight. Another matador appeared, and after several more taunts and flourishes his sword penetrated the heart of the exhausted beast. The bull fell to the ground, twitched his tail a few times, and it was over. The lifeless carcass was pulled from the arena by a team of mules, and nothing remained but a pool of fresh blood that was quickly raked into the sand by two indifferent workers.

"God that was awful," said Alvin. "I don't think I can watch five more bulls being slaughtered like that. This is just too barbaric."

"I suppose it's pretty much like Roman times," I said. "Watching gladiators murder each other wouldn't be much different. Let's get out of here."

A well-dressed Spaniard sitting in front of us turned and said, "Before you leave allow me to ask, how is this different from people in your country shooting wild animals for sport?"

"Perhaps no different," I answered, "but neither seems appropriate in a civilized world."

We had planned to spend the *Semana Santa*, or Easter Holy Week, visiting the south of Spain, but we discovered that this annual religious event was so immensely popular every available bed was reserved months before. Thus, we decided to spend Holy Week in Madrid, an alternate plan that turned out to be nearly as challenging. During this holiest of holidays trains were more crowded than ever. The only way to reach Madrid from Barcelona was by going first to Valencia, and that two hundred mile trip took nine hours. We spent the night in Valencia and for dinner, enjoyed their local specialty, *paella*. The following day we explored the city and by evening were aboard the overnight train to Madrid. Thirteen miserable hours later we arrived in Spain's capital city.

Madrid was impressive with its wide, tree-lined streets and spacious plazas that featured magnificent fountains and statues. We found a charming *pension* for less than a dollar a night and then visited the American Express office to pick up our mail. I had not received a letter since being in Venice, a month earlier. Waiting for me were a dozen letters from family and friends, including every former romantic partner, from Deborah Wolfe to Michelle Garnier. Michelle had just arrived in Paris and would soon be married to her elderly admirer.

"I need some time, Alvin. I've got to read these right now." We found a café, and as I read the letters from my former true loves I uttered a small groan.

"What's wrong?" asked Alvin.

"What's wrong," I answered, "is that I've created an impossible situation, and I don't know what to do about it. My girlfriend in New York will be in Paris in a few weeks, and every other girlfriend from

England, Stockholm, Vienna, Dubrovnik, Rome, and Nice will be there too."

"Sounds like a great problem. All you need to do is plan your time carefully."

"You don't get it, Alvin. Each girl assumes she's the *only* one. How can I convince them that each is a true love? That sounds crazy even to me."

"Calm down, Peter, we'll figure this out. We won't even *be* in Paris for a couple of weeks, and if we continue traveling on Spanish trains it could be months."

I tried to ignore the looming problem as we began viewing the sights of Madrid. We began at the Prado Museum, because their world-class collection was extensive, extraordinary, and we knew it would take several visits. Alvin was in artistic heaven as we dashed from one masterpiece to the next. Among the thousands of paintings were rare examples by El Greco, Velasquez, Rubens, Rembrandt, Goya, and dozens of others. Alvin knew the intimate history behind each painting, and he generously shared those stories. In the next several days we returned to the museum three more times. I became convinced that the Prado was probably the best reason to suffer the prehistoric railway system and visit Spain.

We viewed the endless activities of *La Semana Santa*, including religious processions with floats, candlelight marches, and strange costumes. We also traveled to nearby Toledo one day to visit the Cathedral, the house of El Greco, and more paintings by the master. It was a delightful day with comfortable weather and lovely scenery.

After a memorable week in Madrid we headed for Andalusia. Our first stop was Cordoba, capital of the Muslim Dynasty, where we visited the Great Mosque of Cordoba. We wandered through the forest of delicate columns and marveled at the stunning visual composition.

What a structure! What beauty! What elegance! And what on earth were Ferdinand and Isabella thinking when they drove the Moors out of Spain?

"It's obvious," I said, "the greatest architectural achievements ever produced this side of the Pyrenees were created by the Moors. Wasn't Ferdinand paying attention?"

"I guess he had other things on his mind," replied Alvin.

We next toured the historic neighborhoods of Seville, which were composed of narrow stone streets and small houses with lavishly planted patios. Seville also had one of the largest Gothic cathedrals in Europe. Built on the site of a former mosque, the architects retained the minaret, *La Giralda*, and converted it to the church's bell tower.

"Have you noticed the number of Americans here?" asked Alvin. "The place is crawling with them. I think they're beginning to return to Europe."

Since the end World War II European tourism had been a mere trickle of hearty souls, but in the last few months the situation appeared to be changing. "You're right, and where better to begin than Spain, not only the cheapest country in Europe, but one relatively untouched by war."

Even though Spain's fascist government was ideologically aligned with Hitler and Mussolini, the country remained neutral. Well, not exactly neutral. Generalissimo Franco, Spain's military dictator, provided economic assistance to the Nazis, but on the other hand, he aided Jewish refugees. Apparently, that was his idea of neutrality. When the war ended, Spain was one of the few European countries in relatively sound economic shape.

Our trip from Seville to Granada, about one hundred fifty miles, took eleven hours. Eleven hours! We averaged the blazing speed of around seven miles an hour! That was only a slight improvement over

Robert Fulton's steamboat that first chugged down the Hudson River in 1800! How was it possible, I kept wondering, for anything propelled by steam to travel so slowly?

In Granada we found the second important reason to visit Spain—the Alhambra Palace. The Alhambra was like a small city conceived and built by Moorish architects on the brow of a hill. It was begun in the fourteenth century and was an absolute gem. In fact, Moorish poets referred to it as "a pearl set in emeralds". Alvin and I spent the entire day wandering among the open courts, fountains, and gardens. We were in a state of absolute enchantment.

Muslim art was influenced by Byzantine sensibilities; and the geometric patterns and arabesques were perfectly integrated with the colorful tiles and paving. Clearly, the ancient designers had achieved their goal of "Paradise on Earth". The Alhambra was as perfect as any architectural design could be.

"I could live here," said Alvin. "This place is heaven."

We visited other monuments in Granada, but the Alhambra drew us back several more times, like the artistic magnet it was. After several quiet days we were sufficiently rested to attempt our return to Madrid. We caught the late afternoon cattle car and arrived at our destination seventeen hours later. The first six hours were spent sitting on our bags in the train's aisle, as there wasn't a seat to be had. When a few passengers disembarked around midnight, suddenly there were two seats available on an unforgiving slat bench. It felt like we were sitting on steel reinforcing rods, but at least we were off the floor.

We returned to our old *pension*, in Madrid, and spent the remainder of the day trying to purchase tickets to Paris. What a battle that was! You would have thought we were booking a trip to the moon. Finally a sympathetic railway employee provided what he claimed were "the very last third class tickets" for the overnight train leaving the following day.

We had won the battle, but the war was far from over. I fell into bed that night exhausted and slept for twelve uninterrupted hours.

"Last chance to visit the Prado!" was the way Alvin awakened me late the next morning.

"I'd rather sleep," I said.

"You'll sleep when you're dead."

We visited the museum, treated ourselves to an expensive dinner, and boarded our traveling torture chamber by eleven that night. The train was crowded, and sleep seemed unlikely, but we were finally on our way to Paris, a city I had wanted to visit for years. I felt elated.

"Tell me truthfully, Alvin, is Paris as great as I think it will be?"

"Peter, you have no idea. It's more wonderful than you can possibly imagine!"

CHAPTER TWENTY-THREE

Paris

We knew the trip from Madrid to Paris was long, over six hundred fifty miles, but how could we possibly know the journey would take nearly three days? We reached the border at noon, after spending a sleepless night in an agonizing third-class compartment. I doubt that any victim of the Spanish Inquisition had suffered more. Further discomfort awaited us at the border; Spanish customs officials had prepared a fiesta of red tape.

"What was the purpose of your trip?" the officer wanted to know. "Are you carrying any exposed film? Did you exchange money at less than the official rate? Have you ever been arrested?" And on and on the questions went. Most of our answers were half-truths, but it didn't seem to matter. The officer's objective was to check off each item on the printed form, not evaluate the answers. I imagined that an anarchist who just planted a bomb under the Prado Museum, but provided an answered for each question, could have strolled across the border with little trouble. The officer was like a robot, performing his work deliberately, but at the speed of a slug.

"Excuse me," I said, "can we speed this up? Our train to Paris leaves soon."

"We must follow government procedures," came the bureaucratic reply. "Be patient."

When we finally finished, our patience was exhausted and our train had left the station.

"Damn those idiots!" exclaimed Alvin. "Now what do we do?" The choice was clear; we would wait for the next train, which was scheduled to leave six hours later. French customs was a breeze, compared to the ordeal on the Spanish side of the border, and we were left with several hours to kill. With little more to do we sat at a pleasant café, ordered coffee, and tried not to hate every officious, moronic bureaucrat who worked for the Spanish government.

Our third class French coach, compared to its counterpart in Spain, was like the difference between a new Cadillac and a 1928 Model A Ford. We sped across France through the night averaging almost three times the speed of a Spanish train, and by early morning we were in Paris. Finally, Paris—at last!

Alvin Jacobs spent six months as a student in Paris, and he knew the city intimately. Thus, I put myself in his capable hands. We took a bus to Montparnasse and checked into Alvin's old hotel, *les États-Unis*, which translates as "the United States".

"Did you choose this place because of its name?" I asked.

"No, that's just a bonus. I spent several months here. Loved the room and the area."

"Bonjour, Monsieur Jacobs," cried the concierge. She ran out of her office with a wide grin on her face and embraced Alvin. She was old enough to be Alvin's mother and hugged him like she actually was. They chatted for several moments until Alvin said, "Madame Boulet, I'd like you to meet my friend, Peter Newman. Peter and I have been traveling for the past month and we hope you've saved a room for us."

"I have a very agreeable room for you," she said in her thick accent. "It is the same room you had when you were here a year ago with Monsieur Elwood." Madame Boulet was short and a bit thick around the middle, but she had an attractive smile and vivacious personality. In her youth she must have been a beauty. We settled into our room on the fifth floor, and after going two nights without a bed I was ready to collapse. But I didn't have a chance.

"Come across the street with me," Alvin insisted, "I want to introduce you to *La Coupole*." A block away, just across the Boulevard Montparnasse, was the art-deco brasserie famous for the clients who patronized it during the 1920s. Artists, writers, and intellectuals like Matisse, Picasso, Hemingway, and Jean-Paul Sartre spent hours here eating, drinking, and exchanging ideas. We had lunch, and then I said, "Sorry, Alvin, I can't keep my eyes open. I have to go to bed." I slept a solid, dreamless sleep, through the afternoon, right past dinner, and well into the following morning.

"Today," began Alvin, "we learn how to get around Paris without getting run over by a Parisian driver." Alvin and I were at a small café near our hotel having breakfast. We were standing at the bar having a buttery croissant and a cup of powerful coffee. Standing at the bar, I just learned, cost less than sitting at one of the small tables.

"Believe it or not, there's only one stoplight in Paris, and it's on the other side of the river. Now here's what else you should know. The Metro is convenient and the fastest way to get around Paris. But you're underground and see nothing. Buses are good, but not always convenient. Avoid taxis unless it's an emergency. Taxi drivers hate Americans, and their meters are either rigged or broken. My preference is walking. Walking in Paris is the cheapest way to get around and one of the great delights this city offers. But you must watch out for drivers; they're crazy and dangerous. Early on I learned that pedestrians have no rights whatsoever, except—possibly—the right to flee. So be careful crossing streets. Now, let's go pick up our mail."

It was an April day made for walking. The air was crisp, the sun was bright, and it seemed that all of Paris was alive with activity. I thought of those Yip Harburg lyrics, *April in Paris, chestnuts in blossom . . .* And here I was in Paris; it was April, the chestnut trees were in bloom, and I felt like dancing down the street like that other American in Paris, Gene Kelly. We crossed the Luxembourg Gardens and headed for the Pont St. Michel. I stopped in the middle of the bridge and watched the traffic on the Seine. And then I saw the towers of Notre Dame.

"Alvin, I can't just walk by; I have to see the most famous cathedral in the world." We approached the church from the spacious open plaza, and I stopped to marvel at the delicate façade, the arches, and carvings. Then we stepped inside, and the soaring space became apparent.

In the past months I had seen some of the greatest spaces ever conceived: Hagia Sophia in Istanbul, the Pantheon in Rome, and the Alhambra in Granada. Notre Dame was equally as thrilling.

We continued wandering in the general direction of the Opera House and finally reached the American Express office, every American's mailbox away from home. Awaiting me were eighteen letters, a few more than Alvin. One of his, however, contained a delightful surprise. Alvin had sold a painting! His father reported that a friend bought a canvas that Alvin painted three years earlier, and a thirty-dollar money order accompanied that news.

"I'm rich!" he shouted, "and no longer an amateur. I'm a real, goddam, professional artist!" Thirty dollars would keep Alvin going for weeks, and the thrill would last as long as he lived.

My letters, too, contained surprises. The most dramatic of these concerned my least-favorite, most-boring-person-on-earth, widowed uncle John from Chicago. He was the one who insisted I call Henry Bergmann in Stockholm, which led to one of my true loves, Monika Eklund. Uncle John would be in Paris in two weeks. He had purchased a car to go touring, and he presumed I would be delighted to act as chauffeur. He suggested I pick up the car, meet his ship in Le Havre, and drive off for a splendid few weeks together. I was in shock!

The sad truth was this: uncle John had no idea we were not friends. Yes, he was my father's brother, but that's where the relationship ended. A year ago, when he heard I was going to Europe he sent me a discouraging letter explaining why this was a rotten idea; *The continent is in shambles from the war, it's dangerous to travel alone, it's a waste of good money*, and so on. I had no idea how I would handle this situation, but I feared it would not end well.

I was prepared for the other surprises but had no plan to solve those problems either.

Deborah Wolfe would be in Paris in ten days appearing with the American Drama Theater at the Théâter Montparnasse, right in my own backyard. Monika Eklund was coming to Paris in three weeks to attend a convention of medical students. Laura Ross wanted to know when I'd be free, because she was planning to visit from Rome. Michelle Garnier, my true love from Nice, wrote to give me her address and phone number and hoped I would call *"the moment you arrive"*. Anne Cleary wrote from Iowa to say her planned trip was doubtful, because *"There's a good chance I will be married this summer"*. My Yugoslavian partner, Karolina Novak had scored a visa to visit England, but was unsure if she could get a visa to visit France. And finally, Astrid Obermann from Austria claimed she loved me dearly, but her parents felt she was too young to travel to Paris by herself. So, the final score was four probables, including the engaged Michelle, two doubtfuls, and one dropout. Combined with the latest news from uncle John I saw nothing but chaos in my future.

After digesting this new information and discussing it with Alvin he said, "Let's not be hasty, Peter. There's a solution here somewhere.

First, let's make a chart; we're visual people and a chart will make everything clearer." That afternoon I created a chart with names, dates of arrival in Paris, and a column for comments. We stared at the chart for several minutes. This was followed by a long silence. Finally, Alvin said, "Sorry, Peter, you're screwed."

I decided to forget my predicament for the moment and call Michelle Garnier, the only true love who was already in Paris. We made a plan to meet at her apartment late that afternoon.

"Michelle," I said, "you look wonderful." She embraced me for the longest time and finally said, "So do you. You know, I've missed you. You may not realize it but you awakened something in me, and I have not been the same since we were together."

"But here you are in Paris," I said, "and you're engaged to be married. How wonderful!"

"I am being married because I know I must change my life. And the man I will marry loves me and wants to take care of me. Sadly, I am not really in love with him."

"Does he know that?"

"Yes, but he thinks I will learn to love him."

"What do you think?"

"I don't know."

We sat quietly for a very long time. I heard a clock ticking in the hall, and I was becoming uncomfortable with the silence. "You once told me you were not sure you believed in love."

"I wasn't sure," she answered. "You tried to convince me otherwise, and now I think it may be possible. But I am going to be married, and I can't think about that. I must think about that kind man who has agreed to care for me."

"Why did you want to see me, Michelle?"

"I don't really know. Perhaps I feel love for you, and that seems odd. I have never been in love. But I liked the feeling, and I had to find out if it was real. Will you stay here tonight?"

"And your fiancé? Won't he mind?"

"Leave that to me." And then she came closer, took my face in her hands, and gave me a deep and loving kiss. "Please stay here; this is important to me. It will be our last time."

It was an incredible night of love, and when we parted, we were both in tears. Michelle decided to marry for security, not love, and we both felt the heartbreak of her choice. The following day I crossed her name off the chart. I suddenly dreaded resolving my other relationships.

Several days later I decided to explore the great monuments of Paris. During my first week—a time spent recuperating from ten solid months of travel—I had seen little more than my picturesque neighborhood. I hadn't even glimpsed the Eiffel Tower! It was now time to become a tourist.

Seeing Gustave Eiffel's Tower recalled the shock I felt visiting the Great Pyramids; I was stunned by its size. It was absolutely immense! I walked around the Tower for an hour and marveled at the delicacy and power of its design. In the following days I visited the Louvre, several other museums, and a handful of religious buildings. I also noticed—along the way—Parisian women, probably the most alluring and chic in the world. With fine weather, blue skies, and a city in bloom, romance was everywhere. Lovers on park benches embraced one another in a most unselfconscious way. Someone once said, "At any given moment half of Paris is making love to the other half." Ah, Paris in the spring—there was nothing to compare to that magic.

The day I received the message that Deborah Wolfe arrived I got a letter from my uncle John informing me that he would arrive in Le Havre on another ship a week later than originally planned. That would pretty much coincide with Monika Eklund's appearance, but at least it gave me some breathing room.

"See," said Alvin, "I told you it would all work out."

"It's not at all worked out," I replied. "We're just postponing the moment of truth."

I met Deborah at her hotel in Montparnasse the next morning.

"It's so great to see you," she said. "It feels like we've been apart forever."

We were hugging and I said, "Six months only feels like forever. You look terrific. Tell me, how long will you be in Paris?" I was visualizing my chart of true loves.

"We rehearse one week and then have a week of performances. Then off to Brussels."

So far so good, I thought; Deborah would leave Paris about the time Monika and uncle John arrived. But what will I tell Laura Ross in Rome? And what if Karolina Novac gets a visa to visit France? And if Anne Cleary in Iowa doesn't get married, well, maybe I should just leap into the Seine right now and save Madame Boulet the job of mopping up the blood.

"Why do you look so worried?" asked Deborah.

"Oh, it's nothing, really. My uncle is coming to Paris and I have to pick up his car."

We had dinner that evening and then Deborah suggested we go to my hotel. "I have a roommate, you know, the fellow with whom I've been traveling. Can we stay here?"

I have a roommate too—another actress. Maybe I can get her to stay with someone else."

Everything in Newmanland seemed complicated these days, but where there's a will . . .

We spent the night together, and it was like the first time—tender and gentle, but exciting. I genuinely liked Deborah; possibly, I was in love. She touched something within me, and I felt guiltier than ever that I had created a world-class dilemma with no simple solution.

My uncle had purchased a Hillman Minx, a British car with four doors, four cylinders, and a four-speed manual transmission. I had never seen a Hillman before I entered the showroom on the Avenue des Champs-Elysées. The salesperson had a letter from my uncle directing him to release the new car to his trusted nephew. I was given a twenty-minute orientation, a handbook, and a full tank of gas before I left the showroom. I had not driven a car in nearly a year and did not look forward to driving among crazed Formula One drivers on a busy Parisian boulevard. Somehow I made it back to my hotel without incident, if you don't count the endless horn honking and dirty looks from half the drivers in Paris.

Alvin was standing in front of our hotel as I drove up. "Need a lift?" I asked.

"Look at you," he said, "sitting behind the wheel of a shiny bowl of split-pea soup." I, too, wondered what my uncle was thinking when he chose that nasty shade of Hillman green?

"Look, it's new, it runs, and it's free. Now, do you want a ride or not?" We drove to the Bois de Boulogne and enjoyed the freedom that can only come from having total control over your means of transportation, something I hadn't experienced since leaving home.

I continued seeing Deborah during those rare moments when she was not acting, and our romance seemed to blossom. Perhaps it was our fantasy existence—being in Paris during the loveliest of all seasons, eating delicious food, and being surrounded by the beauty of the city. Or was it—quite simply—that we satisfied so completely each other's needs? When Deborah was working, Alvin and I visited museums, churches, and galleries. And on Deborah's day off Alvin and his old girlfriend, Annie Debizet, joined us as we piled into the Hillman and drove to Malmaison, Napoleon and Josephine's chateau. We were having the time of our lives, while I was still trying to ignore the looming problems ahead.

Those problems, as Alvin predicted, began to fade quite suddenly. I received a letter from Anne Cleary who confirmed her plans for marriage. "*You will always be the love of my life,*" she wrote, "*but Milton, my fiancé is here in Iowa, and who knows where you will be next? I must be practical, as my parents say, and do what is best for my future.*" Like Michelle, Anne opted for practicality. I was a bit sad, but greatly relieved by her decision.

On the very same day Karolina Novak wrote that she was unable to get a visa for France, and she wondered if I could meet her in London instead. I quickly informed her that would be impossible, but I added that she would always remain my true love. My list was quickly shrinking.

On the following day I received a note from Laura Ross in Rome. "*I am disappointed not to hear from you, but trust you are all right. I plan to visit Paris and see you, and I hope that will not be a problem. I will arrive next Monday and will call when my train arrives. I cannot wait for us to be together again. I send all my love to you.*" Back to the chart. Deborah was off to Brussels Sunday afternoon. My uncle and Laura Ross were arriving Monday; and Monika Eklund would be in Paris on Tuesday. Time was running out. I needed to come up with a plan—and fast!

CHAPTER TWENTY-FOUR

The Low Countries

I struggled for hours to devise a solution that would satisfy Laura, Monika, and my uncle John, without actually compromising every ethical principle I still held dear. It was impossible, I thought, unless at least two out of three would end up seriously hating me. Then Alvin, old clear-headed, life-saving Alvin, came up with a plan.

"Here's what you do, Peter. You go to Le Havre on Monday and pick up your uncle. You really can't get out of that. You're driving his car, and he's expecting you. At the same time, I'll pick up Laura at the train station. She knows me from Rome; I'm a familiar face. I'll tell her about uncle John, so you'll be off the hook. I'll also arrange to get a room for myself from Madame Boulet so you two can share the room we have. How does that sound?"

"So far, so good," I said, "but what we do about Monika on Tuesday?"

"Tuesday morning you pick up Monika at the train station, tell her, 'Surprise! I'm taking you to see the tulips in Holland. And, by the way, this is my uncle's car and he's coming along." Then pick up uncle John at his hotel. From there you all drive to Keukenhof. It's the height of the tulip season, and what a great treat this will be for everybody!"

"Monika and my uncle in the same car for days? Are you crazy? Within thirty minutes she'll hate us both, and after an hour she'll probably leap out the car while it's still moving."

"Listen, it was your uncle who insisted you call Bergmann, and it was Bergmann who introduced you to his niece, Monika. This will be like a family reunion."

"You're nuts! And what about her convention? She has to be in Paris five days later."

"You'll return in five days, no matter what. Make up an excuse, get a migraine, fake an injury, whatever. Once you return, Monika will attend the convention, Laura will be available, and by then uncle John will probably look forward to being on his own."

It may have been a good plan, but somehow I felt the quicksand dragging me down.

The French line's S.S. Liberté arrived in Le Havre thirty minutes later than scheduled. I had made the hundred-mile trip early Monday morning and was patiently waiting for passengers to disembark. I spotted uncle John among the Cabin Class passengers and shouted his name. When he recognized me he smiled—something he rarely did.

"Peter, old boy, how good to see you."

"Same here," I lied. I helped him with his bags, and we lugged them to the car.

"So this is my new Hillman Minx," he said. "So shiny and new." I had washed it earlier.

"Yes, and she drives like a dream. Just outside of Paris I had her doing seventy." I knew at once I had blundered.

"Now, let's be clear; we're not out to set any speed records."

On our drive back to Paris, John spoke of my parents, other relatives, and friends. Then he asked, "So, what plans have you made for us?"

"I'm dropping you off at your hotel, and then I'll return to take you to dinner."

"Remember, Peter, dinner is on me." *What? Did he actually think I would pay?*

"Then tomorrow we're going to Holland to see the tulips, just as you requested."

"Isn't that rushing it a bit?"

"Well, if we don't hurry they'll wither up and be gone, and you'll miss the whole show." I figured I would mention Monika tomorrow. Let him have a good night's sleep, I thought.

I returned to my hotel where I found Laura Ross waiting for me and. looking lovelier than ever. "What a delight it is to see you," I said. We were locked in an embrace.

"You don't look so bad yourself," she replied. "I know what's going on; Alvin explained about your uncle and the tulips, and I really do understand. So don't feel bad about it."

"I can't help it; I do feel guilty. Alvin has agreed to show you around Paris, and before you know it, I'll be back from Holland and devote myself entirely to you."

We renewed our old acquaintance that night, and it brought back memories of our time in Rome. Laura was most agreeable, and the guilt I felt was becoming painful. Many times during the night I expressed my regret about how things had worked out. "You deserve better," I said, but unfortunately I could do nothing about it.

Monika's train arrived at Gare de l'Est the next morning, and we stood on the platform for several minutes hugging and kissing. Finally, I said, "I have a wonderful surprise; we're going to Holland to see the tulips in bloom."

"When?" she asked.

"Today, right now. I have a car, well, actually it's my uncle's car—the uncle who knows your uncle and who was responsible for our meeting in Stockholm. By the way, he's coming along."

"Oh, Peter, I've been traveling for nearly a full day. Can't this wait?"

"Afraid not. My uncle insists we see the tulips in full bloom. He's kind of nutty that way."

"You know my medical meetings begin in five days. I can't miss that."

"You'll be back in time; I guarantee it."

We drove to uncle John's hotel and found him in the lobby in his three-piece suit, bow tie, umbrella in hand (though the sun was out), and a felt fedora that covered his totally bald head.

"Uncle John, let me introduce Monika Eklund. She's Henry Bergmann's niece, and it was because of you that we met last year in Stockholm."

"Is she coming to Holland with us?" my uncle asked apprehensively.

"Yes, isn't that wonderful? Monika is a medical student, so if there are any health problems along the way, well, we're in good hands."

"A pleasure to meet you Miss Eklund. I've known your uncle for more than twenty years, and I am very fond of him."

"He has also spoken highly of you, sir."

"Please, call me John." I breathed a bit easier; the worst, I hoped, was over.

We drove to Amiens, site of the purest realization of French Gothic cathedral architecture. I had recently neglected my other true loves, so it was satisfying to view again great architecture. By late afternoon we were in Brussels, where we had a wonderful dinner and spent the night. Much later that night I visited Monika's room. "Alone at last," I said. "I thought it would never happen."

"I've not been in a real bed for a long time, Peter. So if I fall asleep, please understand."

She drifted off in my arms, and it was still dark the next morning when I felt her lips near my ear. "Let's make love," she said. "I've missed you."

Our next day was a visual treat as we traveled through the glorious countryside filled with windmills, canals, and all manner of colorful foliage. The low countries were so named because much of Belgium, Netherlands, and Luxembourg were at or below sea level. Thus we viewed picturesque bridges and canals that pervaded that area. We reached Amsterdam and found a comfortable hotel. By this time, my miserly uncle John barely winced when paying bills for the three of us. Monika had so ingratiated herself with him he seemed nearly happy to be our sponsor.

That afternoon we visited the Rijksmuseum where we viewed some of the greatest Dutch paintings in the world, including Rembrandt's masterpiece, the Night Watch. The day was cloudy and cool, so we walked among the old narrow buildings and canals, had an early dinner at an Indonesian restaurant, and retired to two of our three booked rooms.

After a substantial Dutch breakfast we drove the next day to the Keukenhof tulip fields in Lisse. It was the most spectacular display of tulips one could imagine. Acres upon acres of bulbs were in full bloom, and the colors ranged all over the map, from pure white to a deep, almost black purple. It was an absolute visual delight!

"I'm so glad you planned this trip," said Monika. "I could not imagine missing this."

"And, uncle John, is this as impressive as you thought it would be?"

"You know, Peter, I have lived many more years than you two. I have sailed to Hawaii and been through the Panama Canal; I attended the Chicago World's Fair and the one in New York as well. In other words, I've been around. Perhaps I'm not as easily impressed as I once was."

Now what the hell kind of answer was that? If poor, old, boring uncle John couldn't be impressed by the greatest tulip show on earth, there was little hope for this pathetic man. I suddenly wanted to return to Paris as quickly as possible.

We drove to The Hague the following morning and saw an extraordinary exhibit of Van Gogh paintings at the Municipal Museum. Uncle John was not particularly interested in art, but Monika and I delighted in every canvas. I was so glad she was there. Without her this trip would have ended after the first twenty-four hours.

We continued to Rotterdam, one of World War II's most devastated cities. In the spring of 1940, the Netherlands fiercely resisted the German invasion. In an effort to demoralize the Dutch, Hitler ordered an aerial blitz. Shortly before the planes took off, Netherland surrendered. The bombers, however, never received the message. Thus, more than a hundred German bombers of the Luftwaffe attacked an essentially defenseless city and leveled the heart of Rotterdam with tons of bombs. More than a thousand civilians were killed, and the city of Rotterdam nearly ceased to exist. Much damage remained, but reconstruction was in progress everywhere.

That afternoon I suggested we return directly to Paris. "If we begin early tomorrow," I said, "we can make it back to Paris by dinnertime."

"What's the rush?" asked uncle John.

"Monica has medical meetings to attend," I said, "and I have places to see and things to do."

"What sort of things, Peter?"

"I have obligations to the University. They're financing my fellowship, and I feel a commitment to uphold my end of the bargain."

"Well, I'm financing your trip to Holland. What about your obligation to me?"

"What are you saying? Are you comparing this trip to my fellowship? You know, I never asked for this. You just assumed I'd be thrilled to pick up your car and drive you around Europe. But you never actually asked how I felt about it. I've tried to accommodate you, but both Monika and I have other commitments. As far as this trip is concerned I'm immensely grateful for your generosity, but I felt we were doing something for one another as relatives, not as business associates satisfying some legal obligation."

"I'm terribly disappointed in your attitude, Peter. Perhaps you've been away from home too long. You seem to have picked up some very foreign ideas." I could see this trip was about over.

"We need to leave early tomorrow." I said. "Perhaps we should have an early dinner."

"Don't worry about me," said uncle John. "I'll have dinner sent up to my room." He frowned, did an about face, and walked swiftly to the elevator.

"I'm sorry you had to witness that," I said to Monika. "It was so unnecessary."

"Family relationships are sometimes difficult," she said. Maybe she's right, I thought, but uncle John had always been a world-class jerk, and I had little hope that would ever change.

It rained the entire next day, and with my uncle still in a sour mood the ride back to Paris seemed dull and endless. Late in the afternoon we stopped to see Reims Cathedral, but uncle John chose to remain in the car during our brief visit. "He's being petulant," Monica observed.

"Too bad," I said, "he's missing one of the greatest Gothic churches in all of France."

It was early evening when we arrived in Paris. I drove Monika to the hotel where her fellow medical students were staying. She thanked uncle John and wished him a pleasant stay in Paris. I gave her a kiss on the cheek and said very quietly, "I'll call you tomorrow."

Then I drove uncle John to his hotel on the right bank. "I want to apologize for yesterday," I said. "Perhaps all this could have been avoided if we had discussed your plans earlier. But I don't want there to be any hard feelings. I hope the rest of your time in Europe is more enjoyable."

"There is one more thing, Peter. I was hoping you could sell my car after I leave, if that doesn't conflict with other plans you may have." I noticed a tinge of sarcasm.

"I'd be happy to help you out. Do you know how much you want for the car?"

"Speak to the Hillman people. Whatever they suggest I will accept."

"Goodbye for now," I said. "Call me when you return to Paris." He gave me a stiff hug and then I turned and walked through the light rain towards Montparnasse.

Thirty minutes later I was at les États-Unis, where I immediately spotted Alvin and Laura. They were sitting close together in the small lobby, and they were holding hands.

"What a pleasure to see you both," I said. "The last few days have been incredibly stressful."

"Speaking of the last few days," began Alvin, "there's something you should know."

"Is it bad news?" I asked.

"Depends. We think it's pretty good news. The fact is—Laura and I are in love."

"What? You're in love? All this happened in just five days?"

"We didn't plan this," said Laura. "It just happened. And it might have happened even if you didn't go to Holland."

"You know I love you both," I said, "but this is a shock. I don't know whether to be happy for you or mad as hell. But trust me, I'm trying to be happy."

Actually, the news of my two friends was not exactly catastrophic. Having lived along the edge of the cliff for so long, I suddenly felt relief. Laura and uncle John were now out of the picture. Deborah was off on an extended tour, Anne Cleary and Michelle Garnier were getting married, Karolina was stuck in London, and Astrid Obermann remained in Vienna. Only Monika Eklund was still available, and she would be attending meeting and seminars. I felt at peace for the first time in a month and finally free to concentrate on the reason that brought me to Europe in the first place. A giant burden of my own making was suddenly lifted off my shoulders.

"Have you had dinner yet? I asked.

"No," they said in unison. "Let's eat."

I thought about my true loves before drifting off to sleep that night. I had created a terrible situation, a real mess actually, and I had no one to blame but myself. I believed I could have it all, but that was not only unrealistic, it was arrogant and conceited. In retrospect I was ashamed to have manipulated so many lives. *Starting tomorrow*, I thought, *I will become a better person.* I only hoped I could.

CHAPTER TWENTY-FIVE

Paris Encore

I must have been incredibly dense *not* to realize that Alvin and Laura were perfectly suited. Both were charming, attractive, and bright; that much I knew. But what I didn't recognize was what they had in common. They were part of the American community in Rome for months, but had not met before I introduced them. And enlisting Alvin's help in solving my personal problem was another blunder. So, consciously or not, I was the one who threw them together. On the other hand, no old world village matchmaker could have done a more perfect job. Apparently, they agreed.

"I can never thank you enough," said Alvin, "for introducing me to Laura. I hope some day you'll forgive us for the way we got together. I know if I were you, I'd be plenty pissed."

"No question about it, Alvin, you acted like a real jerk. But on the other hand, maybe I had it coming; it certainly feels like retribution. How could I possibly believe that every girl I met represented true love? What was I thinking? Well, this has been one hell of a lesson. From now on, no more rushing into love affairs; maybe, no more love affairs at all."

"Forgive me if I don't believe you," said Alvin. "And by the way, does all this mean you and I are okay? I mean can I cancel my one-way ticket to Siberia?"

"I suppose so; what's done is done. Anyway, we have some unfinished business. When Laura leaves and my uncle returns, we're still doing the chateau trip we planned."

The next couple of weeks were relaxed and enjoyable. I had been in Paris for more than a month and had become relatively comfortable with the language. I also knew my way around the city and easily disregarded the occasional hostility Parisians aimed at tourists. During the week Laura and Monika remained in town we shared a few meals together. Laura's transition from lover to loving friend was difficult, but it was made easier by her kindness and understanding. It also helped that Monika was there. If she suspected that Laura and I were ever more than good friends, she never let on.

We frequently walked to our favorite neighborhood place, Le Bonne Table, meaning "good food", which its owner produced with remarkable consistency. After all these years I can still taste their signature dish, *Escalope de veau Normande*, which was a tender veal cutlet smothered with mushrooms and a delectable cream sauce that was a bit of heaven. This was accompanied by perfectly seasoned *pomme frites*. Following that was a salad of butter lettuce coated with dressing as light as a whisper. And that Parisian bread! It was like a confection. Add a glass of *vin rouge*, and it became a feast of which I never tired. I would happily pay a small fortune today to have that same meal.

My relationship with Monika was pleasant, but cooler than before. Our time together was limited because of her meetings. She generally attended seminars each morning, classes in the afternoon, and was often obliged to meet fellow students at her hotel in the evenings.

"What is to become of us," she often asked.

"I have no idea," I would reply. But that was not entirely true. I could no more live in Stockholm than she could abandon her life for the U.S. We were as geographically incompatible as an Aleut fisherman and Zulu princess, and that was unlikely to change. So we existed in a delightful limbo, playing out our limited relationship in the world's most romantic city.

It is also true that memories of Deborah Wolfe occasionally rattled my consciousness. I thought of her fondly, and at times, genuinely missed her. She corresponded often and always with enthusiasm about her experiences with the American Drama Theater. *"We had great success in Brussels,"* she wrote, *"and are now heading for Amsterdam. After that we may go to Switzerland. Why don't you surprise me and visit one day. I can promise you a real nice time—wink, wink."*

Despite my recent dedication to a celibate future I was ready to jump on the next train. Instead, I concentrated on my other true loves and continued to explore the charming city of Paris—its structures, monuments, parks, and of course, the people. Alvin frequently joined me as we walked through a particular neighborhood and studied every obscure feature. Often we sat for an hour or two at a local café speculating on our futures. I had become quite close to Alvin, and the more time we spent together the more I admired his delightful outlook on life. Often he would whip out his sketchbook as we spoke and do instant caricatures of patrons. His talent was astounding.

"Come on, Peter," he would say, "let's see what you can do." He would pass me the pen and pad and I would sketch nearby architectural details, like cornices, balconies, or other decorative building elements. Then he would become the critic and say, "You know, you have real ability. If this architecture thing doesn't work out, you should consider becoming an artist?"

"Thanks," I would reply, "but I prefer to go down with the ship that got me here." There were times when I chose to wander the streets of Paris alone in my thoughts. One evening I walked across most of Paris, from the Basilica of Sacre Coeur—high atop Montmartre—to my hotel in Montparnasse, a distance of eight miles. It took nearly three hours, but it was like traveling as a character through a Parisian travelogue.

Eventually, Monika's medical convention ended, and it was time for her to return home.

"Being together has been wonderful," she said, "and I will never forget you. But I suspect this is the end of us. There are too many obstacles to our happiness."

"Perhaps you're right," I answered, "but knowing you has been a dream come true."

It was a sad separation; we both felt a deep loss. We said goodbye at the train station, and before the train began to move we were fighting back tears, thinking about what might have been.

My uncle John returned to Paris nearly three weeks after he began his motor trip.

"It was a most enlightening tour," he said, "but now I'm ready to return home. My ship sails the day after tomorrow. Perhaps you will drive me to Le Havre."

"Of course," I said.

"And, by the way, I just got a message from my niece, Lisa Berger. She's in town and has invited us to see the Ballet Theater tomorrow night. She's a dancer with the company."

"What? A relative of ours is a dancer? How come I've never heard of her?"

"My wife didn't get along with her sister—Lisa's mother—but when my niece learned that she and I would be in Europe at the same time, she arranged this meeting."

I had to admit, my least favorite uncle was full of surprises. Who knew there was a ballerina in the family? And if she was like any ballerina I had ever seen, she was certainly worth meeting. My excitement was tempered, however, as I realized that the new me was still toying with the concept of celibacy.

I met my uncle at the theater box office, where Lisa had provided us with excellent seats. The ballet was *Swan Lake*, and when the melodic Tchaikovsky music began and the corps de ballet appeared I asked, "Which one is Lisa?"

"I can't be sure," he whispered, "all the swans are dressed alike." Some help *he* was.

The ballet was immensely enjoyable, and as the final curtain fell I couldn't wait to meet the attractive dancer to whom I was more or less related. We went backstage and almost immediately I heard a pleasant voice calling, "Uncle John, over here." Lisa Berger was still in her tutu, looking absolutely angelic. She kissed uncle John, and then he said to her, "I'd like you to meet my nephew, Peter Newman. He's my brother's son."

"I'm happy to know you," she said. "I had no idea you existed."

"You're a bit of a surprise as well," I replied. "But I must say, a lovely surprise."

I asked my uncle, "Why haven't we known about each other?"

"You know, family disputes, injured feelings, that sort of thing. There were many subjects my wife and I could not discuss. But Lisa and I have always remained in touch."

The three of us were sitting at a local café late that evening, and as we finished our drinks my uncle said, "I must go now. I have to pack for my trip tomorrow. Perhaps you should get some rest as well, Peter. We have a long drive to Le Havre."

"How long will you be in Paris?" I asked Lisa.

"One more week."

"Perhaps I can show you some of the city."

"I'd like that," she said. "I've seen almost nothing. When do you return from Le Havre?"

"Tomorrow, late afternoon. I'll call when I get back."

We sped to the dock with my nervous uncle clutching the door handle and uttering sounds of disapproval all the way. After a hurried goodbye, I was back on the road by early afternoon. At four thirty I called Lisa. "When can we meet?" I asked.

"Come right now," she said. "I have a couple of hours before I'm due at the theater."

Two hours, I thought, what can we see in two hours? We walked first to the Cathedral of Notre Dame, then around the corner to Sainte Chapelle, and finally ended up at a small café on the nearby Ile St. Louis.

"You've now seen the finest Gothic church in Paris, the greatest stained glass in France, and we have enough time left over for a snack in one of the most picturesque corners of the city."

"You're a wonderful guide, Peter, and I really appreciate this. Now tell me, why haven't we met before? And by the way, are we actually related?"

"I don't really know. This situation is just as confusing to *me*. But tell me about you; I've never met a ballerina before, and I'm in awe of anyone who can do what I saw you do last night."

"I'm flattered, but I'm sure dancing is no more difficult than being able to do what you do. We've both trained for a long time, we both have some skill, and we both love what we do."

"When can we meet again?" I asked. "There's so much more I want to know."

"Come to the theater after the performance tonight. You can walk me home."

"I'll be there, but I have a better idea. Have you heard of the Bar de l'Abbaye?"

The Bar de l'Abbaye was located on a short street just behind the oldest church in Paris, Saint-Germain-des-Prés. The place was no larger than a small living room, and tables were even smaller, as if designed to hold no more than two wine glasses. The room resembled a natural cave with walls and ceiling roughly plastered and painted black. Lighting was minimal, as most light came from dozens of candles throughout the room. Some considered the space claustrophobic, but others, including me, saw it as cozy and romantic.

"I love this place!" said Lisa. *Just the right reaction*, I thought.

On the small platform that served as a stage were two guitar players, American expatriots, who sang romantic French and American songs. They harmonized beautifully and played with amazing skill. At the conclusion of each number patrons showed appreciation by snapping their fingers. Applause in such a tiny space would have been deafening, but the snapping of fingers was consistent with the tranquil atmosphere. If I had taken Lisa to the Folies Bergere, at ten times the cost, she could not have been more impressed.

"Oh, Peter," she said. "This is the most marvelous place I've ever been!"

There was no ballet performance the following night, so I suggested we have dinner. The place I had in mind was also on the left bank, inexpensive, and as uncommon as the Bar de l'Abbaye. It was called Roger la Grenouille. Roger was the owner, and *grenouille* means frog—their specialty. The restaurant was not only small, but also narrow and quite long. Think of an airplane interior with a slightly higher ceiling. Along one wall were tables for couples and tables for four were on the opposite wall. The room width was no greater than ten feet. The menu was written in small letters on a chalkboard at the far end of the room. Thus, each table had, in addition to salt, pepper, and mustard containers, high-powered binoculars enabling patrons to read the menu.

"I can't believe this place," said Lisa. "How did you find it?"

"Friends," I said. "I can recommend the frogs legs, if you feel adventurous."

The conversation became more personal as we began to learn more about one another.

"What you do," I began, "is so exciting, I imagine you have dozens of fans everywhere."

"Then you imagine wrong. We're never in one place long enough to have a relationship."

"How about when you perform in New York, your home base? No boyfriends there?"

"Two years ago I had a relationship that ended badly. I'm not sure I want to repeat that."

"Fortunate for me. I recently had some bad luck as well, and right now I'm considering a life of celibacy. What a pair! Two lovely people with hardly one decent future between us."

"I didn't say the future was hopeless; it's just doubtful."

I walked Lisa back to her hotel. It was a warm and fragrant evening, and the city looked as magical as ever. "Thanks for a wonderful time," she said. I hope I can see you again." And then she kissed me. It was a warm and tender kiss, and we embraced for a long time.

"Is this a test?" I asked. "You know I'm on the verge of entering a monastery."

She laughed. "I just want you to know that I appreciate everything you've done for me. And, not so incidentally, I really like you."

When he heard my story Alvin didn't exactly say I told you so, but his eyebrows arched up to his hairline. "It occurs to me, my friend, you don't even know how to spell celibacy."

I saw Lisa nearly every day the Ballet Theater was in town. We walked the city by day, and several evenings were spent at the theater watching her perform. On two occasions I saw the performance from backstage. What a thrill that was!

Eventually the week ended, and the troupe was off to Switzerland. We met after the last performance and sat in a café talking until three in the morning.

"I'll miss you," she said, "and I won't forget how special our time was in Paris."

"Perhaps we'll meet again," I said, "if not Europe, then New York. Who knows?"

We stood in front of Lisa's hotel in a firm embrace. "I don't care if we really are cousins," she said, "I love you, and not because we may be related." We kissed one last time, and she disappeared into the hotel lobby. I turned and walked back to Montparnasse. *I'm not so sure,* I thought. *Maybe I should reconsider this celibacy business.*

The next morning Alvin and I embarked on our motor tour of the great chateaux of the Loire. I looked forward to a couple of weeks of travel and architecture—those other true loves. No doubt about it—plenty of excitement remained in my future.

CHAPTER TWENTY-SIX

The Last Tour

It was mid-June. I had been traveling for almost a year and had spent nearly all my fellowship money. I hoped to stretch the funds for another few weeks—perhaps until the beginning of August—before catching a ship home. But my fellowship year was definitely coming to an end, and a visit to the chateau region would be my last tour. I had always wanted to explore the chateaux of the Loire Valley. Those magnificent structures, built by the most powerful people of their times, represented some of the finest architecture, lavish furnishings, and magnificent gardens ever devised.

How wonderful it was to have a car, the ultimate symbol of personal freedom; and I was grateful to my least favorite uncle for providing me with the Hillman. I promised to sell it for him, but not before I put another few hundred kilometers on this delightful Minx. A word of explanation: Rental cars in Europe did not exist in 1953. Thus, some tourists—like my uncle—purchased a car, drove it for several weeks, and then sold it before returning home. These transactions often involved black market dollars, so the cost was little more than using public transportation. Gas was more expensive than in the U.S.; however, when purchased with black market francs, it was manageable.

Speaking of the black market, before leaving Paris I exchanged some dollars at my favorite moneychanger, "Pierre". The name was hardly imaginative, but it protected his real identity and—so far—had kept him out of jail. During my first week in Paris, Alvin gave me the following directions:

"Go to the Café Bouquet in the Marais district. Select a table at the very rear and order a glass of white wine, not red, white. When Pierre appears you will say *bonjour* and give him a traveler's check. Say nothing more. He will soon return with an envelope. You will shake hands, say, *merci*, and then leave. Do not open the envelope until you are outside." I often felt like a character in a spy movie, but that's the way you purchased French francs at a twenty-five percent discount during the early post-war years.

Alvin and I headed south from Paris and within an hour reached Chartres, site of the marvelous twelfth century Gothic cathedral. We noted the odd front with its two dissimilar towers that were built hundreds of years apart. We also viewed the extraordinary stained glass and beautiful sculptures. It was as fine a church as I had seen in France.

We continued toward the Loire Valley, and after another hour arrived at the Château de Blois. It was difficult to believe that this immense structure was designed as a royal home; it was more like a fabulous Hilton hotel from the Renaissance. It must have had a hundred bedrooms. Only a small portion of the building was available to tourists, but viewing those rooms, the grounds, and the famous spiral stairway designed by Leonardo da Vinci took the entire afternoon.

"Let's find a place to stay before it gets dark," suggested Alvin. Within a few miles of Blois we found Le Château de Loire, an ancient castle recently restored and converted to a guesthouse. It was a bit shabby, but the cost of a room was less than a dollar a night. The place also had a restaurant boasting "the finest cuisine in the Loire Valley". That claim seemed unlikely, but we figured the food would be acceptable. We were wrong; the food was superb. What a happy surprise!

"What's a great chef doing out here in the boondocks?" asked Alvin.

"Who knows?" I replied. "Maybe he's in a witness-protection program."

Unfortunately, our room was not on a par with the food, and the toilet was about a half mile down the hall. But, we had to remember; it was less than a dollar a night! We slept incredibly well, probably because we were in the country with no disturbing sounds, except for the mooing of a few cows. Breakfast, which was included with the room, was another revelation—boiled eggs, country ham, cheeses, and fruit. I was ready to take up residence for another month or so.

Fortunately, the other chateaux we planned to visit were a short drive from our hotel. We began the following day with the Château de Chambord, which was semi-fortified in character and had enormous circular towers at the corners. The profusion of turrets, towers, and chimneys made it appear as though its roof were exploding. After a few hours we continued to the Château de Chaumont, another fortress-like structure, which was owned centuries ago by Catherine de Medici. Catherine was fascinated by mysticism and often entertained astrologers at Chaumont, including the world renowned Nostradamus. He was notorious for his numerous dire prophecies, which included earthquakes, plagues, floods, and just about anything else that could go wrong with the world.

"Sounds like the king of disaster," said Alvin. "How depressing to have him around!"

"I think he was more like an entertainer," I said, "since there's no evidence any of his predictions came true. Still, there are people today who believe this stuff, like the ones who carry signs saying the world is coming to an end. It must come from a lifetime of guilt."

The next several days were spent touring other chateaux that were easily reached from our home base. It was a splendid few days with great sights, fabulous meals at our hotel, and perfect weather. Among the other chateaux, we visited Chenonceau, the chateau that spanned a river; Amboise, where Leonardo da Vinci was buried; Chinon, where Joan of Arc solicited the king's support; and Azay-le-Rideau, a masterpiece of architecture built on an island in the middle of the river. Each building was a French history lesson and an architectural one as well.

After a fascinating week we left the Loire Valley. We headed for Germany to visit my old roommate, Billy Heston, and learn if a job was still available in Nürnberg. I had not decided whether to remain in Europe or return home to get a job, and I was torn by the decision. On the one hand, I loved being in Europe, though I realized that soon I would no longer be a carefree student. But working in Germany meant putting off the day I would establish my own practice.

"What do you think?" I asked Alvin. "Should I work in Nürnberg or go home?"

"Tough decision, Peter. You pretty much have to follow your heart on this one."

Two days later we arrived in Nürnberg, where my future was already decided.

"Sorry to inform you," said Billy, "the government is shutting down our operation. I'll be lucky to last 'til the end of the year. It's been great, but with so many troops going home there's little need for the work we've been doing."

"Well, that pretty much solves my dilemma, doesn't it?"

"But now that you're here, why not stay a few days? The attic guestroom is still available."

"Same cost as before?"

"Of course. But now, how about lunch at the Officer's Club?"

Billy and his girlfriend, Caroline Murray, were the perfect hosts. Caroline prepared great American breakfasts, we drove to nearby villages for lunch, and we partied with some of Billy's co-workers at a dinner one night. Alvin got along well with my friends, and he endeared himself to them by doing a series of amusing caricatures. It was delightful reunion, but with nothing further to keep us in Germany we discussed our next move.

"I have to get back to Paris," said Alvin. "I have some business to take care of and then it's off to Rome. I want to see Laura, and I've got to get back to work."

"Of course, but consider this: In all my time in Europe, no matter where I went or whatever route I took, I kept going *around* Switzerland. What's say we spend a week or so there. I know it's expensive, but they've got those incredible mountains, cute chalets, and lots of cuckoo clocks."

"What a salesman!" was all Alvin said.

The next day we drove through a pouring rain to Zurich, where we found a modest hotel for nearly double what any other room in Europe would cost. I only hoped we could last a week.

While walking the streets of Zurich the next morning we noticed a poster announcing performances by the Ballet Theater.

"Isn't that the company Lisa Berger is with?" asked Alvin.

"Yes, she said something about Switzerland but I had no idea it was Zurich. I'd like to find her and say hello."

"Go ahead. But if you don't mind, I'm going to find an American movie."

That evening I waited at the stage door until the performance ended. Out came the dancers, musicians, and stagehands, but no Lisa. After a while I cornered a performer.

"Excuse me," I said, "is Lisa Berger still with your company?"

"She was tonight," came the reply. I wondered if I had missed her. Then, looking up, I suddenly saw her. "Lisa!" I called. She turned and smiled her beautiful smile.

"Peter! What are you doing here? I hope you're following me." And then we embraced.

"The truth is, I had no idea you were in Zurich, but what a happy coincidence! Do you have any plans, or can we spend some time together?"

"Even if I had plans I'd cancel them for you. I've thought so much about you lately."

"Tell me more."

"Well, I think we made a real connection in Paris, and even though we may be cousins, I've had some erotic thoughts about you; even a dream the other night. Does that sound odd?"

"It sounds pretty nice to me."

We found a small café, where we continued the conversation. "I was just wondering," she began, "could we have a relationship lasting longer than one night? I know you have your commitments and I have mine, and for all I know, this relationship is just a fantasy."

"It's true; right now we can't really be together. But who can know the future?"

"Maybe we should just live for the moment," she said. "Not terribly original, but if we risked one night together, would the world stop turning?"

"I don't think the world would stop turning, but I'm not sure that's a good idea. Lately, I've thought a lot about this. The old me wouldn't hesitate for a second; in fact, we'd be lying in bed right now enjoying our beautiful life. But the new me feels you deserve better. I can't believe

I'm saying this. I've never turned down such an attractive invitation. I'm either the most noble person on the planet or the most stupid."

"You *are* noble, and I love you for that. I also understand how you feel."

"You'll always be a true love, Lisa, and I will never forget you. Perhaps there will be a chance for us another time, but not now."

We embraced and kissed and held one another for a long time. I had no idea whether I was doing the right thing or not, but I felt both honorable and miserable.

The following morning Alvin and I climbed into the Hillman and headed for Interlaken. We discovered that everything in Switzerland was incredibly pristine; the roads appeared freshly paved, the fields looked as though someone recently mowed them, and there was not so much as an errant chewing gum wrapper to be seen anywhere. I had the feeling the Swiss bathed several times a day. Switzerland had a long history of neutrality; they had not been at war since 1800. And having sat out World War II, the country was in great economic shape. Money, it appeared, was spent to benefit the people, not the military. Thus, the Swiss were a happy lot of comfortable, well-organized, and slightly dull people. It's possible they didn't even realize their homeland was the most expensive place on earth.

We drove to Interlaken because it was the nearest access to the Jungfrau, a major peak in the Bernese Alps. Its elevation was thirteen thousand feet, and a cog railway ran as far as Jungfraujoch, which was two thousand feet below the peak. If you wanted to go beyond that point you'd have to be an experienced mountain climber—or perhaps crazy.

The railway took nearly an hour to reach its end, and its cost was a whopping ten dollars, equivalent to my general expenses for about three days! Once you arrived at the highest railway station in

Europe, however, the view was extraordinary. Sitting atop that glacier we could see several other countries. Despite being mid-summer, the temperature was below freezing. We had been warned to wear our warmest clothes, but since we had so few clothes we wore everything we owned. Nevertheless, I nearly froze, even though I was wearing my bulletproof tweed jacket.

Thick clouds moved in shortly after our arrival, and the view slowly disappeared.

"Do you think we can get a partial refund?" asked Alvin.

"I wouldn't even suggest that," I said. "If you make trouble you might have to ski home."

Among the facilities at Jungfraujoch was the Ice Palace, an actual cave carved out of the glacier, where visitors could rent skates and go ice-skating.

"Ice-skating inside a glacier!" I said. "We've got to try that."

"I'll watch," said Alvin. "There are easier ways to make a fool of myself."

I skated for about a half hour, at which time my feet, hands, and every other extremity was painfully frozen. We returned to Interlaken, had a delicious but costly dinner, and slept in the car that night. We figured it was necessary if we wanted to stretch our money until the end of the week.

The next day we drove to Bern, the capital of Switzerland. The city was surrounded by the Aare River, perhaps most famous for its frequent appearance in crossword puzzles. Bern's medieval old town was virtually the only sight of distinction. It was charming, for sure, but except for the famous clock tower, it resembled similar medieval towns in Germany and Austria.

Our final destination was Lausanne, located along the shore of Lake Geneva in the French-speaking part of Switzerland. It was an attractive city, but again, it lacked any notable architecture.

Was it a coincidence or did I know the American Drama Theater would be in Switzerland? Deborah Wolfe's letter may have mentioned that possibility, but my recent life was so convoluted I couldn't remember. Yet, when I saw a poster announcing the company's performances my heart skipped a beat, and I began to speak faster and louder."

"Calm down, Peter," said Alvin. "You're practically frothing at the mouth. Honest to God, you're acting like a bull at a stud farm. Have you forgotten Paris? Have you learned nothing?"

"This is different," I said. "I'm beginning to think Deborah may be the one."

"Nonsense! It's always the same; every one is the one true love."

"I'm sorry, Alvin, I know it sounds crazy, but I have to find her."

It wasn't difficult to locate the theater and, after the performance ended I watched the performers exit the building. There she was, as lovely as ever. She saw me staring at her and rushed to meet me. We embraced and kissed.

"Tell me you're not a mirage," she said. "Tell me it's really you."

"It's me, and I'm so happy to see you. I didn't know you were here; you never told me."

"So how did this happen?"

"Coincidence, destiny, dumb luck—who knows? But I do know this, I want to be with you."

"That might be difficult; we're leaving tomorrow for London, and in about three weeks we're sailing home."

"That's about the time I'll be leaving Europe. Do you know what ship you're on?"

"The new one, the S.S. United States."

"Incredible! Me too! I made a reservation two weeks ago. I cannot believe this is happening. We're going to be shipmates! Someone must be watching out for us."

I walked Deborah to her hotel and we said goodnight and goodbye. We promised to meet on the boat train in three weeks, and neither of us could wait for that to happen.

The next morning Alvin and I drove to Paris. It was wonderful to have the convenience of a car to roam the villages and countryside, but now it was time to sell that pea green Minx. I only hoped a buyer would appear in the next two weeks. Otherwise, I feared, I might have to drive home.

CHAPTER TWENTY-SEVEN

Over and Out

On my first morning in Paris I took my uncle's car to be serviced and washed. Then I went to the offices of the Herald Tribune and wrote an ad, which boldly stated: *Extremely Rare 1953 Hillman Minx—Low mileage—Excellent shape—$1200 dollars U.S.*

"What makes it so rare?" Alvin wanted to know.

"Well, for one thing, it's color. Who but my uncle would have ordered that bilious green?"

Two days later I received three responses, every one of which thought the price was too high. "For two hundred dollars more," said one disgruntled person, "I could buy a new one."

So I modified the ad to read: *Best Offer.* A week later the best offer was $1050. The buyer was a gentleman from Havana, who not only bought me a great dinner at an expensive restaurant, but also threw in a Cuban cigar to seal the deal. He must have believed he was getting an incredible bargain. I thought the price was good enough, and strangely, so did my uncle.

Bastille Day celebrations began on the night of July 13, the eve of the actual holiday. Streets were blocked off, bandstands were set up, and thousands of couples danced on pavements and sidewalks alike. It was the biggest, nosiest, and most colorful celebration you could imagine. Every section of the city was decorated with flags, colored lights, and crowds of joyful people. It was like New Year's Eve, the Fourth of July, and VJ Day rolled into one night of unqualified merrymaking.

Alvin and I strolled through many neighborhoods, only to discover the most festive celebrations were happening in our own back yard. At three in the morning, when I was ready to fall into bed, there was not an empty seat at any café along the length of Boulevard Montparnasse. The following morning we stood at the edge of the Champs-Elysée and watched the most spectacular military parade I had ever seen. Marching bands, cavalry riders, military equipment, and thousands of uniformed servicemen created a remarkable scene. I have no idea how the partygoers, who were nearly unconscious a few hours earlier, found the strength to show up for the parade, but thousands of people packed the entire length of the Boulevard from the Etoile to the Place de Concorde. It was a stirring display!

I wondered how the French could possibly top that marvelous event. The question was answered that evening as we witnessed the most extravagant fireworks show ever produced. Rockets were set off near the Pont Neuf, and spectators lined every bridge over the Seine to watch the colorful explosions light up the sky. When the fireworks ended, the street dancing resumed, and the previous night's activities were repeated with as much energy and passion as the night before. I never saw so much drinking, dancing, hugging, kissing, and who knows what else, during that Bastille Day celebration. It was an event I would never forget.

A day later I received a charming letter from Woody, my old traveling companion. He now had a girlfriend and a job and, *Life is good,* as he put it. Enclosed was a ten-dollar bill with an attached note that read: *This is for you and Alvin. Have a great dinner on me, and toast the memory of our good times past.* It was a generous and affectionate gesture.

"Ten bucks!" said Alvin. "Hell, we could eat at the finest restaurant in Paris."

"How about the Tour d'Argent?" I suggested.

Later that week we found ourselves at this oldest and most famed restaurant in Paris. They claimed that Henry IV dined there, and a century later Louis XIV would come all the way from Versailles, attracted by the fine food. We were greeted at the ground floor reception room and ushered into an elevator that took us to the top floor. What a spectacular room! We had requested a window table and were directed to one that overlooked the river and the illuminated Notre Dame. Just viewing the cathedral's flying buttresses from that height was worth the price of admission. Waiters were dressed in formal attire and appeared every bit as elegant as the wealthy patrons. We began with a glass of champagne and toasted our generous friend who made all this possible.

"What are you going to have?" asked Alvin, as he perused the vast menu.

"I think we're obliged to try their signature dish," I replied, *"Caneton à la pressé."*

"Is that roast duck?"

"Yes, but like no other, I hear."

The performance that followed appeared to be choreographed. First, the waiter took apart the roasted bird like a surgeon performing before a group of interns. He then carefully sliced the breast meat, and finally put the carcass and whatever else remained into a massive duck press. He turned the wheel slowly until the last remaining drop of juice was extracted. This formed the basis for the sauce, which he then prepared at our table. It was a culinary performance as dazzling as a Jascha Heifetz solo. I wanted to leap up and applaud, but it didn't seem quite appropriate.

"This is really something," said Alvin as each of us began to devour our special bird.

"It's simply delicious," I replied. "Time to toast Woody again," We lifted our glasses for another delicious sip of Beaujolais.

As our meal ended, we sat quietly sipping coffee and staring at the floodlit Cathedral across the river. Our experience was nearly as perfect as that architectural gem. That evening was also a farewell dinner for Alvin, as he was returning to Rome the following day.

"I'm going to miss you," I said. "It's been a wonderful journey."

"Me too," he said. "The last few months were terrific, thanks to you and to uncle John."

I accompanied Alvin to the train station. We shook hands, hugged, and then he was gone. I would not see him again for another year, when he returned to California for his father's funeral.

I spent the next several days revisiting many of the monuments and sights last seen two months earlier. I had become addicted to Paris; the more I saw of it, the more I had to see. I took endless walks along the Seine, crossed every bridge, and explored the breadth of the city from the Eiffel Tower on the west to Père-Lachaise Cemetery to the east. I spent an entire afternoon at the cemetery, walking among the graves of Marcel Proust, Gertrude Stein, Oscar Wilde, and dozens of other notables. I was reminded of an Oscar Wilde remark: *When good Americans die they go to Paris.* I assume he regarded Paris as heaven. So did I.

The days passed quickly, and soon it was time to leave. I had been in Paris—off and on—for over three months and in Europe for more than a year. I was profoundly affected by what I experienced, and as a result, I felt more mature and confident. I thought about that naïve student who arrived in Europe a lifetime ago. Could that have been me? I barely recognized him.

I also thought about Joseph LeConte, the nineteenth century Berkeley scientist who established my fellowship. I hoped if he were looking down on me he'd be pleased with how I spent his generous award. *Thanks, Joe,* I thought. *We never met, and that's too bad, because I'll never be able to thank you. Nor will you ever know how profoundly you changed my life. I will never forget your kindness, your generosity, and how much this journey has meant to me.*

The LeConte Memorial Fellowship's only stipulation was that it should be used *"for further education"*. What a modest goal that was! I felt it had opened my eyes to an entirely new world, and because of that award I would never be the same.

I planned to return to London, spend a few days with an old school friend, Lenny Fox, and then catch my ship to New York. I considered returning to the Student Hostel at Tavistock Square, but Lenny, who was an Air Corps officer, was stationed at Teddington, and he insisted I stay with him. Teddington was thirty minutes from London, but staying with Lenny would save most of my remaining dollars.

The coronation of Queen Elizabeth II took place a month before I returned to London. Lenny Fox picked me up at the train station and drove me around in his new Jaguar so I could see the elaborate decorations that remained on display throughout the city. "This is so good of you," I said. "I'm sure you have better things to do today."

"Not really," said Lenny. "My job with the Air Corps gives me a lot of responsibility, but also a lot of spare time. Anyway, I wanted to see you and hear about your European adventures."

"How much time do you have? My stories could take weeks, but I only have a few days."

"Just tell me this, did you get laid?"

Same old horny Lenny. We met in high school and both of us attended Berkeley. Upon graduation he joined the Air Corps about the time I received my fellowship. Lenny was bright and personable, but as long as we had known one another, he remained obsessed with sex.

"What's the matter, Lenny, haven't you met any willing British girls?"

"Sure, a few, but nothing seems to click."

We reached Teddington and Lenny led me to the spare room in his apartment. It was spacious, comfortable, and the price was right. I dropped my bag and then it was time for dinner.

"Come on, Peter, let me show you how your tax money is being spent. I'm taking you to the Officers Club."

We had an elaborate, multi-course dinner that was the equal of any elegant meal one could find in the States. "How can you eat like this and remain so slender?" I asked.

"I don't often eat here," he answered. "Just on special occasions, like when you visit."

The next day was cloudy and cool, perfect for sightseeing. I took a bus to London and spent the day revisiting the National Gallery, St. Paul's Cathedral, and several other popular sights. I must have walked twenty miles. I also visited the American Express office, where I picked up the last of the letters from family and friends. Lenny had tickets for the following night's performance at the Royal Festival Hall where we saw a British production of *Le Sylphides*. The music and atmosphere brought back memories of Lisa Berger, my Ballet Theater friend. Since our last meeting she had become a cherished memory.

With only two days left before catching my ship home, I decided to visit Oxford, an interesting town I missed during my first visit. The most famous institution there was the medieval university, founded nearly a thousand years earlier. There were other sights, but a persistent rain made it difficult to enjoy them.

Lenny informed me that for my final meal in Europe he was taking me to Rules, the oldest restaurant in London, established over two hundred years ago. Rules specialized in exotic fowl and game, and the menu read like an unabridged encyclopedia of British wildlife.

"I haven't eaten most of these dishes," I said to the waiter. "What would you recommend?"

"You might find the partridge amusing," he answered, "but the grouse is lovely as well."

"They're both good," said Lenny, "but I'm having the fillet of venison."

It was a splendid meal and Lenny insisted on picking up the check. "I have a steady job," he said, "and you don't; so let me handle this."

The following morning Lenny drove me to Waterloo Station.

"How can I thank you," I said. "You've been a generous host, and I won't forget this."

"My pleasure," he answered. "Have a great voyage and stay in touch."

Soon after entering the crowded station I heard a familiar voice. "Peter!" It was Deborah Wolfe, and suddenly I was excited. I looked around the large hall and there she was, halfway across the room. We fought our way through the crowd and finally fell into each other's arms.

"Is this really happening?" I asked. "I don't ever want to let you go."

"Not even if we miss our train?"

Our boat train to Southampton Docks was ready for boarding. Having coordinated our reservations, we were seated together.

"This is how it all started," I said. "We were seatmates; do you remember?"

"I'll never forget it," she said. "You were so gallant; it was my first flight, and you held my hand when we ran into that storm. No wonder

275

I fell in love with you. And then when my cousin didn't show up you shared your room with me."

"I remember sharing a bit more."

"Yes, and it was wonderful."

After reaching Southampton we passed through immigration and customs with little difficulty. It was time to board our ship. Walking up the gangway I thought: *This is it; my travels are ending. My fellowship year is over—over and out.* What a bittersweet moment that was. I knew this day would come, but it was like knowing that some day you would leave this earth. It was not a thought you dwelled on. I felt a deep sadness; I was losing one of my true loves. But on the other hand, I was returning home to see family and friends and begin a career. Talk about mixed emotions; I didn't know whether to laugh or cry. Actually, I did both.

Our ship, the S.S. United States, was almost new; it had gone into service the previous year. On her maiden voyage she set a transatlantic record of three and a half days! Since that record-setting trip, the length of time between Southampton and New York was an unhurried five days. Five days alone with Deborah. What a stroke of luck! But there was a problem. I was booked into a dormitory cabin with three others, and Deborah was sharing her cabin with a fellow actress by the name of Paula Stevens.

"I think I can solve this problem," she said.

Deborah knew that a member of their company chose to remain in London for a few weeks. Her plan, therefore, was to convince Paula to switch cabins and take the place of the missing actress. Her roommate, however, was not easily convinced.

"Why should I?" she kept asking.

"Because it really means a lot to me, and it couldn't possibly make any difference to you."

"But it's inconvenient," said Paula.

"What are you talking about? The other cabin is just across the hall, and you haven't even unpacked yet. If you want, I'll carry your bags across the hall."

"You just want a place to carry on with your boyfriend, don't you?"

"That's none of your business, Paula. Come on, you're acting like a real jerk."

"Well, if I do you this favor, what'll you do for me?"

Deborah scowled and said, "Let me tell you what will happen if you don't do me this favor. I'll make the next five days of your pathetic life more miserable than you could possibly imagine."

"You're just bluffing."

"Oh yeah? What would you think if I tore out a fistful of your peroxide hair right now?"

"Well, if it means that much to you," said Paula a bit nervously, "I'll go."

Deborah found me in the lounge and said, "It's all settled; my roommate is moving."

"How did you manage that?"

"I threatened her with physical force." We both laughed, but only Deborah knew it was no joke. Paula moved across the hall and moments later I moved my bag into Deborah's cabin.

It had taken more than a year for me to realize Deborah Wolfe was my one true love. And it was not because she was the last one standing. It was because she was the most lovable, rational, and delightful person I had ever met.

Our ship sailed that afternoon, and we headed for Le Havre to pick up the French passengers. After dinner that first night, when we were lying in our cozy cabin, Deborah said, "I have one more surprise for you."

"I can't imagine what that could be."

"An agent in London has invited me to Hollywood for a screen test. We'll be in the same city. Isn't that the most wonderful goddam freakin' thing you've ever heard?" I was absolutely stunned to discover that Deborah had apparently conquered her neurotic dread of profanity. And I was nearly speechless at the news. I wondered what I had done to deserve this remarkable life. Everything was falling neatly into place.

So, dear reader, that is how my fellowship year ended—on an incredibly high note. For more than a year I had lived an extraordinary dream. I had seen and done and experienced more than I ever imagined. The promise of my three true loves was satisfied beyond my wildest expectations, and I had memories that would last for the rest of my life.

Late that night I went out on deck. There was a full moon, a sight that always appeared magical to me. The reflection on the water shimmered like the twinkling stars in the black sky above. Our ship was plowing through the calm waters at a steady thirty knots, and a cool spray was blowing over the bow. Suddenly I felt a strange discontent; it was not the happy ending I expected. Then I recalled an old saying: *True loves have no happy endings, because true loves never end.*

And—as it turned out—mine never did.